ISLE OF THE DEAD

BY

JODY NEIL RUTH

DEVIL DOG PRESS

SWANVILLE, MAINE

Isle of the Dead
Jody Neil Ruth

Cover by TalkToTippers

Discover more of my work at
http://www.jodyneilruth.com

Thank you for respecting the hard work of the author.

Dedications

This one is for Cameron.
Live long, son.

This one is also for Rob M. Miller.
Sleep tight, partner.

"*This is the good stuff*"

"*You will not be disappointed!*"

"*What a shocker! Was not expecting that ending!*"

"*Very addictive. Don't make us wait so long for the next one!*"

"*Gripped till the very end and didn't see [the ending] coming*"

CHAPTER ONE

Telling nine-year-old Sarah Purton her father was dead was the shitty part of Sergeant Johnathon Warrington's job.

Telling her he'd stabbed a pitchfork through her daddy's head was something he was going to have to omit.

Warrington stood behind his desk, buttoning up a clean, dark-blue police uniform over his ever-growing paunch. The shirt and trousers worn that Monday morning were now a bloodied, stinking heap in the bin. It had taken enough time to shower clean the blood and mud from his face and hands, but despite the hard scrubbing, he could still see the black-red stains under his nails.

He shook his head.

At least it will stop me from biting them.

"Do you have to get changed in full view of everyone?" Charlotte Lewis scowled as she stacked envelopes at her desk. Despite the relatively few years had on the job—she still seemed cold-eyed about Hangshaw and all its inhabitants, and it would take more than a minor bloodbath for her to feel sorry for the place, even when it involved one of her colleagues.

But Warrington knew better.

He'd been working with her for three years on the island, and he knew—she did care. She had lived on the Isle of Wight her entire life, and he could see their town of Hangshaw was strangling the zest right out of her. He allowed the barbed remarks, knowing it was her way of dealing with problems and not getting overwhelmed.

"Full view? In full view of everyone?" Warrington looked around at the small, empty police station.

She started examining her nails. "The sight of you in your vest offends my view."

"Not used to seeing a real man's body?"

"My boyfriend is a boxer." She raised an eyebrow. "I know what a real man looks like."

Warrington grinned. "How is the local"—he made quotation marks in the air—"star these days?"

Charlotte didn't seem to hear the question. Instead, she sighed and took off her glasses before ripping away a fax that came humming through the machine. "Clarke's bad." She scanned the report on the sergeant's injured junior officer. "Stitches to the face, neck, and hands, plus multiple contusions and lacerations ... as well as the missing fingers." She glanced at Warrington. "What the hell happened at the mill?"

Warrington peered out the window, as if the sun pouring through might cleanse some of the memories. "Teeth." A long pause. "He was bitten—a lot."

Charlotte sat in silence.

For her not to react was unusual.

But then today was an unusual day.

Twelve hours previous, when police sergeant Warrington had finished the night shift, he'd clambered into one of the cells to sleep, too tired to make the journey home. It was something he often did, as an empty home held even less appeal than an empty cell.

It had been a quiet night; the only call out was to investigate a burglary at one of the many cottages gracing the nearby countryside, and although the house was broken into and left in a mess, it was empty, and no valuables appeared to have been taken. A neighbor had called in to report noise and strange sounds from the property, but no one had been found.

Officer Kevin Clarke strolled in carrying bacon rolls his wife had made. Clarke lived two minutes away, so the roll was warm when he put it in Warrington's hand.

They ate as Warrington filled Clarke in on the supposed robbery when the phone rang.

"Hangshaw Police Station," Warrington said between mouthfuls. He felt slightly unprofessional, but the average caller to the station was either a disgruntled farmer he knew well, or one of the many elderly ladies minding somebody else's business.

"Help me! He … he's insane, he bit me!"

"Hold up, son," Warrington barked in a thick northern accent that did not belong this far south. "Is that Greg? Greg Evans? Where are you?"

"The farm … it's Purton, John, he's gone bat-shit!" Evans screamed down the line, breathing hard as he tried to force himself calm. "He kept saying he was ill and was gonna go home. I … I thought he had fallen asleep in his chair. Oh, God, John, I'm bleeding everywhere."

"Okay, kid," Warrington said. "Just sit tight and—"

The sound of glass smashing on the other end of the phone was followed by a scream and a click.

The white Ford Fiesta kicked up dust as Clarke threw it into corners along country lanes then the young dark-haired man turned onto a dirt track that led to Hangshaw's largest spread.

As with most farms on the island, the main building was an old structure, retouched by modern architecture. Rural communities were rife, but thinning on the island, and generations of farmers and their families lived out in the sticks while the many towns on the island expanded and grew. Acres of fields stretched over the hills around the farm, and sheep and cattle grazed in the sun. Warrington had visited the farm enough times over the years to know George Purton's office was situated around the back.

Birdsong filtered from the trees all around them, and animals bleated from behind rolling hills. Warrington indicated with a nod that Clarke should investigate the farmhouse.

Warrington headed for the office, glancing in through the kitchen window as he passed, but it was empty of any signs of life.

A tractor was parked by the barns, its engine chugging. Bales of hay were stacked haphazardly behind it, and the policeman saw a pitchfork sticking out of one.

Mud covered the ground, and Warrington curled his lip as it threatened to engulf his feet. Beyond the two open-fronted barns stacked full of hay was a smaller building, its bricks still fresh and clean in contrast to the rugged original stone walls of the bigger building.

"Mr. Purton?" he called out and heard Clarke do the same from inside the house. "Mr. Evans?"

Warrington momentarily removed his police-cap, wiping his brow and flattening his graying hair. He called out for the farmers again. Wincing, he trod as lightly as he could through the mud, trying not to lose his steel toed boots in the deep puddles.

Nearing the office building, he lowered his head, the peak of his hat shielding his eyes from the sun. He saw bloodied handprints on the doorframe, and the smashed window of the door itself, blood running down the broken pane.

Warrington approached, his boots squelching in the mud. The door was ajar, and he nudged it open, glass twinkling from the ruined frame. Muddy footsteps stretched down a hallway, and he could see streaks of blood lining both the floor and walls.

The gory mess curved into the office, and the sergeant paused at the doorway. "Greg?" He cleared his throat. "Greg Evans?"

He peered around the doorframe and his breath froze in his chest. The small office had been destroyed. Anything that had once lived on the small desk was now broken or stranded on the floor, with filing cabinets upended, and a water cooler's contents emptied onto the ground.

Blood painted the room. It smeared the walls and a window that was half open, covered in bloodied handprints. Blood was all over the floor, mingling with the water and the muddy tracks left by a farmer's boots.

A foot protruded around the desk, but Warrington remained where he was. So much blood could not be lost from someone and they still be alive? Unless it was the blood of more than one person?

He stepped forward, covering his mouth at the sight of Greg Evans. The young man was plastered in his own blood, his hands, face, and neck a mass of deep furrows and gaping wounds. A shock of red hair on his head confirmed his identity. Fingers were missing from one of Evans's hands. Warrington looked around, unable to find them, but more to take his eyes from the macabre scene.

He let out a long breath. He had been a policeman for almost twenty years, covering murders and mysterious deaths, but this was the worst he had seen. He rubbed his chest, trying to keep the bile from rising.

Officer Clarke coughed into his own hand as he stopped in the doorway.

"Christ," he said. "Is that Greg Evans?"

Warrington stared at the body. "We have to find George Purton."

"He did this?"

"We'll know for sure when we find him."

"Let's get out of here," Clarke said.

George Purton saved them the trouble of a search. The door in from the farmyard lost what little glass it had left in its frame as the old man burst through and launched himself at the junior officer.

Clarke raised his hands to protect himself, the farmer's fingers clawing at Clarke's face, teeth gnashing like a wild dog.

Warrington lunged, grabbing Purton around the waist. but between them they pinned Clarke to the wall, Purton's fingernails digging deep furrows into Clarke's face as the three of them wrestled in the tiny corridor.

Warrington slid in the mud and blood, his knee hitting the ground. Clarke howled as Purton's teeth found his fingers and bit deep, tearing one away. Clarke's other hand clutched the bloodied stump and Purton was on him again, teeth chomping on the digit in his mouth.

Blood oozed from between Clarke's fingers. He had no time to react before Purton's teeth were on his neck, the maniacal farmer's fingers locking around his skull. The policeman screamed again as a thumb pushed deep into his eye.

Scrambling to his feet, Warrington grasped Purton's head and pulled backwards, using his weight as leverage. How can he be so strong?

Purton's teeth took a chunk of flesh from Clarke's neck and Clarke screamed. Warrington turned the old farmer as best he could in the confined area, pointing him at the doorway and half-running, half-shoving him through, sending him sprawling into the mud outside.

Warrington moved for his colleague. Clarke was on one knee, his good hand pressed hard against his bleeding neck, while blood squirted from the stump that was once his finger. He thrust the injured hand towards Warrington, and it took him a moment to realize that Clarke was trying to point with a finger he no longer had.

Pointing at something behind Warrington.

Warrington spun to face George Purton as the old man got to his feet. Covered in mud and blood, Purton's eyes were wide, but glazed, blood foaming around his mouth as he chewed on Clarke's finger.

Purton's eyes set upon Warrington. The farmer moaned and started towards the officer. When Purton was upon him, Warrington grabbed his attacker's outstretched arms, holding him at distance. Purton leaned towards him, mouth snapping, blood spraying from his teeth. They danced, shifting weight backwards and forwards, slipping in the mud. Warrington pushed him back to put space between them, trying to keep him as far away from the injured Clarke as possible.

The noises coming from Purton were like nothing Warrington had heard before. They were primal … angry. The moan accompanying the sounds seemed to emanate from the soles of Purton's feet and up through his thin body. Blood covered the old man, but the skin that was visible was discolored and pale. He looked ill and feverish, although when Warrington had grappled with him, Purton's skin was cold to the touch,

Purton's eyes were covered in a milky film, and Warrington could see a dark pupil beneath, working furiously.

Purton lurched forward, slipping in the mud and landing on his knees, hands clawing through the dirt at Warrington's feet. The policeman stepped back, carefully making his way around the tractor. The machine was still chugging away unattended, a steady cloud of exhaust fumes dissipating into the sky.

"Come on, Purton," Warrington said, trying to concentrate on the man on the ground and his own footing. "This way…."

The pitchfork Warrington had passed earlier still protruded from a bale of hay. He hurried towards it as fast as the mud would allow, the unsure ground equally hindering him and Purton.

Grabbing the tool, he spun on his toes, just as Purton found his footing and momentum, charging at Warrington.

As George Purton rushed him, the prongs of the fork touched Purton's chest, with Warrington stepping back. Despite being attacked, he did not want to injure Purton, but Purton pressed upon him so hard, the tips of the prong pierced the old man's chest.

And Purton still kept coming.

As the fingers of the pitchfork sunk into his attacker, the tines scraping past bone, Warrington gritted his teeth. He stepped back, trying to tug the prongs from Purton's chest, but Purton pushed forwards, completely impaling himself.

Purton fought on, his hands reaching for the officer as Warrington pushed on the shaft of the fork to keep the farmer away. Warrington turned his head as Purton writhed and snatched at him, the farmer gnashing his teeth as blood-filled spittle flew from his mouth.

Clarke tackled Purton with a cry of his own pain, the policeman's shoulder taking the farmer in his midriff as the two then skidded across the barn floor.

The pitchfork wrenched from his hands, Warrington lost his footing and fell backwards.

Purton was already on Clarke, biting at the officer's sleeve. Clarke pushed with his forearm, trying to force the man away, but Purton sank his teeth into the offered limb.

Clarke fought for his life. Warrington grabbed Purton by the neck, and between them, threw Purton clear.

The farmer snarled, sliding through the mud on his backside as his fingers wriggled for purchase with the pitchfork still buried in his chest.

"Get out of here!" Warrington ordered his colleague. It might already be too late. He could see the color draining from the younger man's face.

Clarke remained on his knees, bleeding heavily, his skin looking similar in color to that of Purton's, who was now back on his feet.

Warrington lunged and grabbed the handle of the fork, inadvertently pulling it from the farmer's body. The prongs withdrew with a sucking sound, and thick, dark blood stained the fork, with parts of Purton's innards coming out from the puncture wounds.

Purton did not falter and set upon Warrington.

The policeman slid backwards, the fork pointing at Purton's face. The policeman cried out in horror as Purton blundered onto the piece of barnyard equipment, skewering his face as a prong slid along the side of his nose and pierced his eye. A sharp crack as the fork broke through the back of his skull, and only then did Purton cease his attack. His body fell limp and he folded into the mud, wrenching the pitchfork from Warrington's hands.

Warrington stared at Purton, a part of him half-expecting the maniacal old man to get to his feet again. Clarke moaned, stealing his attention. He rushed to his fallen colleague's side. The younger man was also on his back in the mud. Clarke's eyes fluttered as he sobbed in agony.

Warrington pulled him upright, easing one of Clarke's arms around his own shoulders, helping him to his feet. They slid through the mud like ghoulish skaters, before finding slightly more solid ground at the edge of the farmhouse. The two of them headed for the police Fiesta parked on the driveway. He helped Clarke into it, and the younger man lay himself across the backseats, eyes closed.

Inside the vehicle, Warrington snapped the radio attached to his chest to ON. During the tussle, he did not have the time to call in for backup.

"Charlotte?" he said. "Do you read me?"

"John?" said his secretary's voice. A police station as small as theirs meant they often dispensed with radio protocol. "What the hell is going on? Clarke's radio kept turning on and off like he was mucking around with the mic."

"He's been attacked, and hurt bad. Can you alert St. Mary's and let them know we're on our way?" he asked. "I'll put my blues on and get him there as fast as I can."

"I'll try," she replied. "But I've had no contact with the hospital for a while. There was a traffic incident with several vehicles involved, including a bus and a gas truck, out on Coppin's Bridge. A lot of people were hurt, John. I was trying to contact you, but both Newport and Ryde branches are at the scene."

That's most of the island forces tied up at one place, Warrington thought. He hoped there would be no more dramas for the rest of the day.

The wheels of the Fiesta spun, lights flashing and sirens wailing, digging grooves down the gravel driveway as it moved out onto the main road.

If Warrington had looked in his rearview mirror he would have found the dead Greg Evans emerging from the farm's office into the daylight.

Warrington and an orderly carried Clarke into the ACCIDENT & EMERGENCY ward of St. Mary's Hospital in Newport. A doctor he was familiar with, but not by name, told him they would see to his colleague as soon as they could, that the hospital was overrun with injured people. The policeman did not have a chance to ask the medical staff what was happening, and was ushered away by nurses and doctors as he fired questions at them.

"What's going on?" he asked Charlotte as he left the hospital. The car park around him was crammed with vehicles parked on grass verges, and illegally on yellow lines. A traffic warden was busy slapping tickets on windscreens. He smiled at Warrington, but the officer told him to go fuck himself.

"I've never known so many reports of assaults," she

said. "It's like a civil war has broken out on the island. We had so many calls over domestic violence, and attacks in the streets that I couldn't keep up. And I can't get through to Ryde, Shanklin, or Newport police stations."

As Charlotte spoke, Warrington watched an ambulance park behind three others at the entrance to the hospital, its back doors covered in bloody handprints.

"I kept radioing them until I got a reply, and was told that all of their officers are on call-outs."

"How many call-outs have we had?"

"Too many," she said. "I've had to take the phones off the hooks. Without you, Kevin, and no backup, there's nothing we can do."

Warrington stood by his vehicle. All around him he could see thin plumes of rising smoke, and the road before him was full of vehicles heading towards the ferry port in Cowes.

"John," she pleaded. "Can I please go home?"

Passengers and drivers in the log-jam of cars heading away from Newport climbed out of their vehicles—bags and/or children in hand—and started hurrying on foot towards Cowes, at the northern peak of the diamond-shaped island. He knew that the distance was approximately four miles.

What had the island-folk so panicked?

"Sarge?" she repeated.

He spoke into his mic: "I need you to stay put while I go to the Purton household and tell a little girl her daddy is dead."

She sighed down the communication-line before replying, "You think you'll find any answers there?"

"I don't know," he said. "But I've got nothing else

to go on. I'll take you home afterwards. If the island is going to shit, I don't want you walking alone. I'll be back soon, anyway." He looked down at his blood-soaked clothes. "I need to change my shirt."

Warrington turned his hat over in his hands as he exited his car outside the Purton residence. He quickly smoothed out a crease-line in his clean shirt, before slowly treading the steps leading to the front door.

A thicket of trees provided a picturesque background to the two-story building. It was a beautiful, elegant home, with stone pillars guarding the door and an open twin garage with a family saloon parked inside.

Warrington took his cap off and tucked it under his arm before straightening his tie. His steel toe-caps clacked loudly up the porch steps. His hand paused as he reached for the large brass knocker.

"I'm sorry, Mrs. Purton," he rehearsed. "I'm afraid I have some bad news."

His hand lingered at the door, and then withdrew as he noticed it was ajar. It wasn't unusual for homes out in the sticks to remain unlocked while the family went about its business inside, or if they were out tending the grounds, and the Purton estate stretched for a few acres behind the back-line of trees.

Still, Warrington didn't want to walk in like the Friendly Neighborhood Lawman and tell them he'd killed the man of the house with a pitchfork.

He thumped the knocker against the door, the same hand then smoothing his graying hair as he waited.

No answer.

He knocked again—louder.

Placing the cap back on his head, he pushed the door open. "Mrs. Purton?"

He stepped into a vestibule with a patterned wooden floor. Rooms branched off in different directions, and a hallway extended beneath the spiral stairway and into a kitchen. The sound of a television playing filtered in from another room.

Upturned furniture blocked a doorway, the sound of the television growing as he approached it.

Blood soaked the carpet as a television played out Scooby Doo and The Gang searching for a monster.

A coffee table had been smashed and streaks of blood led from the room through another doorway.

"Mrs. Purton?"

Charlotte Lewis's voice made him jump. "We have a problem."

Warrington thumb-clicked the CALL button as he stepped on blood-free patches. "You're telling me. There are signs of a struggle at the Purton residence."

"There's only one body at the Purton Mill."

Warrington's foot stopped in mid-air. "Say again?"

"The coroner only found the body of George Purton where you said it would be. Greg Evans's body was not there."

"Did he look in the office out back of the farmhouse?"

"Sarge," replied Charlotte. "I gave him the same directions you gave me. He says there's a lot of blood in the office, but no body, and there are tracks leading out into the field behind the mill."

"Then someone must've dragged the body out that way," he said. "Look, let me deal with this, and then I'll get back to you ... unless you want to go check it out for me?"

"Fuck that, sarge."

Warrington flicked the switch on the television and the room fell silent.

Had George Purton gone mad and attacked his family? Had Greg Evans been having an affair with the man's wife? Why had no one called the police, and where was the rest of the Purton family?

None of this makes any sense, he thought, entering the kitchen. A dining table chair had been knocked over, and apart from some small blood splatters there were no other signs of anything untoward.

Open patio doors at the back of the kitchen allowed him to see dog bowls full of food.

Putting his fingers in his mouth he whistled.

No pet responded.

The garden beyond the room was beautiful. Flowerbeds blazed color, and the trimmed hedges had no leaf or branch out of place. A rock-feature sprinkled water in several directions as large koi carp swam in circles.

Warrington replaced his cap to shield his vision from the sun. His blues eyes scanned the tree-line around the garden, as his nostrils soaked up the smell of the surroundings.

He dipped his hand in the pond and wiped it on his face before taking his cap off and turning his head towards the sun.

Why is everything going so wrong on such a

beautiful day?

Charlotte Lewis stirred her coffee with the stub of her pencil as Warrington debriefed her on his findings at the Purton residence. The waning sun fell through the window blinds as he talked.

She listened as he spoke, her green eyes switching from man to coffee mug as she nibbled on a long red fingernail. "No matter what way you look at this, it just doesn't work out. If George Purton had attacked or killed his family, where are they? Where are the bodies? And why then drive to the mill and attack Greg Evans?"

Warrington swirled his tea in his hand. "There's also a chance that Greg Evans attacked the family and Purton followed him back to the farm for revenge, but—again—where is the family?"

"Do you think Mrs. Purton and Evans were sleeping together?"

Warrington shrugged. "Whatever happened, we need to find Angela Purton and her daughter, then try and figure out who would want to take Evans's body, then we might get some answers."

Charlotte rubbed her eyes before running her hands through her raven-hair and stretching her back. She had been the only person manning the station all day and had to deal with a flood of phone calls and panicking village-folk banging on the doors of the station before sending them away without any news or words of advice other than to stay at home.

Warrington looked at the darkening circles around her eyes, and she could see the same on the sergeant's own face.

"Come on." Charlotte pushed her chair away from her desk. "Let's go and see how Clarke is getting on. Everyone around here is either holed up at home, or on their way to the ferries."

The drive to St. Mary's Hospital was brief, as were most drives anywhere on the island. Hangshaw was situated just south of the main town, Newport, but the island's twisting roads and the blockages that piled up that day made the trip much less than straightforward.

An artist's colorful cone-shaped monument sat outside of the gray, faux-metal sided building, and he had to use his lights and sirens to drive on the wrong side of the road to avoid the unmoving traffic to reach it. The double-parked/abandoned cars seen earlier had grown in number, and he cut across a grass verge before parking the Ford in a doctor's bay. Charlotte cast him a disapproving look.

They entered the reception of the building, pushing past a clamor of patients awaiting treatment, and those trying to find relatives. Warrington waved at an elderly nurse on reception duty as they passed, but she called him back.

"I'm sorry, John," she said, mouth downturned. "But Kevin's condition has deteriorated. I've been trying to contact you, as Doctor Leppard would like to speak to you, urgently"

"Come on, Crystal," said Warrington, stepping closer to the desk. "I brought him in myself, both of us covered in his blood. If he has something, then surely I do as well?"

Charlotte retreated a step away from him.

Crystal West's eyes watered. "He's gotten real sick in the last hour, John." Her hand found his. "His injuries are badly infected. I'll call Dr. Leppard and let him know you are here."

Moments later, a middle-aged doctor entered the reception area, weaving in-and-out of people and patients without looking up. The man studied a clipboard as he routinely pushed his glasses back up his sweat-covered nose. He saw the policeman and tucked the clipboard under his armpit, grabbing Warrington's hand and pumping it fiercely.

"Hello, John."

"Well, if I were contagious I guess we wouldn't be doing this," Warrington said while nodding at their linked palms.

Leppard smiled and released the grip. "We're not exactly sure what we're dealing with." He indicated they should follow him. "But your colleague is one very sick man."

"How sick?" Charlotte asked.

"He's been quarantined." He placed his glasses back on his nose.

Warrington. "You don't know what's wrong with him, do you?"

The glasses came off again. "I'm glad you've come

back, officer," the doctor said. "If there's anything more you can tell me about the attack, it might just help Mr. Clarke."

Warrington recounted that morning's events as Leppard led them to an elevator. The doctor's brow furrowed as he listened during their ascent to the third floor of the hospital.

"And there were no chemicals or unidentified substances on the ground or at the farm?" asked Leppard, the glasses always either on-or-off.

"No, Doc," replied Warrington. "Just a shitload of mud and ... er ... cow shit."

"Animal waste?"

"It's a farm." Warrington smiled. "The coroner has George Purton's body, so maybe he'll come up with some answers."

"Maybe, but that doesn't help Mr. Clarke right now." Leppard rubbed his brow. "As it stands, I can't diagnose what he has and act upon it."

"You have no ideas?"

Leppard briefly met Charlotte's gaze, and then looked at his clipboard. "I haven't come across anything like this in my twenty-eight years of practicing medicine. He definitely has an infection, and it's killing him. His body is not responding to any treatment or drugs, and we don't even seem to be slowing his condition at all.

"I'm going to allow you to see him, John," he continued as he reached a set of plastic-coated doors, with QUARANTINE emblazoned upon them.

In the room, a facemask-wearing nurse lifted her eyes from a monitor, a bank of machines next to her beeping and expelling hisses of air. Wires and tubes snaked across the floor, and under a plastic partition separating the room from a tent-like structure beyond. Inside the tent, they could see the prone body of Kevin Clarke.

Charlotte gasped.

Clarke was covered with a bloodstained sheet up to his waist. Wires and tubes pierced his body, bandages covered his head, forearms, and hands. His chest was a patchwork of scratches, stitches, and dark bruising, but it was the color of his skin that troubled Warrington. It had little natural skin color, and was a dull shade of gray.

A green line hummed across a monitor, slowly peaking and falling. Leppard saw the policeman looking, but said nothing. Charlotte, however, wanted to know.

"His heartbeat," answered Warrington. "It's almost non-existent."

"The human heart beats at an average of seventy-two pulses per minute." Leppard, nodded at the screen they were all watching. "Mr. Clarke's is currently running at eight beats per minute … and slowing."

"He's dying," said Warrington.

"He should be dead." Leppard shook his head. "There is no way a heart rate such as his could sustain his body. It should not be beating at that rate at all. We tried to electronically strengthen his heartbeat, but failed on every attempt. His body isn't rejecting anything; it's just ignoring all attempts at treatment.

"This virus has deteriorated his body to such a degree that he is clinically dead … and still alive. I'm at a loss on how to explain it."

Warrington approached the plastic sheeting, peering through the cloudy partition at the man beyond. He pried the slats apart, and saw Clarke beneath the enclosed tenting of his bed.

His friend's eyes were open, but covered with a milky-film, the irises looking black beneath. Warrington called to him.

"He doesn't respond to stimulae," said Leppard, removing Warrington's hand from the partition. He gave his clipboard to the seated nurse and turned to Warrington. "I would like to take a blood sample from you."

"Sure," replied Warrington. "I didn't get bitten, but take your sample. Plus, I certainly don't feel like Clarke looks."

Charlotte stood by the plastic curtains, chewing at a fingernail as she stared through the partition, listening to their chatter.

"I think we can assume that the infection came from George Purton," said Warrington.

"I'm not in the business of making presumptions," said Leppard, smiling slightly. "But whatever this is, it seems to effect people in different ways. George Purton—from your description—became delusional to the point of attacking people, and his nervous system may well have shut down, causing him to ignore his injuries, or maybe his psychosis was so strong he lost all sense of feeling and morality.

"On the other hand," he said, indicating Clarke. "The virus can also cause someone to become dormant in every way imaginable."

"Purton's body revealed nothing?" asked the policeman.

"The coroner will report to me as soon as the forensic pathologist has conducted the autopsy," replied Leppard. "But…."

"But?" spoke Charlotte.

Leppard rubbed the bridge of his nose, jostling his glasses. "But, from your associate's condition and his failing bodily systems…."

"He's as good as dead," said Warrington.

With morbid timing, Clarke changed from dying to dead.

No one rushed to his aid.

Doctor Leppard took the clipboard from the nurse, made a note on it, and handed it back to her. She rose from her seat and left the room.

"It's better for him this way." The doctor pulled on a pair of latex gloves. "Now, I have some final examinations to make."

Bidding them goodbye, Leppard slipped between the plastic curtains, his fuzzy figure walking around the bed of their dead friend.

They left the room in silence.

The policeman glanced at Charlotte, his hand twitching to envelope her shoulders, but she bit at her lip and wiped tears from her eyes, and he did not want to give her cause to break down upon him.

Or did he?

A scream smashed his train of emotion.

A scream from the room they had just left.

Warrington burst through the doors in time to catch the screaming nurse who fell into him. He gripped her arms and moved her to one side as Doctor Leppard wrestled beyond the plastic quarantine curtain….

Wrestled with Clarke's dead body.

Blood spattered the sheeting as Warrington moved towards it. He could hear Leppard's pleading with Clarke, but the response from Clarke was nothing more than an angry growl, similar to the one he had heard George Purton make that morning.

He threw open the sheeting as Leppard fell backwards, away from Clarke.

Warrington stared as Clarke lifted himself from the bed, dragging tubes, wires, and machinery with him. His milky black-and-white eyes strained from their sockets, veins standing thick on his face and neck. Peeling his lips back, Clarke moaned, his teeth grinding together until one of his lower incisors snapped.

"Kev?" Warrington managed.

"Nurse!" yelled Leppard, as he scrambled to his feet, cradling his bleeding and bitten hands. "Get me a sedative, now!"

Clarke slid from the bed, standing on swaying legs as he surveyed the room. He gave a cursory glance to the tube emitting from his body, then licked at the blood around his lips. When his gaze fell upon Warrington once more, the dull moan returned.

Warrington took a deep breath. "Kev," he said again. "Kevin Clarke…."

The man snarled and stepped forward as the heart monitor following behind clashed with the bed. Tubes popped out of his body, leaving black pockmarks on his skin. Small droplets of blackened blood formed in the wounds, but did not weep.

There was no recognition in Clarke's dead eyes as he moaned at Warrington, the older policeman stepping back, hands raised.

"Doc," he said, his eyes not straying from his partner. "We could do with a little backup."

While one injured hand sprayed blood down his white coat, Doctor Leppard elbowed an emergency button on the wall.

Clarke ignored the sound, instead taking awkward

steps towards Warrington. The IV drip trailing Clarke toppled over the bed before he dragged it to the floor.

Warrington took slow steps backwards, talking to Clarke to divert his attention from the injured doctor.

"What's wrong with him?" Charlotte asked, her voice gaining Clarke's attention.

"Get out of here!" Warrington shouted, and the noise spurred Clarke towards him, arms outstretched.

Warrington grabbed Clarke's wrists and pulled them together, creating a barrier between them.

Black blood spilled from Clarke's wounds, and Warrington pushed the man away as orderlies and nurses filled the room. They grabbed at Clarke, and Warrington yelled at them to watch for his teeth.

A nurse tried to heed his words, but Clarke sunk his teeth into her wrist. An orderly pulled the gray-skinned head backwards, tearing flesh from the nurse's arm. She screamed as the orderly struggled with Clarke, adjusting his grip to slip his forearm under the policeman's chin. The orderly flexed his arm and tightened his grip.

Leppard clutched gauze to his missing fingers. "He's not breathing," he shouted. "You can't choke him!"

As the orderly struggled with him, a nurse plunged a syringe into Clarke's neck. The policeman did not flinch, his teeth biting into the arm of the man holding him. The nurse emptied the contents of the sedative into Clarke.

Warrington released his friend's wrists as the hospital staff pinned him down. Clarke hissed and struggled, teeth snapping, managing to ensnare another nurse.

He bit hard on the upper arm of the nurse who

screamed. She pulled free, and blood spewed from the wound as she left a chunk of herself in his mouth.

Each time any of his captors got within distance, Clarke would bite them hard, tearing flesh away from limb.

Warrington watched the tussle before him, the hospital staff risking injury and probable infection as they attempted to detain Clarke. More sedatives were pumped into the man, and he could see a syringe poking from his arm.

Clarke bit an orderly's hand, and the sound of bone and teeth breaking with the force mingled with the cry of the hospital worker.

The situation was spiraling out of control.

"Hold his head," he said, but no one heard.

He repeated himself.

Louder.

The orderly with the forearm bite heard him, and placed his huge hands around Clarke's skull. Pulling back hard, he squeezed Clarke's head between his thighs as a second orderly and a nurse threw themselves upon him, holding down his arms.

Warrington snatched the IV drip stand from the floor, and turned it over in his hands to hold the curved end towards Clarke.

"What are you doing?" Charlotte called from the doorway.

Clarke whipped his head to one side and bit the orderly's inner-thigh. The man screamed in pain and then shouted Do it! at Warrington as he pulled Clarke's head fully back.

Warrington thrust the end of the stand through the underside of Clarke's chin, penetrating the skin and jamming Clarke's mouth closed. Warrington's shuddered as he felt the metal grind on teeth.

Clarke grunted as black liquid poured from his wound. He struggled, his head unmoving from the pressure of the IV-stand and the grip of the orderly.

The blood-soaked orderly bellowed at Warrington to finish it. Charlotte screamed otherwise, but Warrington felt something press against his back and caught sight of Leppard throwing his weight upon him, plunging the IV-stand through Clarke's head, skewering him.

The man fell limp. The staff kept their hands upon him, the lot breathing hard and covered in sweat and blood.

Warrington's fingers ached as he released the stand, the thin metal falling to one side, turning Clarke's head with it. The nurse knelt next to him moved away, cradling her injured wrist against her chest.

Doctor Leppard was on his feet, barely finishing attaching bandages to his own hands before he was treating the nurse who wailed over her own missing fingers. Warrington stared at her slowly changing skin color.

It was becoming gray.

"What the fuck is going on?" Charlotte asked, pressing the back of her hand to her mouth as her green-eyes stayed on Clarke.

"Go home," he said. "There's nothing you can do here."

"Then you can drive me," she said, staring at him. "There's nothing you can do here."

Warrington folded his arms on the roof of the police car, resting his chin on them. Charlotte lifted her face to the autumnal sun as she wrapped her arms around herself.

He stared at her from beneath his pepper-colored eyebrows.

Her own eyes were circled with fatigue and stress when she opened them, but she met his gaze. They stared at each other, unspeaking for a moment before getting into the car.

"What will happen about Kev?" she asked as he started the vehicle.

Warrington stared down the bonnet of the police car as he weaved through the claustrophobic spaces of the hospital car park. "I'll hand myself in when the time comes."

She put a hand on his arm. The gesture was small, but coming from her allowed him to set his jaw straighter. "Something strange is going on." Charlotte looked back at the hospital as they drove onto the main road. "I know people die here on the island all the time, but to have George Purton and Kevin—" She cleared her throat. "Something isn't right."

Warrington nodded. "If they'd died natural deaths through this disease or virus, then it would be more understandable."

"Doctor Leppard said they did have a virus."

Warrington stiffened. "The rest of the Purton

family … what if they are out there right now, spreading this thing? Maybe one of them infected George Purton." He urged the car faster down a clear dual-carriageway towards the town center.

"Are we going back to the police station?" asked Charlotte as she looked across the central median at the logjam of traffic heading out of town, and the people and families exiting their vehicles to flee on foot.

"You're going to your house, where you'll sit tight until I come and get you."

"I'm not going anywhere." She folded her arms. "Not until Aaron gets back."

Warrington glanced at her, and found her green-eyes boring into him. He had seen the look many times before. He gave up any hope of arguing. "When is the superstar due back?"

"He's been fighting up in Salisbury, so will be back on the boat soon." She glanced at her wristwatch. "Actually, he should be back now. Do you think he got over on the boats? Or have they been stopped?" She pulled her mobile out of her blouse pocket, wrinkling her lip at the lack of display on its screen before sliding it back.

"Right," he said, rubbing a calloused hand down his face. "We'll go to his—yours—wherever, get him, pack your stuff, and get off the island."

Charlotte raised an eyebrow. "You think things are going to get worse?"

"I think things are already getting worse," he replied. He wiped his brow on his sleeve. "On an island like this, we might get one murder every few years—I can think of only two in the last ten—but I've killed that quota already today, and I don't think that's the end of it.

"Leppard told me he's going to quarantine everyone who was bitten by Kev, and any civilians that come in off of the street with bite wounds, or any other virus indicator."

"Do you think there will be a lot of … of—"

"Victims? Contagious people? I don't know, but we have to prepare for the worst. We have to assume Greg Evans is out there spreading this plague."

"Greg Evans is dead." She slumped in her seat. "But then so was Kev."

Warrington drummed his fingers on the steering wheel, staring into the distance. "Were there many more deaths today?"

"There were no more murders," she said, brow furrowing.

"What about natural deaths? In the last few days? Don't you usually bump into that old guy when you're getting lunch?"

"Nick Galloza? The funeral director?" A small smile took the dark from her face. "Sure, every time I see him in the deli I ask him what he's having in his sandwich, and who the fuck he's embalmed that morning. 'Oh, and try not to drop a tomato in a cavity, Nick!'

"Saying that, I've only seen him a couple of times this week. I'm sure he said something about being busier than usual. And didn't Kay O'Grady die a couple of days back?"

"The old dear from the farm?" he asked. "She kept that place running with her son, the … er—"

"The autistic kid." Now it was her turn to stare into nothing. "Maybe I should check out all the nursing homes on the island and see how many people have recently passed away."

"Might also be worth calling the hospital and seeing what sort of figures they're seeing. Although I think they're a little busy up there, at the moment." A pause. "I do think we need to see Galloza." He switched on the police car's siren. "Because his funeral home has newly dead people in it, and if today's dead are anything to go by—"

"Oh, fuck," she said.

The Isle of Wight measured twenty-three miles across and thirteen miles from top to bottom, in a rough-diamond shape. Nowhere was too far away from somewhere. The Galloza Funeral Home was a short drive from Hangshaw, and they would have reached it sooner had it not been for the one-way systems that clogged up the island's pothole-covered roads.

The place was a combination of red bricks, white pillars, and wooden-slatted walls. Few windows adorned its façade, and the home was topped by a duo of chimney stacks. The combination of ornate architecture and immaculately-kept lawns disguised the true purpose of the building as it settled into the darkening night.

"No lights on," said Charlotte as the car pulled to a halt

Warrington unclipped his seatbelt. "Stay here, lock the doors. The keys are in the—"

—

"Fuck you," she said and got out.

They approached the building light on their toes, or as light as Charlotte could go wearing four-inch heels.

Warrington motioned for Charlotte to stay at the bottom of the short stairs to the entrance. The doors before him were shut, and he knocked on them. A few seconds of silence and he knocked louder, but with still no reply. Pushing the door open, he stepped inside.

The hallway revealed nothing but wooden flooring and historical photographs of the building on the red-carpeted walls.

He entered further and found the funeral home's chapel. A raised stage with a projector screen hung from the wall, and rows of benches facing it held wreaths and hymn books.

A door was open to the side of the stage and he took light steps towards it. More wreathes scattered the floor, several crushed, and bibles spread their torn pages between the pews.

A dull light hummed in a corridor beyond the place of prayer. Through this Warrington investigated an embalming room. A cadaver lay upon a gurney, fluid leaking from a tube hanging from its inner thigh. Tilting his head, Warrington could see that it was Kay O'Grady, the old lady Charlotte had informed him of having died a few days ago.

The smell of formaldehyde, ethanol, and other chemicals made him pinch his nostrils.

A small desk lamp illuminated the room, washing the corpse in a yellow light. The lamp lay on its side, and papers were strewn across the floor. A notepad lay at his feet, and he took a knee to read it:

RICHARD CHAMBERLAIN BODY ARR
TUES PM
INFORMED DEATH WAS EARLY TUES AM
BODY SHOWS SIGNS OF EXTENDED
DECOMPOSITION
?BITE MARKS ON BODY?
INFORM POLICE

"Consider me informed," Warrington said.

Skirting around the old lady's body, he kept his distance from it. Too many dead people had already attacked him that day.

On the other side of the gurney lay an upturned table; a blood-soaked sheet and embalming equipment covered the floor.

"What happened?" Charlotte stood in the doorway, heels dangling from her hand.

"Looks like Nick Galloza encountered the same problem I did with Purton and Kev. Whoever he had been working on here"—he bent down to pick up a chart—"a 'Mr. Michael Ellison—died in a car crash.' Well, it looks like Mr. Ellison woke up and attacked Galloza."

Warrington dropped the chart at the foot of O'Grady's gurney and followed a blood trail to an open fire exit. Blood splashed the steps before disappearing into the grass.

Warrington looked at Charlotte. "Galloza and Ellison make for two more missing bodies."

"What do we do now?" Charlotte asked as the Fiesta moved away from the funeral home.

"We need weapons." Warrington pushed the car deeper into the country roads.

"Where are we headed?" She buckled her seatbelt as they took a small bridge fast enough for the wheels to leave the ground.

"Ol' Johnson has a shotgun."

Warrington stopped outside a bungalow a few miles east of Hangshaw. The narrow lane gave no room for the police car to turn, so he left the flashing roof lights on so they could see the home. The blue lights strobe-lit the house as he made for the front door.

It was unlocked and opened as he pushed it. No sounds echoed within so he stepped inside, feeling Charlotte's hand on his back as she followed.

"Mr. Johnson?" he asked, one hand searching the wall for a light switch.

Warrington walked through the hall, peering into each room they passed.

Reaching the final door on his right, he opened it

to reveal a sitting room hosting an elaborate bookcase, a flat-screen television, and a tall metal cabinet. The doors of the cabinet were locked, so he emptied pots and ornaments until he found a small metal key inside a china dove. The lock clicked with the key, and the doors opened.

He withdrew a shotgun from the cabinet. Rolling it over in his hands, he pumped the chamber and looked inside it—checking it was empty—before squeezing the trigger.

"You look like you know what you're doing," Charlotte said from the doorway, glancing at the front door as she spoke, biting her lip.

"I used to have one." He held the gun up to her. "Same as this, a Winchester 1300 Defender."

Warrington found a box of cartridges in the bottom of the cabinet, and inserted seven of them into the weapon. The others he slotted into a side-saddle attached to the stock, and the rest he stuffed into the pockets and pouches of his stab-vest.

"You can use that thing alright?" Charlotte asked as he walked back into the hallway.

"It's been a while," he replied, checking that the safety was on.

He flicked it off as Steven Johnson blundered through the front door with a groan.

His skin was gray, and his mouth dripped black-blood. A torn shirt revealed lacerations and bite wounds on his body, soaking his jeans in blood.

Charlotte covered her ears as Warrington fired.

The shot took Johnson in the hip and his body buckled. His lips curled as a moan bubbled in his throat. Despite the injury, he regained his footing and charged the policeman. Warrington set the

Winchester's stock against his shoulder, the shotgun already pumped.

The red shell ejected from the shotgun as the buckshot left the muzzle, striking Johnson's cheek, spraying the walls with blood, bone, and brain. The man fell to his knees, his eyes rolling as his jaw flapped down from one cheek.

Charlotte looked away as the next shot disintegrated the man's skull into pieces.

Policeman and secretary held their breath as they stared at the body.

"Can we get out of here now?" Charlotte asked, visibly shaking.

He nodded slowly. "I got a feeling this noise may bring on some others, anyway."

He was right.

They just had enough time to get into the Fiesta before two more walking corpses were hammering on their vehicle.

Warrington drove.

They arrived back at the police station, despite Charlotte's concerns over finding her boyfriend. Warrington told her that Drury may well have gone to the station to find her. Either there or the hospital.

"Fuck the hospital," she said.

A group of people were gathered by the station doors, all hurrying towards the vehicle as it pulled up.

Their voices mingled together as they shouted questions at the policeman. Thrusting the shotgun into the air he commanded their silence.

"Keep your noise down," he said, looking into several scared faces. "Please. It's important."

The crowd quieted as he saw Charlotte exit the car and survey the street around them.

"I know you're all here for answers," he said. "But I don't have any. The only advice I can give is that you return to your homes and barricade yourselves in until the Army arrives—"

"Are they coming?" a man carrying a cricket bat asked.

"They'll fucking have to," Warrington said.

"Can't we all shelter in there?" someone asked, and voices murmured their agreement.

"It's too small," he said, looking at Charlotte and then nodding at the building. She slipped around the car and started for the steps.

"It's better than anywhere else!" the man with the bat said, his voice wavering.

"Believe me," he said. "You'll be safer at home. The station is too small to hold us all comfortably. And we'd make too much noise."

"W-why shouldn't we make noise?" a lady asked, holding her young son. "Is it because of those … people?"

The voices of the crowd stopped, all eyes upon him.

Warrington took a deep breath. "Yes, because of them. There is something wrong with them … something … they have a virus—"

"What kind of virus?"

"Like the flu?"

"Ebola?"

"AIDS? Oh, God, is it AIDS?"

"Enough!" he snapped. "I don't know what it is, but I do know it's dangerous, contagious, and that you should all get off of the streets. Now!"

They dissipated around him, casting wide-eyed glares between their numbers. He could see some of them were injured, covered in cuts, grazes, and bite-marks.

"Wait," he said. "You must do your best to avoid being bitten—"

"I've been bit!" Cricket Bat said, tugging at his blood-soaked shirt.

A man held up an injured hand, and another spoke up about his injuries. Others joined them in revealing bite wounds.

Warrington's tone was steady as he spoke. "You all need to lock yourselves in your homes, away from other people." Questions filled the air once more, and he placated them by raising his voice. "Anyone bitten is infected and must be quarantined away from the others. Try and secure yourselves in a room until the Army arrives, and I'm sure their medics will be able to help." He caught Charlotte's eye and she looked away, nibbling at a nail.

The throng rained more queries at Warrington, but he brushed past them, telling them to go home. A woman grabbed his arm, pinching his skin as she harassed him with questions. He pulled free, turning to remonstrate with her, but he saw a man behind her fall to the ground, clutching a savaged upper-arm.

Shoving the woman aside, Warrington leveled the shotgun at the man as he rolled across the pavement to the bottom of the station steps.

"What the hell are you doing?" someone behind

him asked.

The man on the floor was still for a moment before his hands spasmed. The crowd went silent as they watched the man jerk his body on the pathway, before he slowly got to his feet. His face was lowered and Warrington could see blood slowly dripping onto the chest of his T-shirt.

The policeman pumped the shotgun.

A woman in the crowd screamed.

Charlotte backed away up the steps until the station doors pressed against her rump.

"Get back," Warrington said.

The man wobbled on his feet, his back facing Warrington. Charlotte stared down at him, and he up at her.

The man took a step towards the secretary as she thrust her hands into her pockets, searching for the key to the doors.

"Hey … HEY," the policeman yelled, but the man continued his clumsy ascent towards the woman.

Warrington moved, the muzzle of the shotgun inches from the back of the man's head. He called another warning and was ignored.

His finger applied pressure to the trigger

A cricket bat struck the barrel of the shotgun, pushing it downwards and causing Warrington to unleash a shot into the tarmac. He swore at the bat-wielding man, turning the gun on him for a moment.

"You can't shoot a man from behind!" Cricket Bat said, his body shaking.

The man who was now on the stairs growled, turning towards them at the sound of the shotgun and the arguing. His cheek carried lacerations which hinted at molars beneath them, and scratches stained his clothes with blood. A rip in his sodden shirt allowed broken ribs to protrude from the fabric.

Gasps exploded from the crowd.

"Can I shoot him from the front?" Warrington asked.

The man hissed, taking a step towards the policeman, who fired twice into him, the first striking the top of his skull, and the second severing his head from his body.

The people screamed and ran.

Warrington joined Charlotte at the top of the steps. She stared at the head that had rolled into the gutter, and Warrington pushed her through the station doors.

Charlotte turned to him. "You know by telling those people to lock themselves in, you're condemning them?"

"I know," he said, watching the people disperse before closing the blinds of the window.

"What about the families who lock themselves in with them?" she asked. "They'll all be attacked, bitten … infected."

"It's for the best," he answered quietly.

She sighed as she sat on the edge of a desk. "It's to contain the virus, isn't it?"

He said nothing.

"You're going to send people to die, to try and save the town," she said. "To save the island."

He looked at her, the moonlight haunting rings around his eyes, and turning the lines on his face into chasms

"I'd say my actions would condemn me to hell." He smiled wryly. "If we weren't already there."

Charlotte locked the windows and doors of the small building as Warrington pulled a dust-covered radio from a storage cupboard and began attaching wires and plugs to it. A low hum of static sounded when he turned it on, and a dial on a dull-yellow screen fluttered and then fell.

Charlotte sighed and slumped into a chair, her face buried in her hands.

"I know you're tired," he said, without looking at her. "But—"

"But nothing," she snapped, hands slapping her thighs. "I'm stuck here because you've kidnapped me." Her voice quieted. "And I don't even know where Aaron is because the fucking phones won't work."

"And it's my fault I didn't give you time off to go watch him?"

"Fucking right." She sank into the uncomfortable chair.

Warrington adjusted radios settings and put a thick set of headphones on.

Moments later Charlotte asked from behind closed eyes if he had found anything.

"Just a couple of guys in Newcastle talking about football."

She frowned. "That means people have no idea what's going on down here."

"It seems it hasn't spread to the mainland—yet."

Charlotte crossed her arms against the chilling

night and walked to a window that allowed lamplight to spill over her. The yellowness enveloped her and she closed her eyes. Warrington stared at her until she opened them.

He turned to the radio. "This is Hangshaw Police Sergeant John Warrington issuing a mayday to any military units out there." He released the trigger on the microphone. As he did so the lights and hum from the radio ceased, and the street lights outside flickered off.

"The whole street is out," Charlotte said, peering into the blackness outside.

Warrington unclipped a torch from his belt and used it to navigate his way to the back of the room. "I've got to turn the generator on."

"Are you fucking kidding me?" she asked as he shone the torch at her, before removing it from her green-eyed glare.

"We need that radio on," he said, snatching the shotgun and disappearing into the hallway leading to the station's two cells.

A small utility room housed the washing machine containing his bloody uniform from that morning, but without electricity, it was as inoperable as everything else in the station.

A door led outside, and he took a set of keys from a hook as he paused at the exit, ear pressed against the door.

Warrington cracked it open, hesitating as he waited for the exterior light to illuminate the car park. Then he remembered the reason he was going outside was because there was no power. He called himself a prick, pulled the door open wider, and shone his small torch across the asphalt, the small LED lights showing him nothing other than his old Vauxhall Vectra sitting in a corner since the beginning of the month when the battery had died.

He stepped out, his back sliding across the wall extending away from him. Using the keys from the hook, he opened a small fenced-off area and opened a shed with a petrol-powered generator sitting inside. Grabbing the pull-handle, he yanked it three times—swearing each time the engine failed to ignite—before it caught and fired into life with a rumble and splutter of fumes. The exterior light blazed behind him, and he saw a ghoul crossing the car park, almost upon him.

He swung the shotgun at its skull, swaying it, but not stopping it, and stomped his boot down on its knee, felling the creature.

Warrington pulled the shotgun above his head, to swing upon the beast, but more shadows stumbled across the tarmac towards him, the noise, and the lights.

Warrington returned to the station and locked the door behind him.

Charlotte had found another torch when he re-entered the office area. She shone it at him until he covered his eyes.

"Do NOT leave me here again," she said as he sat down at the radio.

Turning off his torch, the set illuminated his features with a pale orange light as he worked the dials back into life.

"Was there anyone out there?"

"Yeah," he said, and she sat down next to him, turning her own torch off.

Shuffling footsteps and groans seeped through the walls, and the secretary folded her arms across herself.

"Go and get a jacket from the supply cupboard," he said as she shivered.

She stared as shadows crossed the windows, moans penetrating the mesh-glass.

"Charlotte … go and get us both a jacket."

Her eyes found his, and she let out a low breath. "Sorry, sarge." She half-smiled. "It's been a long day." She got up and headed for the rear of the room.

A voice sparked from the radio, making him jump.

"… Frost of the Brit—"

The voice was lost in static and Warrington retuned the radio to search for a clearer signal.

"This is Sergeant Warrington of the Hangshaw Police requesting assistance," he said, and outside a groan responded.

"What's your position, sergeant, over?"

"We're in Hangshaw's police station on the Isle of Wight," said Warrington as he turned the radio volume down following a slap against the window before him. "We could really use some help."

The frosted glass shook as more hands beat against it.

"They're responding to my voice," he said.

Charlotte edged nearer the back of the office, away from the windows.

"We have units headed for the island, sergeant. As soon as—"

The voice stopped and Warrington moved to

retune the radio, but a new voice stopped him.

"Sergeant, this is General Sean Pegg. I have a few questions for you."

Warrington looked at the windows shaking in their frames.

"They're sounding the dinner bell," Charlotte said.

Warrington nodded and clicked the microphone. "Okay, general, but things are getting a little noisy on this end."

The doors to the station rattled as the cacophony grew. Charlotte put her hands to her ears, staring wide-eyed at the policeman. She backed into the thicker-walled and smaller-windowed holding-rooms.

"Do you know what is happening on the island?" the military man asked.

"Well," Warrington said, rubbing his temple and preparing his words. "I know there are dead people killing living people and making them dead people."

Pegg replied, but his voice was lost in the surrounding noise. Warrington asked him to repeat himself.

"Can you hear me?" General Pegg asked.

"I hear you," Warrington said, pressing his ear against the speaker of the equipment.

"We intercepted a call to St. Mary's Hospital confirming that a man had been attacked one mile east of Hangshaw," said the general. "Were you aware of this?"

"I was the officer who attended the incident." His brow furrowed. "But you know this. And why were you monitoring calls to hospitals?"

Pegg ignored him. "I need to know as much as you can tell me about what is happening on your island."

"How many other places are infected?"

Warrington asked, holding the microphone close to his lips. "Is it just Hangshaw? The whole Isle of Wight? Has it spread to Portsmouth or Southampton?"

"If you do not help me I shall end this transmission," the general said.

Warrington raised the microphone above his head, squeezing his fist around it as he grit his teeth. He cast a glance at the faces smeared against the station doors, and the hands slapping all around before taking a breath.

"What do you want to know?"

"There was an attack at the Simmonds's residence at approximately 6 AM," General Pegg said. "Were you aware of this?"

"How do you know this and I don't?" Warrington replied. "I was called out to George Purton's mill at 11 AM, where a young lad that worked there had killed Purton … who then killed my junior officer…." The words fell from numb lips.

"How wide is the area-of-effect, sergeant?"

"You don't sound surprised that the dead are attacking the living."

"How wide is the area-of-effect?"

"Far!" the policeman said. "Everyone alive on this island is in danger."

"Have you been bitten?" the military man asked.

"Ha!" But Warrington had not laughed down the line of communication. He ran a hand over his graying hair and sat back in his seat. The thumping on the windows matched a throbbing in his skull.

He pressed the microphone to his mouth. "No, I haven't been bitten. I'm locked inside the station with my secretary."

"We have units on the island," Pegg said. "We have

set up stations in locations which we will attempt to draw these people towards. The power to the island has been nullified, and floodlights are being mounted at strategic points."

"Like moths to a flame," Warrington said, and Pegg replied in the affirmative.

"When will this happen?"

"As soon as my men are in place."

"How many men do you have?"

"A few hundred, well-armed," Pegg answered.

"General," the policeman's brow furrowed, "are you sure that's enough? There are a lot of those things around and its spreading pretty damn fast."

"We're shutting this down, officer," he said, and Warrington could hear the patronizing pride in his tone.

A window shattered under a fist, contained only by its wire meshing. He stared at it before pulling the microphone trigger. "Send more men, General Pegg, 'cos you're gonna need them. And for fuck's sake, get us out of here!"

"Floodlights are on now," came the response, and a glow filtered past the bodies gathering outside, and in through the station windows.

The commotion stopped. He could hear feet shuffling as the groaning moved away.

Leaving his seat, hc padded towards the doors leading outside and peered through the frosted-glass. Shapes moved in the dark, and he could see spotlights blazing from nearby, possibly up on The Downs—a series of hills and natural conservation areas that overlooked a large section of the island's rolling hills and wide fields.

He drew the bolts, securing the doors.

"What the hell are you doing?" Charlotte hissed from behind him.

"The military is drawing them towards The Downs."

Charlotte pulled the oversize police jacket tighter. "How many do you think are out there?"

He hesitated before answering. "Too many."

Heels in hand, she took quiet steps towards him. "What's the Army going to do?"

Warrington stared at the kaleidoscope of white light through the starred window. "I'm guessing they're gonna lure them in and throw a lot of bullets at them."

"Think that will work?"

"I hope so," he said. "We need to get rid of those fucking things before they swarm all over the island."

"John," she said, placing a hand on his arm. "A lot of those fucking things were our friends … people we know."

He looked at her hand on his arm. It was an unexpected move coming from someone who was usually so cold and calculated. Her blue eyes blazed at him in the dark, more powerful than any floodlight outside.

"We can't think of them like that anymore," he said. "It's bad enough knowing that there are families turning on each other out there." He shook his head and rubbed at his eyes.

"My boyfriend is still out there."

He nodded. "He's a tough kid, Lewis. He'll be fine."

Gunfire began to echo from the hills.

CHAPTER TWO

Aaron Drury stared at the empty signal bar on his mobile phone before throwing it onto the empty seat beside him. The other youths on the coach had similar problems and were unable to reach family or loved ones.

"What the hell is going on?" asked one of the younger boxers, tapping the screen on his own phone.

Drury's attention was caught as yet another ROAD CLOSED sign flashed past on a side street.

"Alright, can it!" Chris Ettritch—the head trainer—bellowed. He sat behind the coach driver, his large bulk twisting as his once muscular neck strained to allow his throbbing, red face to bark at them. "The phone companies are obviously down at the moment. I'm sure everything is fine, and you'll be tucked up in bed with your mummies soon enough."

"Are the closed roads anything to do with the phone signal?" Drury asked.

No answer.

Ettritch struggled from his seat, one meaty hand holding onto a ceiling bar and the other grasping a beer. He surveyed the young faces before him. Less than three hours ago, they had left South London after four of them had taken part in a boxing tournament. Three of them had lost, and only Drury had won. The majority of coach passengers cradled beers of defeat. Drury sat alone on the backseat, drinking water and rubbing a cold iron underneath one eye. It had been the only punch his opponent had landed before being knocked out in the first round.

They had boarded the ferry back to Yarmouth and were traveling on one of the island's winding country roads on their return to Hangshaw Boxing Club. The roads had been strangely bare, even this late at night, and numerous country lanes had barriers set across them. The driver had tried to tune the radio in, but all they received was static, and nobody's mobile phones worked. The faces on the bus were downturned, eyes looking either to their trainer, or staring out into the night.

Ettritch had to revive their spirits, and he did so in the best way he knew how.

Beer.

Singing at the top of his voice, he shook his can and sprayed it all over the fighters around him, and soon the coach was awash with alcohol and out-of-tune young men waxing lyrical about each other's mothers.

Ettritch sat down, a smile spreading across his face as he took a long draw from his can.

Aaron Drury unpeeled himself from the embrace of two of the other fighters and glanced again at his useless mobile phone, stuffing it back into his pocket he headed towards the front of the vehicle.

He thought of Charlotte, and about getting home to her. He had not seen her for three days, an eternity in young love's terms. It was the longest they had been apart in their three years of seeing each other, and to have their only means of communication taken away gnawed at him.

"Gaffer," he said, wiping the beer of spraying cans from his face as he approached Ettritch.

"Ah, Mr. Drury," his mentor said. "What can I do for you?"

"I just wondered if you'd heard anything yet," he said, indicating the vehicle's radio.

Large jowls swung as the fat head shook. "Nothing as yet, but we'll be back in Hangshaw soon."

"Mind if I try?" Drury asked.

"Knock yourself out," the driver answered, smiling at his own wit.

Drury leaned forward, pressing buttons on the radio as he peered at the dimly-illuminated screen. Cycling through FM and AM settings, he found nothing but static.

"Maybe we should stop and find a phone-box," he said, but was then pitched against the dashboard of the coach as the vehicle braked heavily, wobbling out of control. Smacking his forehead, he managed to get hold of the dash as beer cans rolled along the floor, gathering beneath him as the other youths swore as the wheels of the coach screeched for purchase on the road.

The driver wrenched the steering wheel as thuds emanated from the front of the coach. A cold sweat washed over Drury as he realized that they were driving through a group of people.

The vehicle twisted sharply away from the road, the nearside front wheel hitting an embankment hard. It traveled up the grassy slope before its speed and angle caused it to pitch over, its side smashing into the tarmac in a collision of glass and grinding metal.

Sparks sprayed the darkness as the coach tore through more bystanders. The boxers on board were thrown into each other, falling between seats or out of broken windows.

The vehicle screamed to a halt beneath canopying trees, the following silence unnatural.

Smoke rose from the debris as the sound of glass grinding beneath bodies begun to move.

One of the younger fighters clambered over seats and Drury's unconscious form as he sought an exit from the coach. He tried not to stare at those of his colleagues who lay in twisted and unnatural angles, and managed to fall through the shattered windscreen before vomiting.

His legs buckled as he stumbled away from the crash. The moonlight showed his hands covered in blood, and he wiped them on his jeans. Looking down at his legs caused blood to fall from his face, and he pressed fingers against a wound on his forehead. Shock and numbness from the crash dulled his mind, and it took seconds for him to realize what he held in his fingers was a piece of flesh dangling from his skull. He pushed it back into place and held it there, falling onto his backside as he did so.

Crunching glass made him turn his head, releasing more blood into his eye. He pressed his fingers tighter against his forehead.

A man approached him, tripping over a headrest from the coach. He stumbled towards the youth, and a moan issued from his lips. The youngster held a hand out towards him, asking for help from the man in the dark blue overalls. A mechanic? the youth assumed as they reached touching distance. He could see the man through a haze of pain, blood, and shock, and saw that the mechanic was in a worse state than himself. He was also covered in blood. Had he been hit by the coach? And where was his left arm?

The youngster fell back as the mechanic knelt beside him, the stench of his breath overpowering. With his one hand, the mechanic grabbed the flap of skin from the younger man's head and ripped it away. The boxer gasped in surprise, before the pain took him and his eyes fluttered shut.

The young man was out before the mechanic stuffed the bloodied skin into his mouth. He chewed at it, staring at the youth laid out before him, before taking the boxer's head in his hand and grinding his teeth against bare skull as he lapped at the blood still pouring from the wound.

Others shuffled towards the wreckage, the cries of the injured bringing them from all directions. Along the road and through the fields they came, the number of them growing as the survivors of the crash stirred and called for help.

The first to emerge from the crash were attacked by walking corpses. Their screams alerted those inside the bus, and panic spread. The moans of the dead grew, and the two noises combined in a horrifying melody.

The boxers were all young, fit, and healthy, but dazed and shaken. Some of them fought their way from the bus, while the others trapped inside called out in panic at the sounds of struggle outside.

Drury pushed the body of Ettritch off of him, the old man's head hanging down against his chest as blood gushed from a thick neck wound. The driver was beneath him, his body snapped in two, the upper half hidden beneath the side of the coach against the road.

His friends were crawling out of the main window before him and he called out to them. An ache in his head forced his eyes and mouth shut, and he could hear the cries of the trapped and injured within the coach. He called out to them, telling them he would get help, but his words rung inside his skull like a church bell.

Hands grabbed him under the armpits and hauled him up and out through the open windscreen. "Get the fuck out of here, now!" said a voice.

He staggered onto the road, crunching broken glass under his hands and knees as he fell. He looked up as a girl his age approached, her bottom lip and chin hanging on her chest, her lower teeth gleaming under the moon's rays.

She thrust her hands towards him as blood flowed from her wound and down her naked breasts, one marred with teeth marks.

"Fuck," he said, forcing the fog from his mind. He touched the lump on his head and the pain helped him focus.

The girl grabbed him, fingers digging deep into his collarbone as she gnashed her teeth.

He thrust her away, using his heavier weight to propel her to the ground next to him. She sat stunned, before snapping her teeth at him.

He looked at the girl in the torn floral dress. Black irises hid behind a milky glaze, and her once dark skin was the color of out-of-date chocolate. The thought struck that she would have been beautiful if she had not been dead.

She's dead? he asked himself before wondering how he knew that. She was moving and looking at him with wide eyes, yet she had tried to bite him. But her skin was pale, and blood covered her in torrents. She should not be alive.

Yet she moved for him again, Drury scuttling back from her reach.

Beyond her, he saw figures everywhere in the darkness, moaning as they moved towards the crash. Some of them shuffled, some of them crawled, and some of them were already climbing into the coach, and screams grew from within.

He turned towards the stricken vehicle as he rose to his feet, but a hand grabbed his shoulder and spun him round. Raising his fists, he half-expected to see the girl again, but this time he was locking eyes with one of his fellow fighters. "Ballard," he sighed, before lowering his hands.

The red-headed man grabbed Drury's bloodied shirt. "We've got to get out of here." He pulled at him as he saw Drury look over his shoulder. "Don't go back in the coach."

"But—"

"I mean it," Ballard said. "They're lost and we are on our own right now."

"But—"

"Say but again and I'll leave you here."

Drury's stomach fell, but it helped eclipse the pain in his head. He allowed Ballard to lead him away from the cries of their friends.

"What happened?" he asked as the two gathered with a small group of the other fighters, all open-mouthed at the scene of the crash.

"I was hoping you'd tell us," said Ballard, helping a sobbing lad to his feet. "Weren't you up front?"

Drury frowned as he thought and again pain encased his head. He rubbed his hands down his face, pulling his eyes wide. "Yeah," he said. "I think we drove through some people and then crashed."

"What the fuck are those people doing?" the crying teenager pointed at the coach with a hand that shook. "Why were they biting us?"

Ballard pulled his T-shirt off and wrapped it around the sobbing youth's bleeding hand. "I don't know," he said as he tied it off. "There's something wrong with them."

"They were all biting people?" Drury asked.

Several of them nodded and begun telling of incidents that they had witnessed in the coach, ranging from small children attacking the boxers, to badly wounded people, such as the girl who had attacked Drury, biting those inside.

"They all looked like they'd been attacked somewhere before," one of the more heavily built fighters said, taking steps away from the carnage. "You can't talk sense into them. They don't listen. They just attack. They're like zombies, mate... in fact, they are zombies. It's the only thing they can be."

His words sank into the group. As ridiculous as he sounded, there was no other explanation.

They took nervous steps behind the heavy-set man who had spoken his zombie-theory, eager to get away from the yells for help outside.

"We can't leave them," Drury said.

Ballard. "We will leave you."

Screams sounded through the night, all coming from within a coach that lay on its side like a dying animal. Drury looked at it, feeling his feet wanting to take him towards it, but Ballard slapped him on the arm and shook his head. The red-head jogged away, Drury falling into step behind him, still gazing at the wreckage over his shoulder.

Soon, he was lagging behind, the lump on his head pulsing, causing him to close his eyes and stumble blindly onward. Despite his fitness, he could not seem to match the slow pace the others had set. He felt Ballard slip under his arm and hold him up, supporting his weight as he helped him increase speed.

"Just leave him!" a voice cried ahead of the heavyweight fighter, putting distance between himself and the group.

Ballard raised his own voice. "We could have gotten more of us out of there. I didn't see you busting a lung to save any lives."

"Those things were fucking eating us," the man said, and somewhere in Drury's foggy mind he recalled the man's name as Yarranton, one of the older, more argumentative fighters.

"C'mon," said Ballard. "Yarro might be a dick, but he's right. People died back there and we were next."

They continued, Drury fighting to stay conscious as Ballard took most of his weight.

A cry of They're coming and a slap from the other man snapped him to attention. He winced and took his arm from Ballard's grip.

"Don't let go," the other man said, but Drury held up a hand to stop him.

"I'm not concussed," he said. "I'm just dazed. Let me clear my head."

Ballard slapped him again.

Drury blinked. "Better."

Ballard grabbed his shirt collar and pulled him away from the growing moans.

The sounds of those trapped inside the wreckage or being attacked echoed through the night. The moon lit their only means of escape—a back road that split from the carriageway.

Several of the party were injured, one so badly two of his companions made a seat with their interlocked fingers and carried him.

"There's a cafe down the road," someone panted ahead of them. "We can hole-up there."

The group followed his lead without a word.

They rushed for several hundred yards, the outline of a building appearing in the dark. A dusty car-park contained a solitary vehicle, and lights flickered from between blinds over the windows. Drury looked up and found the street-light above was out. He guessed that the dim glow in the building was from candles.

His head ached, but his vision was clearing, and Ballard did not need to support him as much, although he continued to jog by his side.

Drury looked over his shoulder and could see several figures in pursuit. The moon was not strong enough to reveal their details, but their moans gave their identities away, and they were keeping pace with the boxers.

Yarranton reached the door of the one-story building, rattling it with force when he discovered it was locked. He beat his palms on the window, and was joined by a colleague, and then another.

Drury could see a man with rolled-up shirtsleeves standing on the other side of the doorway, a long metal fire-lighter in one hand, as he issued expletives that Drury could easily decipher.

"Let us in!" Yarranton shouted.

Drury pushed past him and pressed his face against the window. "Sir," he said. "There's been an accident and we need help."

The man in the checkered-chef's trousers rubbed his free hand on a tea-towel, looking them up and down.

Slowly he stepped forward and unlocked the door. The men pressed through, barreling past him. He grabbed one of the youths by the shirt. "What the fuck do you think you're doing?" he asked, jabbing the fire-lighter at him.

Ballard shut the door behind the last man, and Drury flicked the latches to lock it before turning towards the chef. "Mister," he said. "Where's the key to the door?"

"Get out!"

The first of the dead shattered the glass behind Ballard. The mesh in the window pane held it together and prevented the red-haired man from falling into their clutches, but the cook could see the bleeding and dead faces through the starred glass.

Drury leaned his weight against the door with Ballard. "Lock the fucking door!"

More bodies hit the door and windows. Hands and fists hammered around them, and one of the younger fighters hid under a table. The cook paused before pulling a key from his pocket and locking the door behind Drury and Ballard.

He turned to a waitress hiding behind the counter,

her shaking hands covering her mouth. "Daisy," he said to the dark-haired girl. "Go lock the back door." He had to repeat himself before she scurried away.

The cook turned back towards the gathering of battered men, the small flame in his hand dancing erratically. "Now what the hell is going on?" he asked. "The electric and phones are down and I want to get out of here." He looked at the shadows behind the blinds.

"People are getting eaten," Yarranton said, slumping into the seat furthest from the door. "By the living dead. By zombies." He laughed at his own words, looking around at the group. "Isn't that fucking ridiculous?"

The cook stared at him before setting his gaze on Drury. "What is this bullshit?"

Drury glanced at the door as he moved away from it. "I wish I could tell you."

"I just fucking did," said Yarranton, banging a fist on the table, knocking over a salt shaker. "Those things out there aren't alive and just ate half of our fucking friends!"

The cook glared at Yarranton, shaking his head before turning back to Drury. "Tell me nice and simple," he said as the glass around the diner rattled. "Just what the hell is going on." He turned to a couple of the fighters who were still on their feet. "And you boys, go round and close the blinds. Looks like your friends out there are a little over excited about you being in here."

The youths did as instructed, and Drury told him as much of the crash as he could remember, as well as the attack upon them, the men filling in other details. The story sounded ridiculous coming out of his mouth and he understood why Yarranton had scoffed at himself.

"Were those people on your bus?" the cook asked.

"No."

"Then why is that kid wearing the same shirt as the rest of you?"

Drury looked out of the door and saw a man pounding on the glass among the others. Scratches covered his shaved head and face, soaking the orange and white Hangshaw Boxing Club T-shirt he wore.

"That's Danny Partridge," said a teenager with intricate patterns cut into his hair. He moved for the door. "Let him in!"

Drury put himself between the youth and the exit, placing a hand on his chest. "Look at him."

They stared at the man who was once Daniel Partridge. The wound on his neck would have been enough to kill him, but they could see he also had fingers missing, and bite marks on his bare forearms. Drury knew Partridge had been sat a couple of rows in front of him on the team coach, and had seen the man fit, healthy, and … alive. Now, at the door before them, was a raging monster, a man with sallow, pale skin, and teeth snapping so hard they looked like they might shatter.

Drury pulled the final blind down over the door. The chef released the trigger of the fire-lighter and washed them all in black.

"What is he?" he asked. "What are they?"

"They're dead," said Ballard.

The cook ran a hand over his graying stubble. He turned as the waitress emerged from the backroom, peering into the gloom at him. "All locked up?"

Daisy nodded, barely perceptible in the dark.

Drury thought he could see her body trembling despite the gloom.

"Okay." The chef turned again to Drury and raised his voice above the commotion that surrounded them. "I think we need to get out of here."

Drury looked at the scattered people in the cafe. They were slumped in seats and staring at silhouettes behind the blinds. Those outside banged their hands upon the glass in an unholy jam; the percussion that beat resounded among those inside, fraying nerves and widening eyes. Several of those inside were injured, especially the man who had been carried in. He lay unconscious on the floor, blood seeping from the bite in his leg into the groves between the black and white tiling like deathly garden snakes. The youngster who crawled under the table hid with his hands over his ears, rocking on his haunches.

"Unless you've got a mini-bus parked out back, we're gonna struggle," Drury said.

"I've got a pickup," the chef said, jerking his thumb towards an alcove leading from the cafe itself to the kitchen. "She's old and rusty, but we can load a few of you in." He paused. "She makes a fair bit of noise, too."

"And will bring unwanted attention," Drury said, looking at the cafe door. "We'll have to move fast."

"What's sound got to do with it?" asked Yarranton, rising from his seat. "They're just brain-dead fucks. All they do is bite people."

"The sound of a coach crashing seemed to draw them out," said Ballard, looking at Yarranton. The larger man bit his lip, looking away and prying some blinds open with his fingers. A hand slapping the window snapped him away.

"What about the injured guys," asked Drury, looking down at the young man on the floor. His skin was gray and his breathing shallow as the bite wound on his calf leaked blood onto the floor. Other scratches and wounds covered his exposed wrists and forearms.

"The site of skin, or flesh, seems to drive them into a frenzy," Drury said, bending down to examine the man's injuries. He watched as the man's eyes rolled back into his head, hands clutching at his chest as his body spasmed.

"Those that are hurt can get in my truck," the chef said. "We could put that lad in the back, and a couple of the others as well, but it will be a squeeze. Daisy and I will ride up front." The waitress stood closer to him and he touched her arm. "Her old man would be pissed if I didn't get her home soon."

"Okay," said Drury, who then pointed at the injured boxer. "Let's get him up and out of here. Any of you others with bad injuries can jump in the pickup."

"What?" spat Yarranton, stepping towards the man on the floor, defying anyone to approach and aid him. "What about the rest of us? Are we gonna stay here and cook some fucking dinner? We are dinner!"

"We're going to run for it," said Drury. "Hangshaw isn't too far away. We can cut across the fields."

"It's dark," said Ballard.

Drury nodded. "And we'll use that to our advantage. The roads are too risky. We need to get back to our families."

"My family lives in Newport," said one of the boxers.

"Can you make your own way?" he asked, the

pressure of decision-making beginning to press on him. "None of us live that way. You'd be going it alone."

The man met his gaze and nodded. "You guys do what you gotta do, but I gotta get home to my kids. I might even be less of a target alone." He managed a weak smile.

"Who the hell died and made you boss, anyway?" Yarranton said, spittle flying from his lips as he aimed a finger at Drury.

"Chris Ettritch," Drury answered without missing a beat. He stepped towards the cook. "You better have your car keys ready and that back door clear for when we come through."

The cook nodded, squeezing the keys in his sweating palm.

"Okay, lads," Drury said, clapping his hands together and talking to them as if he were about to conduct a regular training session. "Let's get up and get moving. This is now your fucking boot-camp. Get him up off the floor, and anyone else too injured to run to be ready, as you're getting a ride out of here. You others"—his eyes met Yarranton's—"will be making a run for it. If we get separated, don't look for each other. Keep moving. Once this is over we can meet at The Crown and talk about it over beers. You all set?"

The group slowly got to its feet, but Drury's words had effect. Chins no longer sat on chests, and they looked each other in the eye, or slapped hands, bumped fists, whatever it took to show that they were ready.

"Wait a fucking minute," it was Yarranton again, bending down at the injured man's side and lifting a coat that covered his wounded leg. Even in the low light, Drury could see the bite wound and the flesh hanging from the calf.

But it no longer bled, and the flesh around it seemed black, even in the darkness.

"He's as good as dead," said Yarranton. "You should let one of us in the truck, someone that has a chance of living."

"And I guess you are offering to fill that spot?" said Drury.

Yarranton rose to his feet, meeting Drury's gaze with his own. "Fucking right. I don't wanna run through the fields like a fucking deer."

Drury pointed at Richmond on the floor. "He goes. You run."

He stepped past Yarranton, their shoulders kissing each other. Drury entered the kitchen where the chef had indicated, and waited until his eyes adjusted to the gloom. It was a small area, and a door, presumably leading out the back, was a few feet away. He turned towards the dining area once more, and his elbow nudged a rolling pin on a cutting board. It began to roll, and he caught it. Bouncing it into the palm of his other hand he felt the secureness of its weight in his hand as he swung it through the air.

A scream from the dining room made him rush back in. The once injured and dying man on the tiled floor had crawled towards the youth hiding beneath the table. Drury could see his fingers digging into the youth's neck so fiercely they had pierced the skin and blood was flowing from the wounds.

The man who should have been dead sank his teeth into the cowering youth's neck, scissoring his head back and forth like a dog with a toy, tearing flesh away before snapping his teeth back into the pumping wound.

The youth's cries turned to a gargle and his body became limp in the dead man's grasp.

Two of the men grappled with the attacker, pulling him away. Dark scarlet washed over them, and one of them slipped on the blood-splattered tiles.

Drury stepped forward and smashed the rolling pin down on the man's skull with a thwack. The dead man fell onto his back, hands flailing before coming to a jittering rest at his side.

No one spoke, open mouths adorning those assembled, distracting them from the growing furor outside.

"Why did no one help him?" asked Drury, pointing at the dead youth under the table.

"No one saw until it was too late," said Ballard. "He must have crawled to him when we were all looking out the windows."

The man with the fractured skull via the rolling pin sat up, everyone recoiling. He wobbled as he pushed himself up.

Drury struck him with the kitchen utensil again. And again. The thin skull-bone cracked and caved as the boxer bludgeoned him to a permanent death. He struck it one final time, the head cracking and spilling its contents on the tiled floor.

"What the fuck?" Yarranton's face was pale, his hand over his mouth.

Drury stepped back, slipping in blood before righting himself. "He wasn't human anymore," he said, dropping the rolling pin. It clattered on the floor and rolled towards the mess he had made.

"He was alive when we brought him in here," said Yarranton, the whites of his eyes stabbing at Drury. "You just murdered him."

"Fuck off, Yarranton," Drury said. "You could see he wasn't normal. He bit the other kid. I'm shocked you're not thankful it wasn't you."

He had taken a step towards Yarranton and kicked the rolling pin with his toe. It skittered across the floor, leaving surreal crimson butterflies that glistened in the moonlight. Drury watched as it stopped at the foot of the table Yarranton sat behind, and the realization of what he had done suddenly swamped him. He closed his eyes, taking long breathes into his nose and out of his mouth. He could hear the figures moving behind the blinds, with hands slapping the glass behind Yarranton as they responded to his voice. He looked at the doorway, a shadow moving behind the slats that covered it. He wondered if it was still his friend, Daniel Partridge. He wondered if the thing that he had become knew Drury, and if it recalled training with him over the last few years, sparring with each other and embarking on team-building exercises, or if it remembered occasional nights out on the town, or setting him up with a beautiful blonde who turned out to boil rabbits in her waking hours.

The thought led him to Charlotte, and inside his chest he ached.

He had to get to her. He needed to know if she was safe, but he was not going to do that while locked in a cafe surrounded by … the dead? The living dead? Zombies? It was bizarre.

Well suck it up, his mind told him, because it's happened. Right in front of your baby blues.

"Sir," he said, turning to the chef whose drained face was visible in the dark. He looked like a ghoul in checkered trousers. "I'm going to cause a distraction, and you're gonna get that motor started."

The chef opened his mouth to speak, but said nothing. Instead, he nodded, turned on his heel, and disappeared into the kitchen. Drury checked the boxing club members that were too injured for a sustained run, and sent them after the chef. Some shook his hand, while some wished him luck.

"The rest of you get in that kitchen and be ready to run," Drury said, ignoring Yarranton's scowl.

He waited until the room was clear, or as clear as possible, with a couple of fighters standing in the doorway as the kitchen was crammed with people. Ballard remained with him, giving him a single nod that he was ready.

He steadied himself, breathing quickly before flicking the blind that covered the door. It snapped to the top, its rattlesnake-noise bouncing off the shattered window. At the sound and sight of him, the undead lunged, breaking the glass more, the mesh wiring bulging inward.

Ballard raised the blind on the next window and received the same reaction, the room filling with moans and shards of glass falling in under dead hands.

"Go," Drury said.

The backroom was unlit, but the back door was open and the moon guided them. A rusty red pickup truck sat full of bleeding and battered men.

The cook gunned the engine and it exploded into action with a loud cough and a cloud of smoke. Inching forward, the vehicle screamed and then stalled. The waitress sitting up front with him stifled her own shriek into her balled-up apron.

"Push!" Drury hissed, trying to be discrete, despite the back-firing truck. He leaned against the back panel of the pickup as Ballard and the others joined him.

Yarranton stared at them, inching his way across the car park.

The pickup gained speed, the chef tried the ignition and accelerator, the engine turned over, the truck lurched, and the young men were left in another cloud of black smoke.

"Jesus," coughed Ballard, as the vehicle screeched out of the car park. "You think that thing will make it?"

Drury hoped so as he led them after the route Yarranton had taken. He stood on the other side of a thin wire fence, and Drury glared at him as he passed. He did not want to reprimand him. He felt he was going to need every breath he could muster as he heard the footsteps of the zombies slapping against the gravel behind him.

CHAPTER THREE

"I give up," said Charlotte as she put her mobile phone back in her blouse pocket. She stood with one hand on her hip, lips pursed, frown lines marring her forehead as they stepped out from the safety of the police station.

Warrington looked around, hands gripping the shotgun as they descended the steps onto the street below. The dead who had surrounded them earlier had dispersed, wandering towards the light and noises flowing from The Downs: the high set of hills overlooking Hangshaw and the vast acres of farmland adorning the Isle of Wight.

General Pegg had been true to his word. His tactics seemed to be drawing the dead towards the floodlight the military had erected. Warrington could see it shining like a fake sun, its beams lost among the thick trees on the side of a hill. It glowed into the night sky, and gave weak illumination to everything around them. All the power in the town had now been switched off, and all that lit their world was the moon and the floodlight.

Gunfire echoed across the land towards them.

"I wonder if these things are all over the island,"

Warrington muttered to himself.

"What?" Charlotte was peering down the darkened road behind them.

"I wonder if it's only Hangshaw infected."

"Maybe they're going through each town and village, one by one," she said. "You can see The Downs from places like Sandown and Brading. Maybe Hangshaw is the most affected area." She paused. "Of course, it's the most infected area. We're in the middle of it."

"Maybe it is," he said, looking back at the hills and counting the shots. There were many.

A zombie tripped over a green waste bin nearby, drawn to their voices. It righted itself and then headed for them at an awkward run, an excited moan growing as it neared them. Warrington bounced the shotgun in his hands before handing it to Charlotte. Pulling a set of brass knuckles from his pocket he slipped them over his right-hand fingers, advancing on the creature as it approached them.

His punch shattered the thing's cheek, the sound causing Charlotte to wince. She had seen her boyfriend punch (and be punched) enough times in sparring and actual fights, but the raw ferocity that Warrington displayed unnerved her. He looked like he genuinely wanted to do more than kill the dead thing.

The dead man, dressed in a sharp suit, buckled under the second punch, its jaw hanging limp as it dropped to one knee. Warrington struck it again, hard, and its hands met the road beneath it. The policeman stood over it; an executioner in a uniform, pulling his knuckle-dustered hand behind him so far Charlotte thought he might fall backward.

The punch he delivered embedded the handheld

weapon into the ghoul's skull, crashing the beast to the ground, slipping Warrington to his knees. From this position, he pounded at its head until it was a dark smear on the blacktop.

Charlotte could hear Warrington's heavy breath over the gunshots in the hills as he stood up and stepped away, pausing before he walked back to her, reaching out for the shotgun.

"You feel better?" she asked, handing it to him absently as she stared at the dead-dead man.

Warrington wiped the knuckles on his trousers. "Yeah," he said in a low tone. "I do. I just didn't want to use the gun in case it bought us unwanted attention. Our voices seem to be doing enough of that."

She looked down at the brains and blood sprayed out on the tarmac.

"No, we wouldn't want that."

They moved out, Charlotte having changed her heels for a pair of old trainers kept at work for whenever she felt the urge to jog home, which wasn't often. She now trod lightly, but Warrington's steel toe-caps echoed a thud with every footfall, so they took to running across house lawns.

They passed solitary zombies, and small groups of them, all moaning and heading towards the hills. Warrington noted that they were not moving as fast as the suited man he had just destroyed.

"I think they're heading for the light out of curiosity," he said to Charlotte as they hid behind a car. "When that guy saw us just now, he couldn't move fast enough. They're clearly drawn by hunger."

"Or rage," Charlotte said. "They always look so fucking angry."

They peered through the car's windows at the

straggling mob bumping into each other along the street, faces tilted up towards the burst of white between the trees.

"There are a lot more of these things than I thought," he whispered, counting over ten in the group. "Could this disease have spread that quickly?"

"Looks like a lot of people were attacked and turned," she said. Her hand clutched his shoulder as one of the undead passed within feet of them. "Oh, Jesus, isn't that—"

He nodded. "Yeah, Richard Robillard, from the snooker hall."

They watched as the creature shuffled past, head tilted back so its milky eyes looked up at The Downs. It was so intent on the attraction it kept walking into cars and tripping over curbs. As it clambered to its feet for a third time, they could see the glint of bare cheekbone and stains all over its once white-and-black Robillard's Pool Palace T-shirt.

"He was definitely bitten and turned," said Warrington.

"I went out with him in high school." She shivered as they watched him disappear around a corner. "Have—" She cleared her throat. "Have you seen many other people you know?"

He looked her in the eye, sinking down to sit on his haunches. "Yeah," he said. "A few. You?"

"Too many." She nodded, her eyes staring at nothing in the gloom.

"I think we should get to the mayor's house," he said, almost tipping her chin with his finger. He needed her to stay focused.

"Why?"

"Because he's higher up the social ladder than I

am, and the military might be at his house to save him," said Warrington. "And right now I'd love to be somewhere surrounded by a big iron fence and potentially stationed by lots of men armed with big fucking guns."

She nodded. "And it isn't far from here, either."

Gunshots sang nearby, making them flinch. After the sneaking through gardens and trying to be quiet, loud noises close-by were a shock to a frayed system.

"The Army?" asked Charlotte as Warrington pulled her closer to the vehicle.

"I don't think so," he said. "That doesn't sound like it came from The Downs."

"Should we go look?" Even in the gloom, she could see the intensity in his eyes.

"No," he said. "Those shots won't be drawing just us in." He began to crawl along the side of the house.

"But what if it's a young kid?" she asked. "Or a mother trying to protect her children?"

He looked at her. "Don't lay a guilt-trip on me. I know I'm the police and it's my job to protect the people, but right now Hangshaw is falling to pieces, and I can't save everyone. There must be hundreds or thousands of people on the island fighting for their lives right now, and we can't help all of them."

She opened her mouth to protest when a group of undead stumbled into view behind them. One of them turned, its head tilted upward as if sniffing the air as another gunshot sounded from nearby. It turned towards them, Charlotte holding her breath as Warrington tried to bury himself into the bricks of the house, before a man's shout drew its attention in the opposite direction.

Warrington pulled her away from the dispersing

group.

Warrington led her through places that the moon could not touch, one hand on the haft of the Winchester shotgun, with the other tightly holding her hand. She tried to pull away at first, but eventually succumbed. Charlotte knew he was trying to protect her, even though she was more than capable of looking after herself … although she was glad that he was with her … and toting a pump-action shotgun.

He led her through streets and back alleys, cutting through gardens behind people's homes. The night had gradually grown cloudy, and a breeze danced through the leaves as a light rain began to fall. The floodlights higher up on The Downs beamed hazily through the rain, and flashes of rifle-fire lit the hills in small pockets.

They paused at a junction where they bizarrely waited until the traffic lights turned green before jogging on. They passed a sign reading BULLEN ROAD and followed a long, straight lane fenced by tall trees with an occasional house set down a long drive. The buildings were large and/or eccentric, and several were segregated from the road by wrought-iron gates. Many of the gates were open, the owners having fled Hangshaw sometime during the terrors of the day.

Warrington and Charlotte flitted between the trees as they made their way to the iron gates that separated

Mayor Parsons' abode from the common citizens of Hangshaw. His gate was more extravagant than his neighbors', black bars with gold-painted tips, and swirls of iron formed the initials AP in the center of the closed half. The other side of the gating was open.

Warrington wrinkled his nose.

He checked the ammunition in the shotgun and Charlotte rubbed the feeling back into her fingers, now free from Warrington's over-bearing grip. She stepped towards the gates, looking inside. Compared to other homes on the island, it was a mansion, an old Victorian building converted over the years to modern standards—complete with pillars on either side of the front doors—and the white-top of a tennis fence appeared ghost-like above the almost-black sprawl of grass before them. A Mercedes sat outside the door and pillars, its nearly-new paint-job shimmering in the rain-flecked moonlight.

"This doesn't look good," said Charlotte, pointing at the open door of the manor as Warrington fixed shells into the shotgun.

Stepping inside the building bought back memories of entering the Purton household. That event had been less than a day ago, but felt like an age away.

Smashed furniture littered the hallway. A picture lay on the floor, gazing forlornly at the space on the wall it had once occupied. A bloodied footprint sat square in its center, trampling an old sailing schooner beneath. Something else obscured the brushstrokes of the artwork, and Warrington saw that it was a finger. He hoped Charlotte had not seen it yet.

"Gross."

She had.

"I think you should wait outside," he said to her.

"I think you should fuck off," she said to him.

Stepping lightly, they moved further into the house. Mayor Aaron Parsons was sat on an extravagant rug in his lounge, pulling innards and entrails from his dead wife's stomach.

Warrington pushed Charlotte away from the scene as she covered her mouth and swore. His feet betrayed him, and he was forced to watch as the thing that had been the mayor devoured its own wife. The policeman had spent an afternoon with them less than a fortnight ago, and had eaten with them at a school fete. His head swam at the thought, and he closed his eyes, concentrating on the sounds his shaking breaths made, trying to use them to block out the slobbering sound of Parsons eating out his wife.

Eating out? Ha.

Mayor Parsons scooped a handful of guts from his wife and pressed it against his mouth. Red stained his whole face, and his eyes were glued together with blood. Parsons chewed noisily for a moment, wrinkling his nose and tilting his head, as if in great thought, before dropping his mouth open and letting his meal slip from his maw.

Mrs. Parsons opened her eyes, moaned, and managed to sit up after a couple of failed attempts.

"That's why they don't eat each other," Warrington said over his shoulder to Charlotte. "They don't want dead flesh."

Mayor Parsons hissed at them, now that his dinner had gone cold. He moved to stand and Warrington sat him down with the shotgun. He used a second shell on Mrs. Parsons, severing her head from her neck and making her fall across her husband.

The lounge was a mess, with Warrington turning

and pushing the secretary out into the hallway.

"John," she said. "I see no guns, no Army, and no young muscled men to save us."

A zombie emerged from a kitchen further along the hall, groaning and heading for them.

The blast from the shotgun was deafening in a more enclosed space than the lounge, Charlotte clasping her hands to her shocked ears as Warrington blinked the muzzle-fire from his eyes.

The dead reacted better than they did, and seemed to pour from every open door that fed into the hallway.

Warrington shot the legs out from under one of the nearer, faster creatures, dropping it and causing the others in its wake to trip and fall. Warrington used the break to their advantage, pushing Charlotte towards the front door of the building.

A woman tumbled down the stairs as they hurried through the hallway, the sound of breaking bones sounding like a child's fire-crackers. Warrington hesitated as the woman rolled to a stop before him at the bottom of the staircase. He wanted to see if she was alive or dead, but when she got to her feet, one arm snapped midway up her forearm, and with teeth chattering at him, he turned and followed Charlotte out of the door and into the rain.

Warrington shut the front door as fists beat upon it. He held onto the handle in fear that the undead had learned basic motor functions other than walking and eating.

"John?" Charlotte said.

"Find me something to jam this shut."

"John—"

"Lewis, please—" He turned and the words evaporated on his lips.

Standing past the Mercedes on the lawn were two figures. The lady of the duo was wearing a red dress with one matching heel, the other had fallen on the wet grass beneath. A figure stood beside her, holding her at arm's length by her neck as she clutched at his hands. She freed one hand momentarily as she reached for Warrington, trying to call for help, but she could do no more than issue a strangled cry.

The other was tall.

Very tall.

Tall enough that the girl's remaining shoe was two feet from the ground. Its face was pale, skeletal, and Warrington could not tell if it was a trick of the moon, or if his eyes deceived him. The skin all over its body appeared taut, and an off-white color that looked deathly in the rain and moonlight, skin stretched so thin that he could see sinews and muscles standing out as lightning illuminated the world. The tall thing was dressed in tattered clothes—almost rags—which revealed much of its body, and Warrington thought that the skin had split in places, leaving raw muscle exposed. The lack of blood, coupled with its parched skin, and pulled-back lips showing jagged teeth, Warrington thought it belonged in a savage desert far away, not someone's pristine lawn in Hangshaw.

Hints of off-color eyeballs glinted from within its hooded brows as it looked from the girl to the man and woman who had burst from the manor. Charlotte's mouth opened, but she was as wordless as Warrington, and he stood there, the shotgun wavering in his grip.

Feet kicking, the girl's eyes begged for help.

Warrington stepped towards them, clearing his throat. "Put her down," he said, his steady voice not betraying the turmoil he felt within.

—

The front door of the Parson household rattled, drawing Charlotte's nervous eyes. With Warrington's attention on the girl and the creature, it was left to the secretary to deal with the undead horde in the house.

She turned and ran for the Mercedes, wishing that the keys were inside it.

They were.

She hoped that the undead were too stupid to figure out how to open the door of the house.

They weren't.

She watched as the dead spilled out, falling over each other and blocking the doorway. Charlotte started the Mercedes, turning on the full beams and slamming her palm on the horn.

Warrington pulled his gaze from the beast and towards the new distraction. With the gathering dead only a few yards away, they would have been on him if Charlotte had not warned him with the horn. He nodded at her, turned back to the unholy beast, and fired.

The warning shot scattered past the lanky creature's side, causing it to flinch.

"Put her down," Warrington bellowed.

The tall man looked him up and down, stepping towards him as it did so.

Warrington raised the shotgun. "No more warnings."

The thing stared at him, black irises swimming in pools of jaundiced-yellow. It stepped forward again, the girl-cum-human-shield swinging from its outstretched hand.

Warrington stared at the girl in the red dress. Her thin form swung rhythmically as the creature carried her towards the policeman, its lengthy strides moving her back and forth, almost hypnotically. Warrington waited as her movement revealed flashes of the beast behind her; each time it planted a foot, she would swing away from it a little.

The creature moved.

The girl swung.

Warrington waited, wondering if the buckshot from the Winchester would injure the girl, but then considered there might be a worse fate on hand for her.

The shotgun blast struck the creature in its stomach, puncturing the skin like old parchment paper. Blood much darker than the normal red Warrington had seen so much of lately sprayed from the wound. The thing clasped a hand to its side, hissing at the policeman.

Warrington pumped another shell and aimed higher. The thing watched him, holding the girl before it as a shield. It stepped forward slower than before, and shook the girl in its grasp.

Is he baiting me? The thought dropped the barrel of the shotgun.

A zombie tailing Charlotte had peeled away from the group and crunched the gravel behind him, making him turn and fire, one side of its face exploding as its neck snapped and its head bounced against its own shoulder before hitting the ground.

The tall creature was feet away when Warrington turned back towards it. It hesitated as the policeman leveled the shotgun again. Warrington peeled sweaty fingers from the Winchester as he adjusted his grip, and tried to remember how many shells he had left … if any.

The girl choked as she tried to speak, fingers pulling at the hand around her neck.

"Don't worry," said Warrington to the girl. "I'm gonna get you—"

The creature snapped her neck with a flick of its wrist. Her hands fell and she hung limp, swaying to the sound of her own death.

Warrington's hands shook. He had wanted to save her ... he had believed that he was going to save her....

The dead girl still dangled between them, and the beast peered from behind her skull, using her as a shield.

"She can't be killed twice," Warrington said with words that felt stronger than his trigger finger... and shot the girl in the face.

Her skull disintegrated, pasting the beast in brains, blood, and bone, as buckshot caught the creature's cheek. It staggered back, but stayed on its feet. Warrington popped the shotgun open and found it was empty of shells. Knowing that the creature did not know this, he closed it, pumped it, and aimed the shaking weapon again.

The thing held one hand to its face, black blood seeping through its skeleton-fingers. Yellow pus oozed from a shattered eye-socket as its teeth clashed together, the thin face contorted and crunched as it shook its head in pain and confusion. It turned the girl around in its other hand, examining the damage with its good eye.

The yellow eye rolled in its socket to look at Warrington.

"Whaaaaat aaaaare yooooou?" it asked. Its voice was a hiss—serpentine—coated with bemused anger. It turned the girl this-way-and-that in its grasp, studying her and the policeman beyond her. It seemed perplexed and amused all at once.

Warrington felt the moisture vanish from his mouth.

It wagged a finger at the policeman, flicking blood into the air as its wounded face seeped fluids down its body. "Yoooou killled heeerrrr."

"Fuck you," said Warrington. "You broke her neck."

"Aaahhhh," it replied with a smile. "But I waassss going tooo bring heerrrr baaaaack."

Warrington blinked at the beast. "You—" He cleared his throat. "You bring the dead back?"

It stepped towards him, the body of the dead girl still separating them.

Warrington moved back, wondering if the empty weapon in his hands was the only thing keeping him alive at that moment.

The Mercedes skidded to a halt between them, Charlotte throwing open the passenger door and shouting at Warrington to get inside. He threw himself into the vehicle.

"What the fuck is that thing?" shouted Charlotte over the sound of gravel being spun and crunched underneath them. Dead bounced over the bonnet, streaking the cracked windscreen with blood.

"I don't know what he is," he said, flinching as hands struck the glass next to him, starring it.

Reaching the gates of the manor, he stole a look back. The tall creature remained where it stood, the girl still in one hand, dangling like a broken toy.

The beast's sole eye stared after the departing car.

Warrington made her pull over once they were a safe distance from Mayor Parsons' house. Turning off the lights and the engine, Charlotte rolled the vehicle to a stop at the side of a quiet road. It was deserted, the moon lighting streaks of rain as the streetlamps remained out of power.

"You called it a him," stated Charlotte. "You think he … it was human?"

"I dunno," he said. "But … two arms, legs … could speak."

"Seven-foot-tall, skin hanging in shreds, shitloads of teeth, kills young girls, and who knows how many others." She stared at him. "I'm pretty sure someone like that would have been noticed hanging around the streets."

Warrington nodded, forcing himself calm. "I think he's the reason the dead are coming back. I think he's bringing them back somehow. He said he was going to bring the girl back."

"The one you just shot in the face?"

His lips tightened. "You saw that, huh?"

She nodded.

"He'd broken her neck by then … I had to do something. I had to shoot him."

"You missed."

"I fucking know."

She paused and he looked at her. "Wait a minute," she said. "Did you just say you spoke to it and it said that it was going to bring her back?"

"Yeah," he answered. "Right after he killed her."

"What the fuck?"

"Don't give me that." He pointed a claret-stained finger at her. "Don't tell me that it sounds ridiculous after all the shit we've been through."

She sat back in the seat, the wipers smearing blood across the screen as a drizzle of rain began to wash it away.

Ahead of them several groups of the undead filtered down the road towards them, their numbers increasing.

"What are we gonna do, sarge?" she asked, tiredness resonating in her words. "Do we kill them? All of them?"

Warrington was loading the shotgun with shells. "That, or get the hell out of Hangshaw and off this island."

"Not until I find my boyfriend."

CHAPTER FOUR

Aaron Drury stopped to catch his breath and rub his bruised forehead. His knees shook and his lungs ached as he leaned forward and sucked in air. His vision swam and the word concussion throbbed in his skull.

He stood and the rain refreshed him, and he lifted his head back to let it fall in his mouth.

All around him fields and hills rolled under the moonlight, the cracks of gunfire surrounding them.

"Gunfire?" Ballard asked between panting breaths.

A youth wiped rain from his dark skin, eyes bouncing as he nodded. "And a lot of it, too," he said. "It's all around. Sounds like the island's at war."

The few survivors of the coach crash let his words sink in. Between the gunshots, they could hear the sounds of the dead growing closer.

"How far behind do you think they are?" asked Anthony Yarranton, looking over his shoulder.

Drury shook his head, his vision clearing. "Hard to tell."

"I think we lost them a while back," said Ade Merchant, the black boxer, rubbing his thighs between the palms of his hands to increase circulation. "But I'm not hanging around. When one of them sees you, they start groaning and it sets the others off. That's what happened back at the bus."

"I think we've put some distance between us," said Drury. "And I don't think they can track us."

"That's a lot of thinking, boss," said Yarranton, setting Drury's teeth on edge. "I don't think those things breathe, so they don't need to take rests. They could still be coming right now." He looked back into the trees they had just emerged from.

On cue, one of the dead stumbled out of the trees and headed towards them at an awkward run, moaning as it did so. It moved faster than the others they had encountered. It was also angrier, spitting bile at them as it snapped its teeth, eyes wide.

More emerged from the trees. They slipped through the mud and crashed through bushes, pushing past each other in their desire to reach the living.

Drury quickly glanced at Yarranton and caught an 'I told you so' look.

"Run," Drury said to the others.

Merchant led the way as they plundered on. As the fittest he set a pace that they needed to keep to.

The moon glistened on wet roofs in the near distance and they headed for them. The wet and mud sucked at their feet, and exhaustion ran with them. The previous day's boxing matches and the bus crash impeded them even further.

The undead did not lag far behind. They did not pause for breath, and broken limbs did not slow them. On they came, slowly closing the gap.

Drury kept throwing anxious looks over his shoulder. The bump on his forehead burned as the blood pounded through his body, and he found his gaze blurring.

"We're almost there," Merchant said, his breathing now as heavy as the others.

"We can hit the police station," said Yarranton, finding his second wind at the thought. "I bet that's where everyone is riding this thing out."

Charlotte Lewis lived not too far from the police station where she worked, but Drury knew her flat was closer to his current position. "The police station is a good idea," he said without looking at Yarranton. "I'm gonna go get my girl and then meet you all there."

"I'd stick with you," said Ballard. "But my mum lives on Warwick Street."

Drury waved away the excuse. "It's okay. We've all got to do our own thing." He saw Yarranton already jogging away.

"Get to your families," said Drury. "And we'll all meet at the police station later."

"Run fast," Ballard said as he slipped into the dark.

Charlotte's home was a mile from where he was.

He jogged through the rain as it soaked his clothes into unwanted extra weight upon his body. His steps grew as thick as his breath, and he slowed to a walk.

He hid in gardens and behind a van to avoid the dead that patrolled the street. The closer to the center of town, the more of them he saw, and the longer he was forced to hide. He was discovered twice, and had to force his body over walls, under vehicles, and across a park as he escaped.

The power in Hangshaw was still off, and the light from higher places coated the small town in an eerie glow. More than once he saw a curtain twitch as the living peered from behind the barricades that preserved their homes. The fools in the buildings that had lit candles or torches were surrounded, the dead attracted to the glows like moths. He avoided those places.

He knew that Charlotte was intelligent enough to survive, and if she was with Sergeant Warrington, her chances of being alive must be significantly increased.

He and Charlotte had been dating for three years, but it was still a new and besotted love. They had met at Waterloo station in London when she had been buying a ticket back to the island after attending a training conference. Her dark looks, green eyes, and slender figure were enough for him to find a weak excuse to talk to her on the train, after making sure he had a seat nearby. Originally, she had balked at the lame attempt at conversation, but his uncomfortable eagerness and handsome physique soon warmed her to him. He had a seriousness and determination in him that—despite him being only nineteen at the time— had impressed her, and they were swapping phone numbers by the time they reached Portsmouth

Harbour. As with all modern relationships, texting was constant, and long late night calls brought on the inevitable romance.

They were rarely apart since, and now he was desperate to reach her and protect her.

He closed in on her flat, a place where he spent most of his time if he was not at the gym, the training hall, or if he wasn't bouncing drunks out of pub doorways.

The sight of her building stopped him. Her flat was in a block, and a car had crashed through the front doors of the building—destroying glass and brickwork—and he could see one undead man wandering around inside the hallway. More staggered around outside as he crouched behind a low wall to prevent detection.

He watched for signs of movement in her flat, or in any of the others, in case the tenants had sought refuge together in one of the rooms overlooking the road. Nothing happened for long moments other than the traffic of the dead as they bumbled and staggered aimlessly, or made vague attempts at listening for the direction of the gunshots that echoed in the distance.

He could wait no longer and dashed for the building, drawing attention as he sprinted around. Reaching the car that had ruined the entrance, he slid across its bonnet and bundled the zombie in the hall onto its back. As each of the dead saw him their moans gathered into one low monotonous sound, punctuated by a hiss or bark of anger from their number. The hallway of the apartments amplified the sound and chilled him.

Drury ran up the (mercifully clear) stairwell and discovered Charlotte's door was locked. Using his own key, he entered and found that the power was also out within the building. Making his way by touch into the kitchen, he found a box of matches on top of the cooker and lit one. He did not want to open the curtains and alert anyone or any-thing to his presence.

Charlotte was not in her flat, and the drawers and wardrobes were still filled with her clothes, so she had not come here to gather her belongings.

The thought of her being attacked—or worse— filled his mind and he shook his head to clear the rising panic.

He flicked the match out and peered around the lounge curtains. The commotion that the dead had made on his way in had caused a crowd of them to congregate outside, falling over each other as they made their way around and over the car that blocked the apartment's entrance. He turned his ear to the flat entrance and believed he could hear their numbers gathering in the hall outside.

He sat down on a coffee table, scattering magazines and property newspapers that he and Charlotte had been looking through onto the floor. He tried to think logically, but fatigue and the groans that vibrated around him made it difficult. His head injury still throbbed.

Striking another match, he entered the bedroom and dug out clean clothes from a drawer by his side of Charlotte's bed. His mind's eye showed him her lithe figure wrapped around the duvet, the girl brushing dark hair from her eyes as she beckoned him to join her.

The match burned his fingers and he hissed as he threw it to the ground. He changed clothes in the dark, before using another match to find a waterproof coat that hung in the hallway. He listened at the front door. The moans were quieter, but he could hear the dead wandering around the stairwell.

He returned to the lounge and looked out of the window. Below lay a lawn and a surrounding hedge, and the fall was not too great. The prospect of jumping did not appeal to him, but he could see no other option.

Drury slid the window open as slowly and quietly as he could. He peered out, hoping he had not been spotted, before climbing out onto the window frame. Taking a deep breath, he jumped before he could think it through, landing on the hedge below. Branches dug into his legs, but the bush cushioned his fall. The noise directed the dead to him, but he was already up and running.

All he seemed to do was run.

The police station was deserted.

Drury skirted around the building and peered in through the shattered and blood-splashed windows. There was no movement and no sound from the shadows inside. He could hear moans from beyond the fence around the station, and knew he could not stay here to see if anyone turned up seeking refuge. People had either already been, or were deterred from taking to the streets by the number of creatures that seemed to be everywhere within the more urban areas.

He jogged up the road a little, and sat behind a

large industrial bin to rest.

Where could Charlotte be? She must be with John Warrington and his deputy, whom he always forgot the name of. Kirk? Clarke? Maybe the police had procedures to follow in extreme circumstances like this, and Charlotte was holed up somewhere with all the other important island figures deep in a safe bunker.

Drury blinked, not knowing where to turn to next. His chin dropped to his chest as his mind blurred its thoughts, and he was dimly aware that he was succumbing to exhaustion.

A zombie fell over its feet on the pavement before him. His eyes wide, Drury's breath caught in his throat as he watched the beast slowly right itself. It did not look his way, and resumed its stagger past him.

Exhaustion had almost meant death, and he knew he had to rest. Maybe he could think straighter with some sleep. Maybe he could figure out where Charlotte and the living were, or find a sign or message telling him where to go.

The curtains of a house across the road from him were open, and he waited where he was long enough to determine there was no one inside.

He rose to his feet, ran across the road, and hugged the sidewall of the house as he searched for its back door. He ran straight into a little old lady. A dead little old lady. She hissed at him and his instinctive response was to punch her in the face, shattering her jaw and cheekbone. The frail bones crunched beneath his thick knuckles and he grimaced at his actions. The dead woman fell on her back, gurgling a moan as she swatted at her own face, as if to shoo away a fly. One blood-soaked eyeball rolled at him and she opened her disjointed jaw to hiss again, but he stepped forward and threw a punch so high and heavy it almost achieved its own orbit around the earth.

The blow sunk the dead woman to the ground, and Drury could not tell if she was dazed or completely dead. Her head was swollen and misshapen, and blood pooled onto the grass around them.

The back door of the house was open and he realized the woman must have been the inhabitant. He ran up the porch stairs, gently closing the door behind him. A key sat in the lock and he secured it. He leaned against the door, closing his eyes and lowering his head. Punching men his own age and strength was one thing, but hitting dead old ladies with haymakers was something he was not sure he could get used to.

There was no window in the door, but he could hear something coming up the steps outside. The same something began to slap at the door.

Drury was suddenly aware that he was now locked in a strange house, unknowing if there was anyone dead or alive inside with him.

He remained motionless, breathing slowly until the slapping on the door ceased. No other sounds came from within the building.

Fishing the box of matches from his pocket, he made a quiet inspection of the place and found it empty. Upstairs he found a bedroom. Dragging a wardrobe across the door, he lay on a bed that smelled of old people. It was strangely comforting.

He was asleep in seconds.

CHAPTER FIVE

It took Warrington a long time to convince Charlotte that their best move was to try and abandon the island at one of the three ferry ports. He told her that Drury and his teammates were probably being held up at a ferry terminal over the water in Lymington, and were as anxious to get onto the island as people were to get off of it.

"In a crisis like this," he said as she drove the Mercedes they had acquired from Mayor Parsons. "Everyone's gonna hit the boats. The problem is that if you want to contain the Isle of Wight, you shut down the ferry system. They did it back in '95 when some inmates escaped from Parkhurst prison."

"Then why are we going there?" she asked, crushing a crawling zombie under the wheels of the car.

"Because we need to start ruling out what options we have, and I want to know if we're going to be allowed off the island."

"I still think leaving Hangshaw is a bad idea."

He rubbed hard at his tired eyes. "That's because you want to see if your boyfriend shows up."

"And what's wrong with that?" she snapped,

rubbing at one of her own eyes. "Just because your ex-wife isn't going to show up looking for you doesn't mean that I have to leave."

Silence.

She sighed, lowering her window slightly, letting the rain cool her face. "I'm sorry," she said. "I didn't mean—"

"It's okay," he said. "We need to get some rest, and we will, as soon as we've been to the Fishbourne Ferry to see what's happening. Pull over and let me drive."

She was too tired to argue. They swapped seats and she was asleep before they passed Purton's Mill, the place the horrors had begun the day before. He stared as he drove by, momentarily chastising himself for not having cordoned the lane off, but then remembering that it would not have made a fucking difference to the rest of the island.

He glanced at his companion and saw that she was already asleep.

The drive to the ferry port usually took fifteen minutes, but they were a mile away when he stopped the car. Along the road before him were cars, busses, taxis, lorries, and vans, all either crashed into one another or abandoned.

A clutch of cars smoldered where they had impacted on someone's once-pristine grand lawn.

Warrington saw the dead hammering on the doors

of barricaded houses, and people gazing out of windows, as brave men and women fought the beasts below. More dead emerged from vehicles and other buildings, joining their vile brethren, pushing the living into shelters. A family beat upon the front door of a house as the dead converged on them, and the policeman's chest thumped as he wondered how he could help. His decision was made when the door flew open and an elderly couple allowed the family refuge before bolting the door behind them.

The undead saw Warrington and clambered over cars and around trucks to reach him. He got back in the car.

Warrington spun the vehicle around and drove away without waking Charlotte.

It took an hour of traversing abandoned cars and undead as he made his way towards the next closest ferry terminal in East Cowes. The roundabout that led into the town was jammed with traffic. He knew that beyond the junction the ferry port would be either shut down or overrun like the one he had just left behind.

Newport was the central town of the island, and East Cowes was the closest vehicle-ferry port. It would have been besieged by locals trying to flee the terrors that encompassed the small island.

That left the boat port at Yarmouth, on the western side of the diamond-shaped isle. Getting there would mean heading through Newport itself, and hoping that the main dual carriageway was clear, which was unlikely. It was busy enough at peak times, let alone run for your life times.

Warrington took the long route towards Yarmouth, avoiding main roads and using his knowledge of the back routes to avoid congestion and dead people. There were abandoned cars and crashes on the lanes he took, but he circumnavigated the worst of them, even driving across a bowling green to avoid one nasty blockage.

The dead were everywhere, chasing him and others that he saw fleeing in cars or on foot. The fields of the island were awash with 4x4s throwing up mud as they escaped the roads and blockages. Warrington could not help but feel annoyed that the Police Department had never financially stretched to getting him anything better than a Ford Fiesta.

The petrol light of the Mercedes was barely above empty, and he frowned as he realized that he would have to go along the Newport Road, via Calbourne. It was several miles to cover due to the longevity of the journey. He hoped that the road would not be too blocked—as it did not lead to any ferry terminals—but it would get him near to the Yarmouth Ferry.

Yarmouth was clogged with cars and vehicles. He could hear a gunfire coming from beyond the dam of cars and buildings ahead of them.

Warrington turned off the engine and sat motionless. The dead concentrated on reaching the gunfire being caused by warm-blooded humans. They paid no heed to the Mercedes sitting idly behind them.

Warrington nudged Charlotte several times until she awoke. Rubbing the sleep from her eyes she asked him what was happening.

"We're in Yarmouth."

"Yarmouth? How long was I out?"

"Over three hours," he said. "Fishbourne was a write-off, and we couldn't get through to East Cowes—"

"What?" she asked. "Why?"

"There are more dead than we thought. It looks like hundreds of them were trapped at the ferries—"

"And?"

"And now they're all dead ... and attacking the living," he answered, closing his eyes and resting his head against the seat. "There's an army of them growing. I see more dead than living everywhere now."

"Jesus."

"Things are a lot worse than we thought."

"So what now?" she asked as more gunfire echoed beyond the crammed cars. Yarmouth was a picturesque place on an island full of beautiful scenery, but now the roads were impassable, and the white-fronted houses were secured with fence posts, while a cottage at the side of the road was encompassed by flames that tore into the early-evening gloom.

"I think the military is here," he said. "That gunfire doesn't sound like a bunch of farmers firing shotguns."

"Do you think the boat is running?"

He shrugged. "It's why we're here."

They waited until the undead thinned out enough for them to try and move with minimal detection. They left the Mercedes—like the other abandoned cars around them—and hurried along a side road. A zombie crawled across the ground towards them, Warrington cutting off its moan by stomping on its skull. It took three attempts to silence it while Charlotte looked away.

The town center of Yarmouth was bathed in blood. The townsfolk and tourists trapped within the shops had been turned by the dead, and the mindless creatures bumped and barged into each other as they funneled down a road leading to a dock. Broken glass from store windows and vehicles crunched beneath dead feet as the rising moon revealed the ghouls filtering out of the square and down a side street.

Warrington led Charlotte onward, staying close to the cars that had been driven into one another and abandoned. The gunfire grew and drew the attention of the dead away from them.

Warrington and Charlotte navigated their way between cars until they were behind the main throng of the dead, who were converging in the narrow street. Beyond them they could see the port, but there was no big-white-rusting-ship in dock.

"Fuck," Charlotte whispered. "Now what? Hangshaw again?"

Warrington shook his head. "No, we need to get some answers to what's happening, and those guys"—he jabbed a finger at the empty dock where flashes of muzzle-fire indicated soldiers—"might be moving people off the island."

The ramp of the ferry stretched across the end of the street, the right hand slope of it descending into the

---

water. Yarmouth Harbour stretched to the west behind it. Warrington could not see any of the boat-masts that usually stretched into the sky.

The harbor was empty.

The crowd of dead were sandwiched between each other and a makeshift barricade involving sandbags and a milk float, and were being busily picked off by two soldiers standing atop a dairy vehicle. They aimed carefully along their sights, squeezing off solitary rounds to drop their targets.

Warrington placed a hand on Charlotte's shoulder, indicating for her to stay where she was. He stepped out from behind a car … and she followed him.

The soldiers clipped away at the dead, and one of them raised his gun at Warrington, who waved his hands in the air to get their attention.

"Wait!" yelled Warrington. "I'm a police officer!"

A few of the dead between them and the soldiers turned at the sound of a fresh meal. The soldiers both looked up from their weapons, one of them sighting Warrington along his gun-barrel before turning to his companion. The military men then began to fire faster into the undead around them.

"Move!" one of the soldiers yelled.

Warrington's shotgun took down an advancing ghoul, then he grabbed the secretary's hand and they ran for the barricade, pushing and fighting their way through as the soldiers destroyed or maimed the dead that were gathering around them.

One of the beasts got close and Warrington had no time to fire, instead, shoving it to the ground. Others pressed in, and Charlotte's heart threatened to leap through her throat. Hands reached for her, and she heard the snap of tooth upon tooth, and then the dead were all around them, one clutching at her sleeve, pulling her from the sergeant's grip, another hand snatching at her hair….

And then she was free. The air around her seemed cleaner, and the moon coated her in its glow. Warrington pushed her towards the milk float and onto the sandbags that had replaced the crates of milk as the vehicle's cargo.

Hands pulled her upward and she slipped at the soldiers' feet on the milk float's roof. She saw Warrington batter a zombie to the ground with his shotgun before reaching up himself.

One of the troops leveled his weapon at the policeman. "Shotgun first."

"Christ, boy," said Warrington. "Aren't we on the same fucking side?"

The soldier shot a young man with fresh blood all over his face as he reached for Warrington. The policeman glanced down at the body, then at the dead surrounding him, before throwing the Winchester up to the soldier. He caught it, handed it to his companion, and then shouldered his own weapon before reaching a hand to the policeman.

The secretary and policeman stood atop the buckling milk float's roof as the military men rained shots upon the enemy. The trooper who helped them up ceased fire and jumped down to the safe side of the barricade. He indicated for them to follow.

"Can I have my shotgun back, please?" asked Warrington as they approached a group of soldiers sitting on assorted vehicles. They were blood-spattered, with dark rings around their eyes as they cleaned and checked their weapons. The soldier holding his weapon ignored him.

"Isn't there a commanding officer here?" asked Warrington as one of the young men stood and jogged over to the barricade to take the shotgun-holding soldier's position.

"Captain Spink went down under one of the first waves," the soldier said, a young lad with a nametag that read: HAYWARD. "We were ordered to defend this port and make sure that no one left the island—"

"Why?" asked Charlotte. "People have died because they're trapped here! The ports were the only escape routes!"

The soldier averted his eyes, and Warrington saw a pile of plastic yellow suits piled next to the water. The lip of the dock was soaked in blood and shattered bodies.

"Are those bio-suits?" he said, stepping towards them. They were blood-soaked and torn.

"Ah," he said, turning to Hayward. "This is being treated as a virus or something, right? No one to leave the island in case infection is spread to the mainland.?"

Hayward nodded.

Charlotte thought he looked like a scared little boy who had mistakenly put on a soldier's uniform and then been thrown into battle. She wondered how close she was to being right.

"There was a full battalion of us here spread over the island," said Hayward as he stared at the barricade. "Around a 100 of us. We had bio-suits and were told that the air was carrying a contagion, and that if any of the hostiles got too close we had to stop them."

Warrington ran a hand through his graying hair. "If the contagion is airborne, then everyone is infected … which would mean that everyone was a hostile." He looked up at Hayward, his eyes wide. "You were shooting the living as well?"

Hayward's youthful looks fell, and his eyes betrayed the tiredness and guilt he felt. "At first—" He cleared his throat. "We killed … everyone … everyone that came seeking help." He looked at his feet, shaking his head at the memories that tormented him. "It caused fucking chaos and some of us broke rank. There was a lot of infighting and Captain Spink had to try and keep us all together. That's when the dead came out of the sea and everything went to shit."

"Why aren't you in your bio-suit?" asked Warrington.

"Why aren't I dead?" countered Hayward.

Warrington nodded. "Because you realized this virus doesn't kill people. Dead people kill people."

"It took a few ripped suits and shooting a few of our brothers before we realized that," the soldier answered. "They smashed us by coming out of the water; we just never expected that. They tore through us before we knew what was going on. And it didn't seem like a random action. Those things were moving as a unit."

"You … you think they were coordinated?" asked Charlotte.

"I don't think it."

Warrington rubbed the bridge of his nose. "I don't suppose there was a tall, freaky fucker leading them out?"

"Huh?" the soldier furrowed his brow. "I don't know. We were holding the barricade and then they hit us from behind—"

"When did the last boat leave?" asked Charlotte.

"A few hours ago," replied Hayward. "The last one was full of people, and we were told the Navy stopped it in the Solent, and that it's still there now."

"There might be infected people on there," said Charlotte.

"There are," said Hayward. "The Navy have packed the channel and are stopping everyone. There was a lot of gunfire out there earlier, but it's stopped now."

"There's always the routes to France," she said. "They can't catch everyone leaving, surely?"

"They've cut the island off," said Warrington. "And if any boats do slip through to France, this thing could hit Europe." He cast his eyes over Hayward and the weary troops. "If the island is infected, I'm guessing no one's coming back to pick you guys up?"

Hayward rubbed a hand over his shaved head. "We were told a couple of hours ago, there's no one coming for us. I figure they're just gonna let the place kill itself off and mop up after."

"Does General Pegg know this?" asked Warrington.

"You know the general? Well, yeah, the information came from him directly," replied Hayward. "He said to sit tight and he'll come get us."

"Have you heard from him since?"

"No," said Hayward.

Warrington's mind recalled the gunfire on The Downs where Pegg was sat with floodlights burning to attract the dead. He glanced at the soldier's frowning face and did not know what to say.

"We're stuck here, aren't we?" asked Charlotte, looking out across the Solent that separated the island from mainland England. She squinted and stepped forward as her attention was piqued. "Where are the lights on the other side?"

"They went out in Lymington a few hours back.

Around the same time they did here," said Hayward. "The only lights we've seen are from the Navy."

"So, are you just going to stay here?" asked Charlotte, surveying the body-part strewn ground. Streaks of blood indicated where the soldiers had dumped bodies into the harbor.

Hayward pointed a gloved-finger at the spot. "We dumped the bodies into the water," he said apologetically. "No one likes having them around us, even if they are dead. I mean properly dead … not fucked up dead."

Warrington studied the harbor and looked around the car park that the soldiers had blocked with Army trucks and civilian vehicles. They had made a good job of sandwiching everything together and filling the gaps with sandbags. Coaches had been parked across the entrances of the car park, and high-sided lorries were scraped against the low walls that separated the area from the nearby shops. The military had reduced the size of the car park with their efforts, and the smaller area was easier for the handful of men to patrol.

"What's your next move?" he asked the soldier.

"Wait for General Pegg and the rest of the battalion."

"What if they don't come?" asked Charlotte.

"What if they do?"

"Look," said Warrington, checking his shotgun. "We're not staying—"

"We're not?" Charlotte put a hand on his arm. "But these boys have guns. Great, big guns."

"I think you're wasting your time staying here," Warrington said to the soldier.

"He'll come," said Hayward, hoisting his weapon onto his shoulder. "Besides, we haven't got anywhere else to be right now." The soldier stuck his hand out and they shook. "Good luck, officer."

Warrington and Charlotte crossed the dock and pass the tired soldiers who barely acknowledged their presence.

"We can't leave them here," the secretary whispered.

He grabbed her hand as a trooper threw sandbags on the ground to make a ramp for them. "We've got to look out for ourselves now," Warrington said as they walked up the makeshift structure and onto a car roof.

"You might," she said as he pulled her up. "I have to find Aaron."

He studied the dark circles around her eyes, patches of tiredness that could not mar her beauty. The green of her eyes seemed to glow in the dark.

"Okay," he sighed. "We'll head back to Hangshaw. If he's as determined as you, then that's where he'll go. But," he added, clutching her hand tighter. "You have to consider the fact that he might be—"

"He isn't."

CHAPTER SIX

Aaron Drury opened his eyes and winced as sunlight poured through the curtains he had left open. Raising himself up on his elbows, he felt his legs ache and his shoulders tighten as the exertions of the previous night pressed upon him.

He wondered how long he had slept and looked at his watch. It was smashed and useless.

He groaned as he sat up. The room smelled old and was decorated in horrid flowery wallpaper, with a dresser covered in family photos and ornaments. He thought he recognized the old lady he had tried to crush the skull of, and turned his gaze away.

His legs wobbled as he came to his feet. He limped to the curtains and stood to one side as he peered out. The sight that greeted him made his chest ache.

Hangshaw burned.

Bodies lay across roads and gardens, too savaged to reanimate, or having returned to unlife, they scrambled around where they lay, or tried to move towards anything moving or making a noise—which was generally other undead.

Buildings burned despite the night's heavy rain, smoke coating the sky. The morning sun poked through gaps in the haze and he could see plumes of more smoke from The Downs nearby.

A stumbling zombie falling across the bonnet of a car startled him and he stepped back from the window.

Sitting on the bed, he pulled off his mud-stained T-shirt. His jeans were sodden, but he harbored little hope of finding trousers that would fit him in the house of a little old lady.

He opened the wardrobe he had placed across the bedroom door and flicked through the clothes inside. There was nothing that he could wear unless he fancied a flowing floral skirt or a woolen shawl.

He scratched at his stubble before feeling the bump on his forehead, wincing as he did so. He tried to forget it by examining his mobile phone, but it was still smashed and as useless as when he had first looked at it after the coach crash. He tossed it onto the bed where it bounced off and struck the wall beyond it, shattering it completely.

The noise was answered by a groan beyond the door, followed by a thump.

Drury froze, and cursed himself as he heard another blow against the bedroom door. He looked around the room for an escape, and—for the second time in a few hours—realized he was going to have to jump again.

Grabbing his T-shirt, he slipped it on and opened the window.

The moan echoed again, and more accompanied it as the beating against the door increased.

As he looked down at the lawn below, he wondered how the dead had entered the house, but did not give it another thought, as the pressure on the door moved the wardrobe resting against it an inch, just as the dead on the ground below spotted him.

Moans directed at him took him off guard, and his fingers caught the frame on either side, momentarily leaning him out over the garden.

Undead from all around responded, the garden filling rapidly as the pounding on the door increased.

A drainpipe ascended past the window, and a garage roof extended out to the side of the building, level with his precarious position. Breathing deep, he snatched for the pipe just as a rotting fist broke through the bedroom door, the wardrobe falling to its front with a smash.

The dead below groaned and hissed, and he saw one or two almost running across the lawn to leap onto the backs of the ones beneath him. The thought that the creatures might be getting faster horrified him, but not as much as when the drainpipe started to peel away from the brickwork.

The plastic appliance made a snapping sound as nails withdrew from the wall. Drury swung his momentum to the other side of the pipe and let go just as it broke from the wall. His body weight carried him onward, and for a split second he thought he would slip and fall into the hands of the dead below.

But he caught the lip of the garage roof. His body slammed into the wall, but his grip stayed true. Fingers brushed his heels as he pulled himself up with a speed powered by survival and fear.

Swinging his feet onto the roof, he rolled onto his back and lay still, listening to the sounds of the dead. Hands slapped on walls and doors, and their moans grew as they attracted more zombies—grew until his skull ached with the sound.

He put his hands to his ears and breathed deep,

using his boxer-training to calm himself.

Drury crawled along the roof. A playing field bore dozens of the undead, all of them hungrily answering the call of their brothers and sisters. They poured through broken fence panels and into the back garden.

Laying on his back again on the rain-soaked roof, he smashed a fist down against his side in frustration——

——and it sank into the roof.

He looked at the mark he had made, a soft indentation in the roof's black asphalt that was already filling with water. Probing at it with his fingers, he found it soft and malleable. He experimented with sections of the roof and found that his fists could make heavy marks in places.

He smashed into the softer sections he could find, and soon was digging his fingers to claw away at the material underneath. He created a sizeable gap and peered within, dropping chunks of asphalt onto the shining metal top of a car. The promise of escape made him dig even harder.

Then he fell through as the structure collapsed under him.

Drury fell the short distance and landed on the car with a clang. The garage door rattled as the walking corpses outside moved their attention along the building towards the noise. He thanked his lucky stars the inside of the structure was devoid of any dead people.

Climbing off of the vehicle's dented roof, he tried the door of the car and it opened. There were no keys in the ignition.

"Now … if I were an old woman?"

The car keys were on a hook by the door that led back into the house. A frosted glass-paneled door. A door that revealed numerous shapes in the kitchen beyond.

He tiptoed towards the door and lifted the keys from their hook. He looked at the vehicle he was pinning his hopes of survival on.

"Ah," he sighed. "I fucking hate Nissan Micras."

Sitting in the driver's seat (complete with lumbar support), he turned the ignition once to reveal it had nearly a full tank of petrol. He also found a garage door remote on the spotless dash, neatly clipped into a holder.

The garage door still vibrated with the force upon its outside, although it had died down somewhat. Still, Drury hesitated to press the door release button.

He knew the noise of the engine would pull in the dead from the kitchen, and the garage door opening would just flood the room with dead from the outside.

He sat silently, fingers dragging his cheeks down from his tired eyes.

An option provided itself to him from a workbench.

Getting out of the car, he picked up the petrol-powered lawnmower and shook it to see that it, too, was full of petrol.

Suspension bounced as he climbed onto the bonnet of the little car and fed the lawnmower up through the hole in the roof. He climbed out after it.

The sun warmed his skin, and he could feel his body succumbing to a cold. The previous night's running in the rain had taken a toll. He needed to find Charlotte as soon as he could, and get themselves to a secure place so he could rest.

Drury took quick breaths and then pulled the cord of the mower. It spluttered once, twice, and then caught on the third try.

He ran to the front edge of the garage and hurled the mower as far across the garden as he could. The engine coughed and choked as it sailed through the air, spraying the dead with leaking petrol.

The zombies pursued the racket as it struck the concrete path, shattering the machinery and knocking the tool out of action.

Drury ran for the hole, sliding down into it, and hitting the Micra's roof again. The dead in the kitchen responded, and one of them fell through the glass door, the pressure from its brothers pushing it through.

He was in the vehicle and furiously pressing the garage door remote as a second zombie burst through the kitchen door, crashing over the undead beneath its feet. For a horrifying second he thought that without any electricity the garage door wouldn't open, but thankfully it either ran off a battery or a backed-up power source, as the shaking, metal door slowly flipped itself outward.

The sound of rubber screaming against the floor filled the garage along with smoke from the tires. The Micra burst from the garage before the door was fully open, shattering the thin windscreen.

But he did not care. And he did not care for the handful of dead that he powered the car through, the lightness of the vehicle rocking as it met the heavy forms of the undead. Nor did he look in his rearview mirror as he left them in his wake.

CHAPTER SEVEN

The sound of Warrington pumping the shotgun chamber woke Charlotte. She squinted as the sun poured through the windscreen of the military jeep they had taken from the dock. No soldier had answered when Warrington asked if he could take it.

"How long have I slept?" she asked, and then saw Warrington's jaw set tightly and realized why he had pumped the shotgun.

There was a blockade ahead of them.

"Please tell me it's not the military again," she said.

"It's the military again."

"What are we going to do?"

"I'm going to ask them to get out of our fucking way." He opened the jeep door, shotgun in hand.

"John, don't!" she cried, and made a grab at him.

He walked around the vehicle, holding the weapon down by his side. His uniform shirt was untucked and creased, and his trousers were covered in mud from the boots up.

She opened her door and stood on the seat to boost her height, leaning out of the jeep. "John," she called again, the sound of his name feeling strange to her—he had always been sarge or boss. "Please get back in the car."

He stopped and she thought it was because of her, but she now saw a figure striding towards them from the blockade, a man in a decorated uniform with his hands empty and above his head.

"Are you Sergeant John Warrington?" he asked. "I'm General Pegg."

Charlotte's shoulders stopped shaking. "Thank fuck we found you." She offered the man a tired smile.

Warrington punched him.

Pegg stepped back, hand to jaw, while the twenty soldiers behind leapt from their vehicles, chambered weapons, and ordered the policeman to the ground.

Warrington did not move, shotgun still held by his side.

Pegg waved the soldiers back. He looked at Warrington with what Charlotte hoped was admiration.

"You can have that one for free, sergeant," he said as he clicked his jaw. He looked him in the eye. "You want to tell me what that was for?"

"You've left the whole island to fight or die," said Warrington, shoulders hunched. "So, here's the fight."

The troops behind the general shifted uneasily. Charlotte saw fingers hovering above triggers as they regarded the policeman. Their eyes echoed the darkness around hers and Warrington's, and she knew that everyone was tired and on edge. The soldiers' dirty cheeks were streaked with tears, blood, or both. She recalled the radio conversation between Pegg and the sergeant, and knew that these men had been on The Downs—using floodlights as bait—drawing the dead to them. They look like they had been attacked like the men at the Yarmouth Ferry port.

Attacked and beaten.

"Officer," said Pegg. "It is not my decision to abandon your fair isle." He cast his arms wide, head nodding at the men behind him. "Can you not tell that we are also in the same predicament?" He lowered his arms, and the tone of his face fell with them. "I learnt that we were as expendable as you while we were mid-skull-fuck up in the hills."

Warrington kept his focus on the general, but the shotgun hung a little looser in his grasp.

"General," Charlotte called, in an attempt to diffuse the situation. "We've had a rough time ourselves, but we did meet your men at the Yarmouth port, and they are waiting for you."

Pegg shielded his eyes, seeing the secretary for the first time. "Please come down, little lady," he said, flashing her a smile that gleamed against the dirt and dust covering him. "I feel it may stop your friend from shooting me … and my men from shooting him."

Pegg had said it with a smile, but the words rang true. Charlotte stepped down and walked towards the two men, Warrington throwing a look at her over his shoulder. Tiredness had replaced the defiance on his face.

"I guess you're infected as well?" she said to the general.

"We were left behind because the island is now a quarantine zone," he answered, straightening his grubby uniform. "I'm afraid that might be my fault. Once I had reported our findings and choppered out a few of the hostiles, the brass informed me that we would not be leaving your little island."

"How long are we all stuck here for?" she asked.

Pegg scratched his gray-flecked stubbled chin.

"Hard to say, ma'am, but it doesn't look good. I imagine they'll leave us here to try and kill all the dead things before they ride in and mop up."

"But we're not infected," she said as Warrington rested his back against the grill of the jeep.

"How do you know?" asked Pegg, eyes unblinking.

"It's easier to harness the problem in a small community," interrupted Warrington. He rested the shotgun on the bonnet of the jeep and Lewis saw some of the soldiers relax their own weapons.

Pegg nodded. "It's a matter of containment."

"What if the hostiles you send over infect the mainland?"

"Right now, Miss Lewis," said the general as he put on a pair of sunglasses and looked up into the morning sky. "That is not our problem. Those are our problem." He pointed behind them.

The dead approached in a cluster, having followed the voices and the noise of the jeep. The sight of people visibly excited them and several broke into shambling runs.

At a barked order from Pegg, the troops fell into position and gunned down the zombies as they neared. Their shots were methodical and lethal, and it took little time to clear the area.

"Sergeant, Miss Lewis," said Pegg, as his men walked towards their enemy with pistols drawn. "We are leaving and I would like you to accompany us."

"Where are you going?" asked Warrington.

"Recon suggested a place called Gatcombe Manor," came the reply. "Shortly before he left my service."

"Set in the middle of lots of land … easy to defend," said Warrington. "We'll come for the ride, unless we get a better option."

General Pegg studied him for a second before nodding. He turned to his men who were dispatching anything that moved among the dead on the ground. "Let's go get the lads from Yarmouth!"

Although it technically belonged to the military, Pegg let Warrington keep the jeep to follow the convoy in as they headed back towards Yarmouth. The men were still there and still fighting, and more than relieved to see Pegg and their comrades arrive.

Hayward acknowledged Warrington with a nod of his head.

"Told you they'd come back." He grinned.

The troops organized their weapons, and loaded themselves into trucks and jeeps.

"Sergeant," squawked Pegg over the jeep's radio. "Are you receiving, over?"

"Sure am," he answered, and then awkwardly added over."

"We've got to pick up some of my men who have strayed from their post here in Yarmouth and have made it to Shalfleet. We're heading through that way, anyway, over."

"We're picking up deserters," said Warrington to Charlotte.

"Don't they usually shoot them?"

Warrington said nothing.

Charlotte's brow furrowed and she played with the hem of her tattered skirt. She gazed at what was left of her tights and mud-splattered legs. It was hard to believe she had dressed for work just over twenty-four hours ago, and was now in the middle of an undead war, still in her work clothes.

"I need a shower," she said. "And, sarge, I know you're all for staying with these Army boys ... but I have to get back to Hangshaw. It's fine if you don't—"

"Don't be stupid," he snapped, and then apologized with an upturned hand. "We'll go with Pegg and get some rest, and then we'll get going. I'm sure Aaron is fine, and I bet he's outrun those things and is waiting at your house with a bottle of wine and some chocolates."

She sighed and stared out of the window. "I hope so."

Gatcombe House sat in vast grass-covered grounds away from the main roads, its perimeter coated with high hedges and tall trees. A farmhouse was situated to one side of a long driveway, and Pegg sent a group of soldiers to investigate it.

The remaining soldiers—Warrington and Charlotte among them—continued the drive to the manor. It was an old Victorian building, square, but elegant, with ivy completely covering the front of the house, but trimmed away from the large white-paneled windows.

"Oh, wow," said Charlotte.

The jeeps and trucks drove across the gravel entrance to the house and onto the perfectly-manicured lawn. Pegg apologized for disrupting the grounds, but added, "Needs must, while at war. Unfortunately, the house will also require some attention."

"What does he mean?" Charlotte asked Warrington.

"I think they're gonna take the place apart and make it a fortress."

He was right.

The soldiers jumped from the trucks and jeeps and broke into the manor, immediately starting to reinforce the downstairs area. Warrington and Charlotte stayed in the jeep as other troops ran further into the grounds and trees behind the building to secure the area.

"What do we do?" she asked him.

"Sit and wait," he said as he slid the seat back as far as it would go and stretched his legs under the dashboard.

It took the men an hour to board the windows on the ground floor. Some of the soldiers traveled to and from the farmhouse carrying supplies, floorboards, and tools that they had commandeered. The trucks were parked by the windows along the sides of the house, and the three jeeps formed a barricade out front. Troops positioned themselves on and between the vehicles.

Charlotte woke Warrington up as Pegg approached.

"If you two would care to join me inside," he said, his shirt sleeves rolled up and a hammer tucked into his belt. "I think one of my men has cooked us some breakfast."

Plates of bacon, sausages, eggs, and beans adorned a massive dining room table that the men sat around. Warrington and Charlotte seated themselves, and took the food that was offered them with thanks.

"We should be safe here for a while," Pegg said to them all. "This place has a lot of food stored in the kitchen, and we have plenty of ammunition." His eyes lowered as he mopped a up beans with a piece of toast. "I just wish we still had the men for it all."

The soldiers ate in silence.

"We need to keep our strength up," said Pegg, motioning for Charlotte to eat. "We don't know what we have ahead of us." He examined his men as they ate. "And we have brothers to avenge."

The soldiers nodded, faces stern, saying nothing as they fed.

"We won't be staying long," said Warrington, waving a fork towards Charlotte. "She needs to find someone and she's not going alone."

Pegg's eyes narrowed as he tipped his head. "Well, I wouldn't recommend traveling anywhere." He smiled at the secretary. "But I do understand. With the communications blackout, my boys have no way of letting their families know how they are. Not to mention the troops I've lost."

Warrington nodded his thanks and finished his

food. Afterwards, Pegg told them that he had been through the house and allotted them a room, which he asked a soldier to show them to. It was a large bedroom with one double bed, but it had a shower-room in which Charlotte disappeared. When she re-emerged, Warrington was on the bed asleep in his clothes, snoring lightly.

She laid next to him, dressed in a bathrobe.

Exhaustion enveloped her.

Gunshots woke them. Warrington was on his feet as Charlotte rubbed heavy sleep from her eyes.

"Are we being attacked?" she asked as she slid her legs off of the bed and gathered her clothes from a chair.

Warrington hurried to a window. Outside he could see undead men, women, and children streaming down the path towards the manor. From his vantage point he could see a sizeable amount of the grounds, and zombies were tearing through the tall hedges that secluded the property from the rest of the island.

Below, the soldiers kept a tight formation as Pegg stood behind them, barking orders and overseeing the defense. The soldiers waited until the closer ranks of the dead were within range before opening fire.

The bathroom door closed as Charlotte ran inside with her clothes, and Warrington left the room. Walking down a hallway he approached the rear of the house and entered another bedroom. The two beds were unmade, and a military kit lined a dresser. From the window, he could see more of the rear garden, and found a number of troops battling the undead. An inspection of the east wing of the building revealed a similar ongoing melee.

Warrington headed downstairs and out of the front doors. Pegg stood behind his men, pistol drawn as he issued orders and spoke to his men in a calm voice.

"Make your shots count, boys," he said, and Warrington caught his eye. "I appreciate your appearance, officer, but I think you may get in our way."

"This is no random attack," said Warrington.

Pegg nodded. "I know. They've come from all sides—in even numbers—and spread my men out nice and thin." His blue eyes were hooded, determined, as he looked at Warrington. "This is an organized attack, make no mistake."

"Can I help?"

Pegg unclipped his sidearm, but Warrington dismissed it. "I want something with a kick, general," he said. "And I saw one of your men out back has my shotgun."

Pegg eyes narrowed before he turned to a soldier and tapped him on the shoulder. The man handed the general his weapon before picking up an even bigger gun from a nearby stockpile.

"This is an SA80," said Pegg, checking the chamber and tossing it to Warrington, who looked it over as Pegg pointed out specific parts of the weapon. "It's a selective fire, gas-operated assault rifle, and will stop whatever you point at, as long as you hit it in the head."

Warrington felt the weight of the gun. Setting the stock against his shoulder, he moved away from the soldiers and aimed at the tree-line bordering the main road. The dead broke through incessantly, Pegg's men bringing them down as they progressed towards the defense-line.

Warrington aimed down the sight and found a bodybuilding zombie clawing its way through the hedge. Its face and hands bled from the exertion, and it stumbled as it emerged fully from the foliage.

The policeman's first shot took it in its tattooed throat, and—as it sank to one knee, hands flapping at its neck—Warrington's following shot destroyed its face and skull.

The policeman heard appreciative murmurs from the soldiers and caught a small smile on Pegg's face.

"Sergeant," said the military man. "Fire at will."

Charlotte watched from the bedroom window. Despite her brief rest, the sight of more fighting drained her.

She buttoned her dirty blouse and unconsciously smoothed her skirt, before checking her phone for the third time that minute. Still no service, and still no way of finding out where her boyfriend was. She traced a finger down the picture of him on her phone's wallpaper before slipping it back into her skirt pocket.

Blinking moisture from her eyes, she left the

bedroom. She determined that she would gather food from the kitchen and be ready for when Warrington told her they would be running. Again.

Bare feet padding along the hallway, she descended the stairs and entered the kitchen. It was deserted, but a big AGA cooker was covered in the pots and pans from their meal.

There was still some bread and sausages among the plates, and she found a tea-towel, wrapping the good pieces of food she could salvage. She tried to ignore the shapes that flitted through the gaps of the boarded windows, and busied herself looking in cupboards.

Pickings were sparse, and she turned her attention to what she knew to be the pantry-cum-cellar door.

Wrapping the tea-towel of food up, she moved towards it, flinching as gunfire resounded from outside the kitchen windows.

She touched the doorknob before releasing it instantly, as if her fingers had been burned.

The doorknob was moving.

And something knocked upon the other side of the door.

A pause, and then another small knock sounded, this time accompanied by a hiss. She recognized the noise, and it made her drop her bundle.

Food burst from its wrapping and splashed her bare feet. She side-footed away from the pantry door, her legs feeling alien beneath her.

Another knock, and the door handle turned. Slowly. The movement grabbed her attention and she rushed to the door, grasping the round handle in both hands and holding it tightly.

"Help!" she cried, but her words were lost amidst the gunshots.

The handle twisted in her grasp and a voice seeped into her soul....

"Knooock knooock,"

"Fuck fuck fuck fuck fuck," she whimpered.

The handle wrenched from her grasp as it imploded inward, and she fell on her backside as the door disintegrated before her.

She crawled backwards as the Tall Man stooped to enter the kitchen. Behind him, in the darkness, she could see the gleaming eyes of the undead following him, moaning as they spied her.

The tall, thin beast stared at Charlotte, holding a hand out behind it to halt the others. Golden eyes squinted as it examined her, before widening in acknowledgement. "Yooouuu...," it hissed, long tongue flicking over razor-teeth.

Numbness soaked her body, her blood frozen. Her mouth opened to say something—anything—but the words were as dead as the creatures before her.

The Tall Man stood framed in the smashed doorway to the cellar, the zombies behind bumping and shoving one another, but none dared to pass their master. It stood, staring at the girl cowering on the ground ... and a smile broke out on its face, a smile more terrifying than anything Charlotte Lewis had ever seen in her life.

She scrambled to her feet and ran, and the Tall Man stepped out of the way of his undead minions.

Charlotte burst through the front doors and fell down the stairs in her haste. A soldier stepped towards her to help, but she pushed him aside and ran. "They're in the house!"

The undead burst through the tree-lines all around, as if her scream was their cue to move. Pegg blinked once, and then shouted at his men to form a circle where they stood.

The sight of Charlotte running towards him, knees scraped and bleeding—eyes and mouth wide with terror—chilled every fiber in Warrington's body. She said nothing as she reached him. She did not need to.

"We have to leave now!" he shouted at Pegg, but the general ignored him as he bellowed orders to the men scurrying into formation.

Warrington threw the SA80 into a jeep, just as Charlotte stumbled into his arms.

"He's here," she said, trying to catch her breath.

He bundled her into the vehicle, casting one last look at Pegg. The general met his eye, shaking his head in disappointment.

The soldiers gravitated around Pegg as Warrington climbed into the jeep after the secretary. He hesitated, wondering what to say to the general and his men that would make them listen, but Charlotte screamed at him to go.

Starting the jeep, Warrington ploughed through the undead that blundered across the long lawn before them, tearing up turf as the tires spun for traction. He steered the vehicle onto the driveway, bodies bumping and breaking as he struck them.

Charlotte buried her face in her hands, unwilling to watch as he cut a swath through the men, woman, and children intent on catching them. It seemed to take an age, but once she heard the squeal of rubber on road and the ride smooth out beneath them, she raised her head.

The dead were scattered along the road ahead, but most were intent on forcing their way through the hedges towards the manor. As Warrington pushed the jeep forward he slowed down.

"What are you doing?" asked Charlotte, shaking.

Warrington held a hand out to calm her. "They're ignoring us."

The dead shambled or ran past the jeep and straight for the hedge and the holes in it. A couple of the zombies gave them a cursory look before sniffing the air, and moving with the rest of their kind.

"I think the Tall Man controls them," he said.

Charlotte locked her door, and then threw herself across Warrington to lock his. "I just saw him in the house."

"What?" Warrington grabbed her arm and forced her to look at him. "Did he touch you?"

"No," she said and pulled away. "He came up through the basement, from the cellar. That's how the dead got into the house."

"Did … did he say anything?"

Charlotte rubbed her arm where he had grabbed it. "Yeah, he said knock knock and scared the fuck out of me." She rubbed her scuffed knees, flicking off pieces of gravel stuck to her bloodied joints.

"We need to find out as much about the Tall Man as we can. I think he uses mind control on the dead. He's organizing them to attack like they did here and back in Yarmouth."

"But why?" she asked, flinching from her window as a zombie smashed against it.

"I think he's growing an army," he said. "I think the Isle of Wight is the perfect place to gather a shitload of dead things to control ... before moving onto the mainland, Europe, wherever."

Charlotte shook her head. "An army? An army that can't be stopped."

Warrington looked in the rearview mirror and saw the Tall Man standing in the road, staring after them.

He waited until they were clear of the area, and the roads were free of the undead.

"Is he following us?" she asked, looking over her shoulder.

"No," he said, unconvincingly.

"Maybe he's following you," she said. "Because you shot him in the face."

A buzzing sound filled the jeep and Warrington looked at the dash. "Great, we're out of diesel," he said. "But I think we can make Newport. It's the nearest garage I can think of."

"What?" she asked, raising her eyebrows. "It would have gone to shit like everywhere else!"

"This jeep is strong and secure and we can go off-road in it," he said. "It could save our lives. Actually, it just did."

"But driving into Newport could end our lives," she said, running her thin fingers through her hair. He thought she looked ready to pull her dark locks out.

"If you want me to drop you outside of town and come back after and get you, I will," he said, slowing the vehicle.

She jabbed a finger at him. "If we're gonna die, I want to be able to look you in the fucking eye and say, I told you so."

He navigated a roundabout and drove the jeep onto a dual carriageway, only to find it blocked with vehicles. Dead flitting in and out of the wreckage headed towards them.

Smoke rose over the horizon, and the smell of burning flesh haunted them. Warrington steered the vehicle between the crashed cars, smashing into the undead when he had no other option. The carnage grew heavier, and he could not press the jeep any further down the road.

The dead moved closer in every direction.

Warrington pointed the 4x4 down an embankment, leaving the road as it slid down a grass verge. Negotiating another roundabout, he found more cars and zombies under a bridge he had planned to go under. The pavement was clear, and he forced the jeep along it, scratching its side on the concrete wall.

The garage was in sight, but more cars blocked its forecourt. The dead were numerous, leaning into cars to eat people who had been trapped within.

The Hangshaw policeman bared his teeth and . drove over a zombie as he powered the jeep between two cars blocking the entrance of the garage. There was one pump free on the forecourt, and he hand-braked the vehicle to a stop alongside it. Grabbing the SA80, he told Charlotte to fill the jeep with gas—fast.

Stalking the dead, Warrington rattled off shots

from the military weapon as Charlotte popped the fuel cap and inserted the nozzle.

"Sarge," she called, her voice wavering. "The pumps are off!"

"Go into the garage," he said, very aware that he had no extra ammunition for the assault rifle. "There should be a fuel pump ON/OFF switch behind the counter."

"I'm not going in there," she snapped, throwing a glance at the building.

"Then we aren't going anywhere," he said, shooting two of the undead.

She groaned as she looked at the darkened garage store before slowly forcing herself towards it. Silence settled around them and she saw that Warrington had cleared the immediate area of any threat. The lack of noise was unsettling.

She paused at the door, and Warrington walking along the outside windows of the store, peering inside.

She stepped into the building.

The store was cool and dark, the electricity having been turned off with the rest of the island. Blood streaked the floor, and she trod lightly between pools of it as she neared the counter. She hoped that the fuel pumps were running off of something else other than the national power grid, otherwise they were in for a long walk. Or run.

The switch was in a small office behind the counter. She turned and told Warrington who stood guard in the main kiosk.

"I'm hoping it runs off an alternate power supply," he said. "Flip it and see if it works."

She did as instructed and they heard a rumbling from the garage forecourt as petrol and diesel pumps vibrated into life. Some of the fuel hoses had been left on the ground and liquid began to squirt over the asphalt.

Warrington ran to the jeep and placed the nozzle into the open fuel port. The sound of diesel filling an empty tank echoed from within. His brow furrowed as he noticed a fuel hose fed through the open passenger window.

Charlotte's bare feet splashed through pools of diesel and petrol as she ran across the forecourt.

"Get in the jeep," Warrington said to her, stepping towards something obscured by a mini-bus. His tone was calm and quiet, and filled her with fear.

She saw the dead gathering in number, their moans echoing around them. She pulled open the door and was covered in a wash of fuel that sprayed from a hose hanging over the jeep's window. Wiping her eyes, she spat the liquid from her mouth, the moisture in her tongue evaporating and making her gag. Her eyes stung and she heard Warrington shouting at someone to keep away from her. She knew they were in trouble, so she felt her way into the jeep, slamming the door behind her.

She wiped her eyes with the sleeve of her blouse, and tried to blink the sting out of them. Outside the window, the blurred shape of Warrington stood beside her, weapon raised, still shouting. She could sense movement all around him.

Charlotte's survival sense told her to get them the fuck out of there.

Leaning across the seat, she reached under the steering column and turned the key still in the ignition. The engine fired and she cranked down her window enough to yell at him to get in.

"Get down!" he yelled.

Her eyes had cleared enough so that she could see the fear in his own.

She looked over her shoulder and her breath caught in her throat. The Tall Man stood across the forecourt—petrol pump in hand—spraying inflammable liquid over the tarmac and across the vehicles parked around him. The creature raised the nozzle and squirted jets of petrol at the policeman, grinning as it did so, its remaining eye gleaming next to the shattered remnant caused by Warrington's shotgun at Mayor Parsons' manor the previous day.

"Shooot meee…," it said.

Charlotte pointed. "Shoot him!"

The beast stared at him from the dark pit of its eye socket, its tongue flicking across its cracked lips. Tilting its head to one side, it watched the policeman slowly open the door of the jeep. As Warrington was getting in, the Tall Man used the nozzle to point at something behind him.

On the other side of the road next to the garage was a grass bank, and while he could not see what was approaching, he could see a plume of black smoke advancing towards them.

"Drive," he said as he fell into the jeep. "Drive!"

Charlotte crunched the vehicle into gear as a zombie in flames stumbled over the verge and onto the pavement, making its way for the garage and the petrol-soaked ground. Warrington yelled at her to move and the jeep spun its thick wheels on the soaked ground.

The flaming dead person—its sex indistinguishable inside the flames—reached the edge of the forecourt and fell, the fire rendering its withered body useless. It pitched forward, smashing its face into the ground, sending a beautiful bellow of multi-colored flames as it touched the petrol.

The wheels of the jeep spun so fast Warrington feared their own friction might ignite the fuel beneath them, but slowly the jeep gained ground and slithered away.

Warrington watched as the fire expanded from the fallen figure in a crescent-shaped wave. It engulfed cars and pumps and swept towards them as the wheels gained traction and Charlotte pushed the jeep away from danger.

But it wasn't enough.

The liquid-flame engulfed them with a whoosh. The tires burned rapidly and filled the cabin of the vehicle with a rank smell. The petrol on the windscreen ignited and blocked Charlotte's vision. The noise of the engine and the flames deafened her, and the loss of vision was disjointing. She pressed the accelerator in panic, bizarrely hoping that she could outrun the flames that consumed them.

Instead, they crashed.

The impact threw Charlotte against the steering wheel as an airbag deployed and cushioned her. Warrington was already slipping into the foot-well of the vehicle and ended up firmly lodged within.

He sat up, scrambling into his seat while grabbing Charlotte's shoulder to pull her towards him. She tried to speak, but the fire ate their oxygen, and the sound was all-encompassing.

The inside of the cabin was a mixture of yellow and orange light, and the heat was immense. Warrington saw the crumpled front of the jeep embedded in the side of another car that was rolling away from them, and down a bank … to a river that ran past the garage and along the side of a supermarket.

Grabbing Charlotte's face, he buried her head under his arm and kicked the door open.

The yellow and orange animal fed upon the inside of the vehicle as the secretary fought against his strength. He dragged her from the jeep as the fire destroyed each of his senses as it burned the petrol covering them.

He could not see, but he felt the slope of the embankment under his feet. Taking two more steps, he succumbed to the flames and fell to his knees, throwing Charlotte Lewis down the bank before him.

She hit the river with a splash as Warrington rolled into her, sending them both under the murky water. Where she had the air burned from her lungs, she now found her throat filling with liquid, and she lost all sense of what was happening to-and-around her.

Charlotte's body flailed, and she did not know what to do. The coldness felt soothing, and she began to struggle less within the confines of the river.

Warrington dragged her up by the scruff of her blouse. Clear air filled her nose and she gasped, coughing dirty water up from her throat. She looked at Warrington who had hold of her in one hand, and was wiping his face clear with the other. They both looked themselves up and down, surprised and shocked they were alive—singed, but alive.

Warrington looked around himself, hoping that the SA80 had made it down the bank with them, but he was in no such luck.

"How the hell did we get away with that?" she asked as she grabbed the back of his tattered shirt and dragged him to the other side of the thin waterway.

"The petrol—" he gasped, taking a deep breath. "The petrol covering us burned, instead of our skin."

The garage exploded in a massive fireball. Bits of cars, concrete, metal, and the dead were thrown into the air, the force of the blast knocking them off their feet and into the water again.

Warrington helped her up as dead bodies peppered the water. He pulled her onto the opposite bank from the now-ruined garage and dragged her to her feet

"Where now?" she asked as she turned to him, the heat from the burning structure already warming them.

He shoved her onwards as the dead bodies in the water began to rise.

"Just run," he said.

CHAPTER EIGHT

Aaron Drury ditched the Nissan Micra in the middle of a road, its dented bonnet trying to contain clouds of steam and failing. He kicked one of its thin wheels and swore.

He had driven around Hangshaw the entire morning, avoiding the dead as much as possible, skirting roadblocks, and stopping to talk to survivors wherever he found them, although they were more and more becoming scarce in their numbers. He learned that most places had been evacuated by the military, who were taking survivors to a nearby high school, so he headed for that.

Ryde High was a public school with long playing fields extending from it. An uneven sports track lay next to a fenced football pitch, and long hedges adorned the outside of the fields. He stood behind one hedge—peering through—taking in stock of the soldiers on the opposite side of the field, near the school building itself.

Attached to the rear of the building were a set of tennis courts—again fenced off—and sat inside the courts were dozens and dozens of men, women, and children, all under the eyes of the military. The soldiers stood before them, weapons raised, but not aimed at them, and Drury could not figure out if they were forcibly being detained, or merely recommended to stay in their place.

He pressed into the hedge to gain a better look, and flinched when a gunshot cracked the air before him. He had been so intent on examining the tennis courts, he had not seen the trooper crossing the field towards his position. The soldier stepped forward, firing again, and Drury stood motionless.

The noise of breaking foliage resulted in a zombie crashing to the grass a few feet away from him.

He sighed. The soldier had not seen him, and had picked off a beast beside him. He was trying to figure out how to gain the soldier's attention without being shot, when another sound stopped him.

The boxer pulled back slightly from his position within the shrubbery so he could survey the small road that extended to his left and right. Numerous undead were walking towards the hedge, stopping as they reached it.

Drury frowned. What were they waiting for? The gunshot alone should have excited them enough to launch an attack. He remained still, watching as more and more zombies came to stand to his left, still as statues, staring at the hedge before them.

Drury heard the sound of dragging feet over his other shoulder, and a glance revealed that he was hiding in a hedge in the middle of dozens of the creatures. Their moans became a combined drone that covered the sound of his own breathing which sounded like an engine roar in his own ears.

He pressed himself as deep as he could into the branches and leaves, every crack or rustle making him grimace. He wanted nothing more than to run, but he risked being shot in one direction, and eaten in the other.

Looking back through the hedge, he saw more soldiers pacing the field, some of them leaving the tennis courts to investigate the dead man that had been shot near Drury.

The people and families in the courts were getting to their feet, and he could hear some of them shouting at the soldiers, asking what was happening. One man tried to leave the sporting area, but a soldier pushed him back. The trooper called to a man wearing slightly different attire to his own—a higher ranking soldier, perhaps—and he stopped his advance into the field. Turning back to the man trying to leave the tennis courts, the official man pointed a pistol at him, shouting. The leaver shouted back, stepped forward, and was promptly shot by the official.

Screams erupted from the tennis courts, and a woman and young girl rushed forward towards the fallen man. The trooper with stripes on his shoulder shot the man on the ground twice in the head. Drury knew it was to prevent the dead man from getting up again.

The zombies around him moaned and swayed in the breeze like dead, rotting flowers. He tried to move his head as little as possible as he looked at them, and almost yelled in shock when he found one of the creatures standing only mere inches from him.

The skin and flesh around its mouth had been stripped away, its milky eyes staring into the branches before it. Blood soaked its clothes, and it stood just behind him. If it breathed, Drury would have felt it upon his neck.

Drury's own breathing was too fast and shallow, and he clamped his mouth shut and sucked air in and out of his nose.

The dead suddenly stepped forward towards the head—as one—like they had all heard a hidden command.

The noise they made after being so quiet for so long was tremendous. The hedge fell apart beneath their combined weight, and Drury fell with it.

The undead paid him no heed as they tore through the hedge and advanced towards the soldiers. The troops raised their guns and pumped bullets into them. The dead moved in waves, the fastest almost running, while others shambled quickly. The sheer number of them caused more than one soldier to flee.

The undead trampled past Drury where he lay as he tried to squash his body as hard into the fallen hedge as he could. Branches dug into him and he could feel sticks penetrating his clothes and skin, but he dared not move.

The troops were greatly outnumbered, and—at a command—fell back towards the high school building. Dead emerged from the school itself, cutting off any escape plans the soldiers had through there. The tennis courts were their only option.

The living bottle-necked the entrance and the far exit of the asphalt courts. The soldiers that stood by their commander on the field fell beneath tooth and clawed hand—several shooting themselves rather than be murdered—and it was not long until the dead started eating into the panicked townsfolk trapped inside the fenced area.

Still, Drury did not move as the dead army continued to pass him. One stood on his hand as it went, and he bit his lip to prevent more panic from overcoming him. It moved off, and he saw their numbers packing into the courts, intensifying the screaming from within.

He remained still, trying not to stare at the stragglers as they passed him. Eventually he felt safe enough to move.

Somewhere distant he heard an explosion, and every single one of the undead in the fields and school grounds stopped moving, all at the same time. Even those feasting on the living.

Drury held his breath as he trembled. His eyes flicked from one zombie to another. They all stood swaying, not looking at anything with those glassy eyes.

And then they all regained their senses. They began to shuffle and move, but without the cohesion and force that they had displayed before. Now they spread out, moving aimlessly like the mindless drones they really were. The screaming, shouting, and moaning from the cluster of living and dead next to the school drew them in.

All except for the zombie standing next to Drury, who looked at him and moaned as it reached down.

The boxer was up and running before many of them had a chance to spot him. He found himself running towards a plume of smoke that he thought was coming from Newport.

Seven miles away, standing next to a burning petrol station, the Tall Man opened his eyelids. Thin yellow skin blinked against the dull gold of its one remaining eye. It stared at the flames surrounding it before turning to the stream that the two humans had escaped across.

It stepped into the water.

CHAPTER NINE

John Warrington pulled at the loose threads of his charred police shirt. He scanned the surroundings as he and Charlotte walked further into an industrial estate—keeping to the rear of buildings and hopping from car park to car park, looking for an open vehicle.

"Can't you just hotwire one of these things?" she asked as he tried the door of a BMW, setting off the alarm.

He dragged her behind an old factory that had been converted into a car wash, and they climbed a small fence separating it from a used car sales lot. Warrington tried the office door, wishing he had the military rifle that he had left in the burning jeep. The door was locked, and he broke the glass front of it with his elbow.

"Can you not do anything quietly?" she chided.

They entered the office and Warrington found a cupboard on a wall behind a desk. His elbow broke it open as well, revealing rows of keys inside.

"Now is not the time to be picky," said Charlotte as she saw zombies on their way to investigate the noise.

"I'd rather a car on the front row rather than one

that's boxed in," he said, tapping his bottom lip as he read the models of cars written above the keys.

Charlotte stood behind the doorframe of the office, peeking out across the car lot and at the undead that moved across the car park of the car wash next door. One tripped over the fence, breaking the flimsy wood, creating an opening for it and the others to walk through.

When the beasts heard no feeding moans, they began to wander and shuffle aimlessly once again, but now some were in the used car lot, flitting between the vehicles.

Warrington touched her arm and she jumped, covering her mouth with her hand. He looked at her apologetically.

"I'm getting sick of running and hiding everywhere," she whispered. "We need to find Aaron and get somewhere safe."

He nodded and moved towards the door, but she put a hand on his arm, turning him so their bloodshot eyes met.

"Please, John."

He studied her face. The once bright green eyes seemed duller, and tired lines darkened her features. Her light-blue blouse was damp and burnt, and her pencil skirt was beyond repair. Her bare feet were black and covered with scratches, and her bare legs plastered with mud.

And yet her straight back and posture conveyed the fight within.

"I understand," he said. "We'll find your boyfriend back in Hangshaw, and then a safe-house to ride this shit-storm out."

"Thank you," she said, then touched his arm.

He looked down at her hand and was about to say something when a moan interrupted them. A zombie in the car lot had seen them. The noise started as the moan of a solitary zombie, but was instantly echoed by that of the undead all around. Heads turned slowly as they sought the source of food, and the ones nearby fell in behind the one that had seen Warrington and Charlotte.

He grabbed her hand and ran towards the front of the lot as he frantically clicked at the key in his hand. A black Honda CRV 4x4 responded with a beep beep and a flash of lights.

They got in and he pressed the key into the ignition, turning it and starting the engine. The Honda hit the road with a squeal from the tires and crushed a dead girl crawling along the road towards them.

Warrington looked around the cabin of the 4x4 as they drove out of the industrial estate and away from the maddening dead crowd.

"Any other time and I think I might buy one of these," he said, admiring the leather seats and trim.

"Ironically, you've just stolen it," she replied. "Will you be arresting yourself, sergeant?"

They passed close to the garage that had exploded and could see plumes of smoke filling the sky. The smell made Charlotte cover her nose and she chose not to look down the road that was crammed with burning vehicles and zombies.

The back roads and outskirts of town seemed safer than the center and they proceeded relatively unbothered. At one point, they were flagged down by a woman and her child, but when they informed her they were heading for Hangshaw, she scooped up her son and disappeared into a nearby house.

"I guess before the military shut everything down the news was saying what was happening in Hangshaw," said Warrington as he drove on.

Charlotte rubbed the bridge of her nose. "Is that really where everything started?"

"I think so," he nodded. "The Purton Mill, plus…," his voice quieted. "Kevin at the hospital." He shivered as he thought of piercing his colleague's skull with an IV-stand. "I think it all stemmed from our little town."

He glanced at her and saw tears welling in her eyes.

"But I think that there were outbreaks everywhere," he added, wanting to ease any burden she may have felt. "There must have been. There's no way that the whole island fell just from a bunch of dead people spreading this plague in Hangshaw. I think that the Tall Man is controlling the dead and was spreading the outbreak himself. He probably had them all tucked up in places waiting for the order to jump out and infect everyone."

She looked thoughtful. "You really believe that he … it … whatever, is the reason behind all this?"

"Yeah."

She buried her head in her hands. "This is all so fucked up."

Hangshaw was in ruins.

Warrington steered the Honda around debris and wreckage with a growing expertise, and had even conditioned himself not to flinch when driving through the undead that got in their way.

Aaron Drury's flat was a smoking shell when they reached it, and the dead milled around outside, before the rumbling vehicle drew their attention.

Charlotte put a hand on Warrington's arm as he put the Honda in reverse.

"Wait," she said. "Just a minute."

"He can't be in there," the sergeant replied. "Plus, this place is full of those things."

He noticed her eyes were not watching Drury's flat, but were scanning the dead that approached them. He cursed himself for not realizing she was looking to see if her lover was one of the undead.

"Okay, go," she said.

He drove to Drury's parents's house under her directions, although she added they were currently away on holiday. The building was dark and empty and a search revealed no one had been inside anytime recently.

Back in the 4x4, Charlotte sighed heavily. "I don't know where else he would be."

For the first time since he had hired her three years ago, Warrington could see she was on the verge of being beaten by something out of her control.

He dropped the vehicle into gear and drove, skirting a lorry that had crashed into a bungalow.

Warrington touched her hand. "Maybe he's looking for you."

Soon they pulled up outside of the police station. Warrington suggested Charlotte try the doors to see if Drury had broken in. He stood by the open door of the Honda, leaving the engine running. It would draw attention, but he did not plan to stay long.

She withdrew her key as she ran up the steps, hesitating as she reached the door. Something had caught her attention and she took that something hanging from the door knob.

"All okay?" Warrington asked as she jogged back down to him.

"Yep," she said, holding up a necklace to him. It was half a gold heart on a chain, and from under her blouse she produced the other half. "He is looking for me." She grinned.

Warrington could not help but return the smile.

"Wherever he goes next, he's going to find that he can't get off the island at any of the ports." He stopped outside a hardware shop. "So, he'll come back here to look for you. We need to leave him some directions."

Charlotte followed him. The store's glass had been smashed and the window-frames covered in blood. Warrington stepped through one of the windows, fanning the shotgun around the darkened area. When nothing revealed itself, he waved for her to follow.

Warrington took a bag from behind the counter and searched the store for spray paints, which he piled into it. Adding some duct tape, super glue, hammers, tools, and nails, he filled another bag with the materials.

"Back in the car," he said as she took one of the bags from him.

They remained undetected as they loaded the bags onto the backseat of the Honda.

"Back to the station," he said. "Let's leave your boyfriend a message."

Warrington sprayed PURTON MILL on the police station doors. Charlotte added her name, with XXX underneath.

"Wait," she said. "Won't everyone that reads this head for the mill?"

"Sure," he answered. "But I figure as long as the person can read, they won't be too much of a danger to us. I haven't seen any dead reading the Isle of Wight County Press."

She nodded. "Alright, but why the mill?"

"It's empty. It's out of the way, surrounded by lots of visible land, and we should be able to hole-up in it pretty well. There's a barn-full of materials we could use, too, and I think we'd be pretty safe there."

"You mean like we were at Gatcombe Manor?"

George's Purton's body had been long removed by the coroner, but blood still filled the muddy puddles in the ground. Tape and markers indicated possible evidence, and broken tape fluttered from the door of the office out back. He peered inside and saw that Greg Evans's body had gone, blood and severed fingers marking the position where Warrington had found him.

The farmhouse was unlocked and he put the bags of supplies on a thick-legged kitchen table. He almost shouted with joy when he found Purton was stashing his own antique shotgun in a cupboard under the stairs. Cramming a handful of shells into his pocket, he loaded it and showed it triumphantly to Charlotte before moving through the house, locking and bolting every door and window.

"What shall I do?" she asked as he disappeared upstairs.

"I haven't had a cup of tea since yesterday!" he yelled down at her.

"Yes, sarge," she said and saluted the empty room.

Loose floorboards upstairs were used to secure the windows on the story below. Charlotte found a set of keys for the tractor outside so he moved it across the entrance of the lane leading to the house. The policeman dragged floorboards against the tractor and sprayed BEEP HORN over them.

"It's a shame the electric is out. I saw some CCTV cameras in that hardware store," he said, rubbing his chin.

"Couldn't we get a generator set up?" she asked.

"The constant noise might attract the unwanted."

She pointed at the sprayed boards. "And sounding your horn won't?"

"C'mon," he said. "We've got work to do."

Her protests continued as they walked back to the house.

They argued whether to light the open fire in the lounge or not. Warrington thought the smoke might lead the dead to them.

"The dead only want blood and flesh," she countered. "They're too thick to know what smoke signifies."

"What about the Tall Man?"

She put the box of matches back on the hearth.

Warrington dozed on a sofa until Charlotte prodded him awake. He did so with a start, one hand reaching for the shotgun on the floor.

"Easy," she said holding her hands up. "Someone's beeping."

He rubbed his eyes and got to his feet. Stretching his aching body, he saw the day growing dim between the slats of the boarded windows.

"It's near dark," he said.

She bit her lip.

Mud squelched under his boots as he walked outside, pulling on a coat found by the door to protect him from the cooling air. He could see a car at the bottom of the drive. He stopped as he recognized the vehicle, an old black Ford Capri, engine purring heavily.

"Sarge?" Charlotte asked as she emerged from the doorway of the farmhouse. "Is that—"

"Yeah," he said. "Stay here."

As he approached the vehicle, the driver's door opened. A smile crossed a young, stubbled-face as the man stepped out.

"Well shit tha' bed," he said in a heavy Irish accent. Adjusting his leather jacket, he walked around the tractor. "If it isn't Sergeant Warrington. I should've guessed the pretty sign-writing at the police station was by your own good hand."

"I'm surprised you could read it, Cole," Warrington said as he balanced the shotgun on his forearm.

"Funny," said Christopher Cole wagging a finger at the other man.

"What are you doing here?"

Cole looked confused. "I thought anyone looking for sanctuary had to come to the Purton Mill," he said. "At least that was what's written across your station doors."

"I meant what are you doing back on the island?"

"I was released from Winchester two days ago." He lifted up his jean leg to reveal a plastic device attached to his ankle. "They let me out with a tag, and I gotta stay at my folks during curfew."

"Then I guess you better run along home before you break tag, son," he said. "And give your dad his car back. He's had that thing since I came to the island."

The smile on the Irishman's face vanished, and he looked as tired as the policeman. "Shall I describe to you exactly what happened to my parents today, officer?"

Warrington bounced the shotgun barrel in the palm of his hand. Their eyes locked, neither blinking.

"Sarge," Charlotte said softly, walking up behind him.

The smile returned to Cole's face. "Ah," he said. "The delectable Miss Lewis. Oh, how I've missed your pretty face—"

"I won't miss—". Warrington started, before

Charlotte silenced him.

"Come on up, Cole," she said. "The more the merrier."

Warrington stared at the vintage motor burbling at the bottom of the driveway. The night air was quiet and he heard Cole and Charlotte talking as they walked to the farmhouse.

"So where have you been?" Charlotte asked.

"At her majesty's pleasure in Winchester," Cole replied.

"Nice place?"

"Ask your boss," Cole replied. "He put me in there."

Warrington listened to them leave before the noise of the Capri forced him to move it. He knew Cole had left it running with the intention of pissing him off enough to move it himself. And he was right. Warrington thought about ditching the car in a nearby stream, but left it in a nearby neighbor's driveway, tucking the keys into his pocket.

Cole and Charlotte were sitting in the kitchen talking when he entered; Charlotte smiled wryly at him while Cole lifted a cup of water, in salute.

Warrington placed Purton's shotgun on the table between them.

"You can stay tonight," he said. "But then I want you out."

"John!" Charlotte snapped.

Cole held his hand up to her. "It's okay. Your boss is pissed that the two times he's chased me, I jogged away both times." He smiled at her, cheeks straining to contain a mouth of perfect teeth. "And he's also upset that his police dogs can't jump fences."

Warrington gritted his teeth as Cole's eyes flickered at him in the dying daylight.

"Easy now, officer," he said. "Things are a lot different now. The law doesn't apply here anymore."

"No," Warrington said as he picked up the shotgun. "No, it doesn't. So if I shot you, no one would give a fuck."

Cole laughed as Charlotte snatched the weapon away.

"Enough!" she said. "Right now things are so fucked up we need all the help and manpower we can get. Cole can help us defend this place until Aaron turns up, and I'm sure that there are others on their way here, too."

Warrington's eyes lingered on Cole before looking at his colleague. He took a deep breath, his shoulders relaxing as he glanced back at the man sitting at the table.

"Fine," he said, teeth gritted. "But you best pull your weight around here."

Cole held up his hands, his face serious. "Look, whatever happened between us happened in another lifetime. Another world. Right now all I want to do is stay alive, and if that means I gotta play Happy Family with the man who put me in prison?" His smile faded. "Then so be it."

They room was silent until Warrington held his hand out to Charlotte. She handed him the shotgun.

"There are more floorboards upstairs that need tearing up," he said to Cole.

The younger man said nothing as he took a hammer from the table and disappeared up the stairs.

Warrington avoided Charlotte's gaze, but she grabbed his shirt sleeve.

"He's not that bad, John," she said, quieter than he had expected her to. "He's just a young man who—"

"He broke my nose," he said, leaning towards her. "He ran from me twice, he escaped police dogs, he was busted for drugs and stealing cars—the man is a criminal and a menace and a liability we don't need."

"How?" she asked. "He's helping us, and by the sounds of it, he's already lost people like we all have. He just wants to survive. If you turn away everyone you've arrested, we might not end up with anyone here."

"I'm just trying...," he said, but turned away from her.

She frowned. "Trying to what?"

He remained silent so she asked him again.

"I'm just trying to protect you."

Cole pried nails from the floorboards in a small upstairs bedroom. The furniture was already piled up on one side of the room, and several wooden planks had already been used over the windows downstairs. He was kneeling down, working the flat end of the hammer under a nail, when Charlotte walked in. He gave her a grin. "Care to give me a hand?"

She folded her arms. "You need to work with me if you want to stay here, Cole."

He held up the hammer. "I am."

"You know what I mean," she said, managing to find a spare corner of the bed to perch on. "We've been through a lot today and the last thing he needs is trouble at home."

Cole rested his back against the wall, the hammer sticking up from the floorboard. "All I want is somewhere to stay. Somewhere I don't have to sleep wit' one eye open and change my pants every time I hear something. When I saw your sign at the police station, I figured that all of the police were sitting here ... not just you two."

"Sorry to disappoint."

He laughed. "It's fine. The fewer people the less noise. I kind of half expected every officer on the island to be shored-up here, drinking tea and eating biscuits."

She groaned at his words and rubbed her stomach. "I haven't eaten since we were with the Army this morning."

"The Army?"

She nodded and told him of General Pegg and the attack on Gatcombe Manor. She also told him about the Tall Man.

He turned his head slightly and looked at her from the corner of one eye. "Are you winding me up, lass?"

She stared. "You're going to question that after seeing the dead eating the living?"

He stared at the uprooted hammer before him. "I guess not. Just sounds a little incredulous."

She smiled. "You swallow a dictionary?"

"English lessons in prison." He grinned. "So, what's the plan, anyway? I mean, after here."

She frowned at him.

"What are you going to do once this place starts filling up with survivors?" he asked. "What if a hundred people turn up ... and what if this tall dude rocks up with his army again?"

Her shoulders slumped and she looked down at her hands. "I've no idea. I'm just following John's lead."

"Is that a good idea?"

"He's kept me alive so far," she said with more conviction. "Which is why you need to listen to him and not piss him off."

"He's only going to keep you alive," he replied. "Not me."

"He'll protect us both," she said. "It's in his nature."

Cole ran a hand through his short black hair and barked a laugh. "You're wrong, Lewis," he said. "He'll ditch me at the first chance he gets. He would prefer it if I were still inside."

"How long did you get?"

"Two years," he said. "But I did ten months, and then they put me on a tag." He rubbed at his ankle. "The prison was so crowded they were trying to free-up some room." He blinked at her, gray eyes seeing something far off. "Jesus ... do you think the prisons are safe?"

She smiled. "They're probably the safest fucking places around."

Cole nodded, absentmindedly pulling at nails in the board again.

"So, what happened to you?"

"You mean what happened to my family and why

am I driving my dad's car without my dad in it?"

"If you don't want to talk about it—"

"It's fine," he said. "My tale probably isn't much different from yours or anyone else. I'm assuming that since you're with the policeman downstairs, that your superstar boyfriend is—"

"He's alive," she said, louder than she had intended as her fingers traced the necklaces beneath her blouse.

Cole regarded her. "Alright, Miss Lewis, I'll start again. I've been staying at my folks's because of the 7 PM curfew I'm under." He checked his watch. "Oops. Looks like I've broken that already."

"Hopefully they'll send someone to pick you up."

He smiled again. The gesture lifted some of the weight on her soul. "So, yeah," he said. "Been staying there, and I went out to see a couple of friends yesterday, and on the way back, thing's started to get really fucked up. I saw a crazy people attacking other people … and I tried to help some of them. One guy kept shouting about how important it was to not get bitten. I had no idea why at the time, but I sure as hell know now....

"Another guy kinda fell in with me and we made our way back home," he said. "I never got his name, but he saved me more than once." Cole rubbed at his eyes. She assumed it was tiredness. "We got to my folks and he passed out … because of his bites...." Again, he stared at something distant. "And then I had to cut his head off with garden sheers."

Charlotte's eyes never left his face.

Cole sighed, sitting upright. "Feels like an age ago," he said, working at the nails again. "Oh, man, that trip back home...." He paused to look at her. "I've seen things I hope you never see."

She sighed. "Unfortunately, I probably have. And I got a feeling things are gonna get worse before they get better."

He nodded, his chin falling slowly to his chest. He remained like that for so long she thought he had fallen asleep. She shifted her weight to stand when he spoke again:

"I ran into the house as the dead chased me." She could barely hear his soft words. "My dad had … he'd killed me mum … and she attacked me while I was beatin' on m'dad with a coffee table."

"I'm so sorry."

His voice shook. "I took my dad's car, and remember feeling upset that he wouldn't be pissed at me for taking it this time." He rubbed his hands down his face. "Man, what a couple of days." He fumbled the hammer and dropped it in a dark gap between the floorboards. Giving up on it, he turned to the secretary. "So, spill. What's your story, Miss Lewis?"

"Another time," she said. "We could end up swapping horror stories all night, but I need to rest."

He nodded.

"I'm waiting for Aaron to get here," she said, rising and moving towards the hallway. Pausing at the door she turned to him. "Try not to piss the sarge off too much ... please?"

He smiled and she left, and then so did his smile.

Outside, Warrington was talking to an elderly couple who had pulled up in their camper van by the tractor. The man leaned out of the window, smoke from his thin cigar dissipating into the growing gloom.

"Town's gone to hell, officer," he said, picking tobacco from his teeth.

"Seen a lot of folks get killed," the woman next to him moaned and held her hands to her stomach.

"Quiet, Elsie," he snapped, looking apologetically at Warrington. "We went to the hospital ... but...."

Warrington nodded. "There were a lot of sick people there," he said, casting his mind to his deputy. "People who couldn't run if the infected got among them. I can imagine what it was like."

The old man turned paler in the fading daylight. "No, I don't think you can. I saw patients and doctors fighting and killing each other. I heard some wards were barricaded and weren't letting anyone in. I think there are quite a few people still alive in that big ol' hospital.

"Anyway," he sighed. "We saw your sign at the station and figured we'd claim sanctuary with the local law enforcement." He smiled a rotting-toothed smile. His wife moaned again and he hushed her.

"Why were you at the hospital?" Warrington looked at the woman.

The old man stared at him and then glanced at his wife. The elderly woman clutched her hands to her stomach. Her head rolled back, revealing graying skin on her neck and chest.

The old man turned his head back to the policeman, but could not look him in the eye.

"When did she get bit?" Warrington asked, shifting the weight of the old shotgun in his hands.

"A few hours ago."

Warrington stepped back from the vehicle and raised the shotgun. "You know I'm not gonna let you stay here," he said. "And I can't let your wife go, either."

The old man's eyes widened. "You ain't killin' my Elsie, you mad man. I know she's in trouble—"

"She's going to turn," Warrington said.

"I know, I know," he said, holding a hand up between them. "But she's been my wife for fifty years, and I ain't gonna dump her by the side of the road."

"She has to be taken care of," the police officer said.

"You can't expect me to kill my own wife." His voice was shrill and loud.

Warrington let out a long breath. "I'll do it for you."

The old man stared at him. "Fuck you, officer. You can keep your safe-house. I'm gonna take my wife somewhere else. Somewhere humane, because it looks like the monsters are getting worse."

The camper van left in a haze of petrol-smoke and squealing tires. Warrington's shotgun followed the vehicle.

"That was pretty fucking cold."

"Don't sneak up on people," he said to Charlotte.

"Don't turn people away."

"His wife was bitten," Warrington said, walking

back up the muddy lane as she fell in step next to him. "She's going to turn any minute."

"Oh," Charlotte said, looking back over her shoulder at the road.

No one else came to the farmhouse that night.

CHAPTER TEN

Drury sat hunched on the pavement, feet in the gutter and his head in his hands. Exhaustion had him, and running through the rain the night before had left him shaking and his nose dripping. He wiped it on his sleeve as he watched a dead man approach, a moan rising from its ripped-chest.

He got to his feet and ran/stumbled away.

His mind asked his body where he was going, but it did not respond. It concentrated on lifting one heavy foot after another, planting them on the road with slaps that resonated in his ears. He was vaguely aware he was heading back towards the police station

Maybe she had gone back there to look for me?

He forced himself to stop and think. He tried to take refuge in a nearby pickup truck, but found it locked.

A driveway behind the truck led to a house—one with an open front door. On the gravel track lay an open suitcase and discarded children's toys. Either the occupants had fled and dropped the case on their way, or they had run outside straight into the walking dead and been forced back inside.

Drury chewed his lip before heading for the house.

He listened as he entered, pushing the front door wide open before stepping inside.

"Hello?" he called out, but his voice cracked. He cleared his throat and tried again.

More clothes and toys covered the laminate flooring and up a stairwell. Whoever had left had done so in a hurry.

"Hello?" he called out louder, and was answered with a noise from up the stairs. It was not a moan and did not sound like the undead—especially not the same sound as the dead man approaching him from behind was making.

He stepped inside the door, closed it, and threw the latch. The zombie slapped its palms against the door. Drury put his back against it and slid to the floor. The door felt strong and secure behind him, yet he pressed against it.

Moments later, he snapped his head awake, amazed at himself for having fallen asleep. His body ached, and he felt his skin burn as illness sank into his body.

He sat still, but did not hear anything within the building.

Getting to his feet, Drury tiptoed towards the staircase, and made as little noise as possible as he ascended. Children's toys littered the floor when he reached the top, and an array of doors surrounded him, some open, some closed.

He aimed for the shut door nearest him, hand shaking as he reached for the doorknob. Behind it he could hear movement ... a familiar sound ... panting?

Realizing what it was, he opened the door and didn't jump as the dog shot out of the room, bypassing him and scrambling down the stairs. Drury watched as the Rottweiler slipped and missed steps in its rush down the stairwell.

Drury walked into the room vacated by the dog. It was a bedroom, and more clothes were strewn all over the bed and floor. The dog had been so well house-trained it hadn't dared foul its master's room.

Movement caught his eye and he looked out of the window into the garden where he could see the dog relieving itself.

Once finished, the dog ran in circles around the garden, jumping on and attacking a large, teeth-damaged soft-ball.

"Stretch them legs." He smiled, and then found his eyes drawn to the large, soft bed.

Moments later he was lying on it, fast asleep, uncaring that there must have been an open door somewhere to allow the dog out....

He had no idea how long he had slept, although the sky outside the window was dark. His T-shirt stuck to him with sweat, and his bones ached. Trying to sit, he found the Rottweiler nestled against his back, adding its body heat to his.

"Scram, pooch." The dog stared, wagged its tail, licked his face. He pushed it away, laughing, but the big dog jumped on him and licked his face some more. Drury's own laughter sounded alien in his ears.

He pushed the lump off him and scratched it

behind its ears as it nuzzled against his stomach. "Alright," he said. "You can stay."

He fell asleep again.

The growling dog awoke him, its black-and-golden fur standing up as it crouched on the bed next to him, growling at the window. He ruffled its ears. "Easy … easy."

The dog jumped from the bed as he moved to the window. He could see a dead man heading for the house. The sun was sitting atop the garden hedge, and silhouettes moved around in the growing darkness.

He looked at the zombie and then at the dog who continued to growl.

Heading downstairs, he looked in a kitchen where he found the back door wide open and the dead man heading for him.

With the dog at his feet, he rushed forward and shut the door, locking it with a key and sliding a latch across. The hound followed as he left the kitchen and the sound of the door being pummeled.

In the hallway, he stroked the dog and gave it a hefty pat on the stomach. The dog rolled over and Drury scratched until its legs spasmed and its tail thumped the floor.

"My very own undead alarm, huh?"

The dog followed Drury as he examined every room and locked all the windows. Drury headed back into the bedroom, shutting the door and dragging a chest of drawers against it. The activity drained him, and he sank onto the bed, arm around dog, head sunken in pillows.

When he awoke, he glanced at the watch that was not there, and then at a bedside clock, which was off, along with all the electric.

The curtains were open and it was night outside. He got to his feet as the dog stirred and lifted its head.

Nothing moved in the garden. All he could hear was his own breathing along with the canine's, his cold making his thicker and heavier than the animal's.

He rested his head against the cool glass and closed his eyes. Where would his girlfriend be?

He turned away, his jaw set, angry at himself for not being with her when the island went to hell.

The dog tilted its head and looked at him. He sat next to it as it leaned forward for him to stroke.

"What's the plan, er—" He found the tag attached to the pink collar. "Zac? For a girl dog?" He shrugged until he caught a glimpse of a little girl in a photo, both arms wrapped tightly around a Rottweiler puppy sporting a pink collar. They looked like the happiest couple he had ever seen.

"Alright, Zac," he said. "What's the plan?"

The dog let out a low wine and lowered its almost-black eyes. Their stomachs rumbled in unison.

Drury held his and grinned. "Dinner time it is."

The garden outside of the kitchen was empty as far as the dark would allow him to see, and Zac issued no warning growls. He ruffled her short hair before searching the cupboards for food.

Back in the bedroom, he opened a family-sized bag of crisps while the dog ate noisily from a bowl overflowing with strong-smelling dog food. Crumbs and bits spattered the bed and floor, and the smell reminded him of old fish, but even the presence of a dog was comfort of a sort. Especially as the only people he had seen lately had been dead ones.

They ate their way through more snacks and tins of dog food he had loaded into a pink rucksack he had found in a child's bedroom. It was already half-empty, and he stored in it two bottles of water he had filled in the kitchen.

He stroked the dog again. "I'm getting out of here. Fancy tagging along?"

Zac tilted her head at him, tail thumping the bed as the big dog licked a chunk of rabbit from its own nose.

The dog followed Drury down the stairs. On a hook hanging by the front door he found a set of car keys for the Golf that had been parked at the bottom of the driveway. The fleeing family must have forgotten the keys in their haste to leave... although surely they wouldn't have forgotten the family pet. Which means they probably hadn't fled anywhere...

He cracked open the front door and peered into the dusk. Zac growled as a dead woman staggered along the pavement just yards in front of them, but a single low word from Drury silenced the dog.

A button on the keys illuminated the vehicle's

indicators and the alarm beeped shrilly.

"Fuck," he said, and ran from the house, Zac at his heel.

He opened the door and the dog bounded in, finding a place on the passenger seat as he slipped the keys in the ignition. The Rottweiler growled at the woman who had turned and headed for them, broken legs buckling beneath her, but not halting her progress. Blood smeared her face and a lace dress hung from her in tatters. Bones poked through both shins, and her hands were a mess of flesh and what he thought were knife wounds.

The Golf started with a thunderous grumble, and he grimaced as he realized the car had a racing exhaust, not ideal for being discreet.

He pulled out of the driveway and turned up the hill rather than passing the dead girl. He saw her mouth of smashed teeth opening and closing, but the noise of the car and the growling of the dog masked any sound she made.

Thankfully.

Drury drove past the homes of two of Charlotte's close friends, but one was overrun, and the other was empty. He had no other option than to try the police station again.

The dog settled down in its seat as Drury threw the Golf down narrow country lanes, knowing that the noisy vehicle was attracting the dead.

He barely saw any of the wandering corpses, and assumed that they had been attracted to other towns or villages, or maybe the shooting he had heard up on The Downs.

Knocking the car out of gear, he switched off the engine and let it roll forward as he approached a small village neighboring Hangshaw, hoping against hope that he would find other survivors, or even his girlfriend.

Instead, he found chaos.

A mini roundabout separated a handful of small shops which had once been the heart of the village. Three of the four roads leading away from the roundabout were blocked with vans and cars in an attempt to seal the area. Judging by the pools of blood covering the road and vehicles someone had failed.

He coasted the Golf towards the barricade; Zac remained silent, tongue panting as the dog stared out of the window.

He left the vehicle and she trotted after him, sniffing the ground, but staying clear of the bloodstains. Drury winced as Zac sniffed at a finger that lay on the road. Mercifully, she left it untouched.

He examined the nearest shop and found the big windows smashed and the place looted. The next store was a sailing-clothes one. He threw his dirty T-shirt on the ground and zipped up a black waterproof jacket over himself.

Drury found the dog sniffing along the blockage of vehicles leading down to a seafront. Across the Solent, he could see no lights in Portsmouth. He stared at the darkness, wondering if the mainland had fallen along with the island.

He investigated the barricade separating him from the road to the sea, and found that a car and van had been wedged together, jammed in so tight the wall on one side was scratched, and the other side was a mixture of glass and wood, as the van had obliterated the front of a small estate agent's.

Looking over his shoulder at the way he had come, Drury weighed his options, retrace his steps and take another longer route to Hangshaw, or move the barricades and take the short-cut.

"No-brainer," he said to himself.

He opened the back door of the small Toyota van that faced him and climbed in. Clambering over tools and buckets, he found the keys in the ignition. He climbed in the seat as Zac jumped into the back of the van.

The engine vomited into life, belching out smoke in a smog behind them. He squeezed the accelerator only to find that the engine revved loudly without moving the vehicle an inch.

The motor screamed its disgust as he floored the pedal, and he started rocking in his seat to give the van some momentum to break free. The tires started to find traction, and the sound of metal-scraping-on metal set his teeth on edge. The dog whimpered as the night was filled with the sound until the van broke free and trundled down the lane, dropping bits of bodywork in its wake.

He turned off the engine and rolled down the hill towards the seawall. He forced open the warped driver's door, and looked up and down the road to see how many dead would answer the racket he had created.

Drury hurried back to the remainder of the

barricade and found Zac rigid and growling. He tried to make out which direction she was indicating, but his head moved backwards and forwards.

They came.

They stumbled down the hill and out of nearby buildings, their moans growing. He already regretted not choosing the longer route.

"Let's go, girl," he said and ran for the Golf.

He held the door open for Zac to jump in. This time the roar of the Golf was not enough to drown out the sounds of the dead.

Heading for the gap he had made in the barricade, he was aware that the Golf was slightly wider than the van he had just moved. With no time—and no room for fucking-up—he had no option other than to shove the accelerator down and hit the gap with as much speed as he could gather in the short distance.

The noise was painstaking, as one side of the car scraped along the wall while the other ruined itself along the other car, with Zac yelping as the dog tumbled into the footwell.

The speed and weight of the Golf powered it through, and he steered it around the van he had abandoned moments before. The car that had formed the second half of the barricade freewheeled down the hill next to him, before heading off at an angle and pummeling into a small ice-cream store, creating more noise and carnage.

He glanced in his wing-mirrors to find they had both been destroyed in his flight. Nearing the road that ran along the seawall, the dead fell out of doors and windows as they sought him out.

A dead girl stood in the road before him and he swerved around her, clipping a boat on a trailer, tipping it over and shattering its hull into splinters.

Following the seawall, he steered the car along the road, skirting the dead and expensive abandoned cars. As he steered his way through a set of wooden pinch-points, an undead threw itself at him, forcing him to steer away from it and shatter one of the wooden pillars.

Drury powered the Golf away from the cacophony of undead, the Golf's one remaining headlight illuminating the way.

He stroked the dog's head in relief. Zac whimpered again, but stayed in the passenger seat, no longer growling.

Turning the remaining headlight off, he allowed his eyesight to adjust to the darkness until he could see the road beneath his wheels. Moving at a steady pace, he carried on towards Hangshaw, the noise from the car bringing the dead out in its wake.

The sea-road continued for a mile until it ran back inland. As the road turned away from the water, it ascended a hill, and at the bottom of the hill lay an overturned three-and-a-half-ton delivery truck.

Drury got out. The truck had hit the wall on one side, causing it to overturn and block the whole road. There were three other cars parked in front of it, the occupants probably trying their luck along the seawall extending miles to his right. He did not like the thought of walking miles along the edge of the beach in the dark. The moon might illuminate the dead, but it would also show him up to them.

Zac sat by his heel, panting. Just past the truck were the open gates leading to a cafe and park. He had visited there many times during his youth, either climbing on the playground equipment as a youngster, or sitting on the sloping hills with his friends, drinking and talking rubbish. Now the black interior of the park promised a different scenario to the one from his youthful memories.

With the road blocked, he knew their only viable option was to cut through the park and then walk the rest of the seawall into Hangshaw. He did not want to risk going back the way they had come—with the following horde of undead already audible over the sea wind—and the Golf would not smash its way past the fallen truck.

He stood at the gates and peered into the gloom. The sound of dead feet striking tarmac mingled with the moaning, indicating the closeness of his pursuers. He put a hand around Zac's muzzle as the dog started to growl. "I know, girl," he said. "But I need you to be really fucking quiet through here."

Zac's growling had already saved him, but this time it might serve as a beacon to the dead.

A cafe loomed out of the black as they walked, its glass doors a wreck, and a barricade of tables and chairs was scattered all around. They did not investigate, and moved as quickly as they dared. The clouds in the sky obscured the moon and its light, but it also caused him to stub his shin on a low fence around a mini-golf course. He bit his lip as he put a hand to his lower leg, the other hand finding Zac's collar to hold the hound close.

They neared the children's play area that once held fond memories, and could see an empty car park adjacent to it, the moon shining on the painted white lines that separated missing vehicles. A breeze ruffled the trees encompassing the park, making trees creak along with his anxiety over crossing the grounds.

He felt that the shadows all around moved. He glanced at the dog, and saw that it was staring at something he could not see.

He jumped when she growled.

Drury's frayed nerves strained even further, and he held his breath. Letting it out, he peered in the direction that the dog was facing, but could see nothing but a black chasm that ate the fading white lines of the parking bays.

He hushed the animal, but found his jaw shook so much it broke it into a shhh-shhh-shhh-shhh.

The dog growled from deep within its chest and Drury could hear a wet, slapping sound. It puzzled him, but the moan accompanying it was all too familiar.

Once the zombie was close enough, Drury found the slapping noise came from the creature dragging itself along the ground, its palms smacking the asphalt of the car park in its pursuit of food.

Its face was a mess of blood and hanging skin, its eyes gouged from its skull. Blood and fluids glistened on its cheeks, and as it pulled itself closer, he saw that it had no legs.

Zac growled, but did not approach the beast. The zombie jerked its head in the direction of the sound, and started hauling its way towards them.

Drury squatted down, trying to keep his

companion quiet. Zac stopped when the man wrapped his big hands around her muzzle.

The undead thing was within touching distance, a trail of thick blood indicating that it had not been dead for very long. Were there more creatures nearby? The ones who had turned this once-human into a monster?

Zac backed away from the zombie, and it followed the sound for a moment before continuing its macabre and sightless journey. Drury watched as it scampered into the mesh-fence of the tennis courts before adjusting course and disappearing into the blackness.

Do they not like animal flesh, he wondered, looking at the dog.

Clicking his tongue, he indicated Zac should follow him. The hound never ran ahead, always staying around his heels, occasionally pausing and tipping her head to listen. Drury's nerves shuddered every time the brawny dog hesitated.

Gusts of wind shook the leaves over his head, and he felt drops of rain on his face. Pulling his waterproof jacket tightly around him, he hurried his pace, trekking across the park using a mixture of poor visibility and a memory of the layout of the area.

A vehicle barrier indicated they had reached the other side of the grounds. He walked around it and up a short slope that led to another cafe on the seafront itself. He could smell and hear the sea as it stroked the beach. The closeness of the noise told him it was high tide.

He stopped just before he reached the small building. Nothing except the trees around them moved, and he could hear nothing from within. He approached cautiously, to find that it was as broken and derelict as every other store or building he had seen lately. It had either been attacked or looted, but was empty now.

The coastal path trailed away in both directions from the cafe, and Drury took the left path towards Hangshaw. It was a walk he had made a thousand times during his years, and when the summer came the beach was covered in swimsuited tourists and locals, soaking up the sun, laughing and playing in the sand and sea.

Now it was a mass of black, the path disappearing into the night, and he could barely see the water as it rolled against the dark-sand before them. The patter of the dog's paws kept him focused on his journey as Zac trotted a few yards ahead of him, no longer staying around his heels. He figured it was a good omen. Not for the first time he was thankful he had found a companion who could see and hear in the dark a lot better than he.

He wiped his nose on his sleeve. The rain fell harder and he pulled the thin, plastic hood up and drew the strings tight.

The dog ran ahead.

The rain was as strong and steady as the wind that pushed at him as they reached the end of the path. A boating lake dipped down a bank at a junction in the road, and they dropped to this lower level for their journey, slightly sheltered from the wind. Drury stifled coughs as they jogged, stubbornly ignoring his worsening ailments.

As they reached the far side of the lake, he stopped and leaned against a railing to catch his breath. Zac growled.

"C'mon," he moaned. "Give me a break."

The dog's nose was pointed towards a row of houses, but they did not stay around to find out what was causing Zac her angst.

The seafront leading into Hangshaw was decorated with tall tropical trees, but more than one had fallen under the weight of busses or lorries that had been used to force their way through the logjam of cars. People had tried to flee towards the bus and passenger-ferry situated at the end of Hangshaw pier, but now the once tourist-friendly seafront was a graveyard of vehicles and dead bodies. Fires that had once raged through the vehicles had succumbed to the wind and rain, but provided him with enough light to see the horrors all around him.

A seawall enabled them to run along its top and they neared the bus station. Several double-deckers were either parked in bays or crashed into walls and other modes of transport. The entire seafront-road was an accordion of crashed cars.

The Rottweiler growled again, but not before he heard the dead making a commotion a few hundred yards ahead. A taxi rank full of wrecked vehicles barred his way, but he could see movement through the rain. Zac's growl rose as the moaning increased.

He knelt down and stroked the canine. "We gotta find a way through." To his left, the hill running up into the town center was cut-off by overturned vehicles and flaming debris. Well-painted and presented shop fronts now gave either side of the hill a lop-sided, broken-toothed smile, punctuated by the backends of cars that had smashed into them. The random fires among the cars highlighted the dead men and women still standing among them, waiting in a morbid dinner line.

"Fuck it," he said, not wanting to trek through the carnage, but knowing it was the quickest way to the station. He hoped the bad weather would mask their ascent.

He looked down at his sidekick. "Ready?"

Inside a car they approached, he could see a dead figure slapping its hands against the window. He avoided its gaze and the growing anger of the hands trying to beat a path to him.

The rain drove down upon them, crashing off vehicles and beating upon his waterproof jacket with a forceful staccato.

Cars pinned bodies between them, bodies that flailed their arms and reached out to him. Incessant moans grew as those around responded to the feeding call.

A hand clutched his ankle, making him jump. He snapped the wrist underfoot, and then told the dog to run.

Scrambling over the bonnet of a car rear-ended by a bus, Drury begged his tired body to jump, slide, and weave his way around and over the obstacle-course of cars.

Another bus barricaded his way to the main street that led further into town. He jumped onto the roof of a car and used it to propel himself onto the bus's single-decked roof. He hit the top of it with his midriff, fingers scrambling for purchase on the wet metal. Managing to get a toehold on the rubber-tread of a window, he hoisted himself up.

Glancing down he saw Zac run around the bus. He could also see a lot of the dead picking their way through the wreckage towards him.

A hell of a lot.

They walked and stumbled from all directions, from the bus station and down the hill he needed to ascend. Cars were smashed and concertinaed together all the way up the slope, and the dead were crawling over the damaged transport as their moans escalated.

Putting his hands on his thighs, he bent double and shook his head. "This was a bad idea."

Was this where he was going to die?

No, Charlotte's voice whispered in his head. You need to find me first.

He opened his eyes, nodded to himself, and jumped onto the roof of a car below.

Leaping from vehicle to vehicle, he picked his way up the bottom of the hill, slipping often, but managing not to fall into any crevasses between the cars. The dead were drawn to him, their noise making his bones hum.

The cars became more tightly packed the further he went, and more dead were trapped between them. Scrambling across the roofs became a horrific game of tag.

A sound eclipsed any noise he could make and diverted the dead's attention from him.

He stopped and looked into the air, the sound of a helicopter unmistakable. He could see its landing and tail lights as the spinning blades filled the air above. It shone a spotlight over the carnage on the seafront.

"Don't shine that on me," he yelled.

The spotlight shone on him.

The dead grabbed at his feet as he teetered on the car roof.

Sliding down a windscreen, he stumbled and put his hands through the rear window of the next car. He crawled out and vaulted over the vehicle, making for the shop front that the vehicle was stuck in. Coming off the bonnet, he landed on a carpet of broken bricks, wood, glass, and a lot of smashed ceramic dolls.

The spotlight from the helicopter revealed the store was empty. It also illuminated his precise whereabouts, so he ran, blundering into a glass case of figurines, which he knocked over and destroyed with a smash.

If the helicopter was not giving his position away, he was doing a damn fine job of it himself.

At the rear of the store darkness engulfed him again, the spotlight having burnt light into his eyes. He pressed on, hands waving in front of him for something, anything that would give an indication of a way out.

Feeling his way behind a counter, he opened a door and entered another room. A flash of the helicopter's spotlight across the shop front gave him a brief flash of illumination which revealed the room to be a near-empty storeroom. It also revealed the dead bundling in through the storefront.

He shut the door between him and them, but found

no way of locking it.

He moved forward knowing he did not have time to let his eyes adjust to the gloom.

His hands found the long bar across an emergency fire door. He put his weight against it, and fell into the back street beyond.

The smaller side road was just as crammed with cars, but the number of undead was considerably less. The helicopter buzzed somewhere overhead, but was still patrolling the main street, instead of this back one.

The spotlight from the aircraft flitted over the back alley, but the buildings provided him with enough cover to remain undetected.

The realization of having lost Zac made his chest ache. For a fleeting second he considered going back for the dog, but sense saw through, the dead pushing sentimentality aside as the ones that were in this back lane called out to him. Zombies squirmed their way towards him, hissing and moaning.

He shuddered, climbing onto the bonnet of another car, using the vehicles as stepping stones to move past the dead.

The rain fell, unrelenting, Drury slipping and sliding his way up the hill.

He found a clear piece of road and ran along it, the movement clearing his nose. His feet slapped into a rhythm he was accustomed to, legs and arms pumping as he powered on. The rain washed his face and the now-even ground underfoot spurred him on.

There were hardly any undead at the top of the hill, the feeding moans from the bottom calling any stragglers away. The light of the helicopter swept the seafront, and a similar aircraft appeared to be flying across the Solent to join the other. Beneath the powerful beam the undead writhed and groaned, arms reaching up towards the scouting helicopter.

Drury squeezed his frame behind a phone-box as the nearest helicopter flew further inland. The dead moved up the hill following the light and noise, and he knew he must move as they thinned out around him.

A dead woman fell from the doorway of a pub as he marched by. Lifting its head from its crumpled position at the bottom of the steps, it moaned and the dead nearing the top of the hill answered.

He ran….

And tripped over a heavyset Rottweiler that bowled into him. Drury laughed and the dog barked. He shook the big animal's head in his hands with glee.

The moaning closed in and they moved on.

CHAPTER ELEVEN

Warrington sat alone at the kitchen table, a cup of water in his hand tilting precariously as his head rested on his chest. His light snores echoed in the room, the shotgun on his lap and all of the doors and windows on the ground floor locked and barricaded. A bird sang outside and the noise jerked him awake, the cup of water spraying the kitchen table. He put it down and wiped his hand on his trousers. He was glad it was not a hot drink he had spilled, but the thought of a nice, hot cup of tea made his mouth water. No electric meant cold food and only water from the tap to drink. Being unable to light a fire because the smoke might lure the dead aggravated him further.

Warrington hoped there would be warm food and safe shelter off the island … but what if there was not? Had mainland England succumbed to an assault like the one on the island?

He studied the kitchen, thinking of the grounds that the farm consumed. If they could erect a decent defense around the land, they could live off the livestock (which the dead strangely left untouched) and find more survivors, maybe establish a small community. Eventually the number of dead would diminish, and then he and Charlotte could….

He knew she would never go for it. Not while there was a chance her boxer-boyfriend was alive.

Warrington admired her devotion to the man.

And envied it.

He had been in love once, married to a beautiful woman who doted on him so much it broke her heart when he worked seven days a week and had no time to gift her a child. He worked so long and put her off so often, that in the end she left. He had not heard from her in over three years.

Not one word.

He had been a constable in the island's central area, quickly promoted to sergeant, and then offered the position in Hangshaw. Originally, he was unsure if he should take the post in such a small district, but his wife had encouraged him, believing that being closer to their home would give them more time together. Unfortunately, Hangshaw's crime rate was increasing rapidly and he worked even more hours than before. He was busy enough to recruit Kevin Clarke as his junior officer, and Charlotte Lewis as his secretary to handle the station while he was on the beat.

Charlotte had only been eighteen when he hired her, but was fresh out of college and eager to work. The others he interviewed were a product of their environment, gossiping, middle-aged ladies who would not keep station affairs private. A few of them were farmers' wives whom Warrington imagined had been sent by their husbands to keep out of their way. Charlotte took to the job and flourished, her telephone manner and attitude polite, if a little cool. Over the next three years that manner was replaced by an iciness that caused people to shy away from her. Warrington knew it was because she was fed up with the island and people and longed for the bright lights of the bigger cities, but she had not found a decent job in any of the locations she had searched, and she had to wait for Drury to finish a sports-therapy course at college along the coast in Bournemouth.

Drury had been back on the island for a year now, finding employment as a builder for a short time. His current job-searching was peppered with irregular semi-pro boxing matches; he won them all, but the purses did not grow any bigger.

They never had enough money to move away, although the unfortunate death of his grandmother bankrolled the flat he lived in. It was put up for sale months ago, but like most small property on the island, it remained that way. Charlotte rented a house and they spent most of their free time there together.

Warrington weighed up Drury's likelihood of survival. He was young, physically fit, and nobody's fool, but the police chief had seen trained soldiers and his own officer bought down by the dead.

"Morning, officer," Christopher Cole said as he walked into the kitchen, interrupting his thoughts.

Warrington looked, but remained silent, wiping the spilled water from the table and his trousers.

Cole walked around him, smiling as he picked up a glass and ran it under a tap. "I managed to find a bedroom with half of its floor intact. The bed was a little small, but I slept alright, thank you for asking." He pulled a stool to the table. "I don't think much of the room service, though."

"Zip it," Warrington said.

Cole's smile fell. "Look, I've paid for my crimes." He put his glass down heavily enough that it added its contents to the water already on the table. "Why don't you and I just get along until we can ride this shit-storm out?"

"Because a loudmouth like you will get us killed," Warrington replied, rising from his seat.

"Or I might be the extra eyes 'n' ears tha' saves your arse."

Warrington studied him. All he saw before him was a criminal, whether he'd paid his dues or not. He saw a man he had chased through the streets of the island on-and-off for almost five years. The last time he had captured him, Cole had accidentally broken his nose and been sent to Winchester prison. Now he was out and on a curfew that did not hold any power.

"Just stay out of my way," Warrington said as he scooped up the shotgun and opened the outside door.

Dew settled on the farm as he stepped outside. The ground was soft and muddy, the same as it had been the morning Warrington had killed George Purton on the very same grounds. A barn stood a short way off, coroner's markers sitting brightly in the mud where he had impaled Purton on the pitchfork.

He moved on, feet sinking as he patrolled all around the outside of the farmhouse, shotgun resting on his shoulder.

Cole strolled into the sun, eyes closed, face raised as he let it warm him, hands stuffed into the pockets of his leather jacket. "Tis a fine morning," he said. "Well, wha' wit all the dead people an' being stuck indoors with an angry policeman."

Warrington continued walking.

Cole continued following him.

"So what's the plan?" the Irishman asked, staying slightly behind Warrington and avoiding wherever the shotgun pointed.

"Staying alive," Warrington said.

"Good plan."

They walked, Warrington scouring the surroundings as the light grew and Cole chattered behind him. He paid no attention to the other man, his thoughts far away. He looked at the steep hills and trees around him, knowing that beyond them was the sea....

The policeman stopped and Cole almost bundled into the back of him. Without a word, Warrington turned and headed back for the farmhouse.

"Chief?" Cole asked.

"We're gonna need a boat."

"Not without my boyfriend," Charlotte snapped as the three stood around the table.

"I think he has a point," Cole said, arms crossed, glancing at the policeman. "Maybe getting to one of the harbors to see if there are any boats left isn't a bad idea."

Charlotte looked straight at the policeman. "You said we would wait for him."

"I know," he replied. "But you have to prepare yourself for the fact that—"

"He's alive!" she shouted. "He has to be. You go and jump in a boat all you want, but once you get out onto the Solent, the Navy will blow you out of the water, anyway. Remember what the soldiers told us in

Yarmouth?"

"She has a point," Cole said and was told to shut up by both of them. He shrugged and walked outside.

"He should be here by now," Warrington said, his voice low.

"He may have been held up," she said, leaning on the table. "It's hardly a walk in the park out there."

"Exactly. That's why you have to try and consider that he might—"

"Enough!" she almost screamed, holding her hands near her ears. "He left his necklace on the doors of the station, so he is looking for me."

Warrington could not match her gaze.

Finally, he succumbed, rubbing his hands down his face and sitting on a stool. "Alright," he said. "We'll give him until nightfall and then we're out of here."

Charlotte opened her mouth, but he raised a hand.

"That's more time than we should give him," he said. "We need to get off this island and take our chances on the water. If your boyfriend can't get to us in the next twelve hours, we have to go."

Her eyes closed and her shoulders slumped. She sat down herself. "I know," she said quietly. "I know…." Her voice was almost inaudible. "He has until tonight."

Warrington nodded. "I'm going to go and check around…," his voice drifted away. "Where's the shotgun?"

Charlotte looked at where he had left the old weapon on the kitchen side, but it had gone.

"Cole," he said, and ran from the kitchen.

"This is going to be a long day."

"I wasn't gonna go walking armed wit' a bread knife," Cole complained as Warrington snatched the shotgun from him.

The policeman checked the weapon, teeth grinding. "This is mine."

"Technically, you stole it," Charlotte said as she stood in the doorway of the farmhouse.

Warrington turned and looked at her coldly. "It could save our lives."

"You stole it?" Cole laughed. "Talk about pot calling kettle."

Warrington glanced from Charlotte to Cole and then stomped away, mud splashing up his legs. He disappeared around the back of the farmhouse. He told himself it was to check his temper.

He was angry at Cole simply because he did not like him, and he was angry at Charlotte because she would not listen. He could not imagine Drury having lasted this long on his own, and he did not want Cole tagging along on any escape attempt.

Would he leave Cole if he slowed them down at all? In a heartbeat.

And Warrington had seen the way that Cole had looked at Charlotte.

The thought slowed his pace. Was he jealous? Had he really seen anything between Charlotte and Cole?

He shook his head. No, he was just protecting his friend and colleague. She was young enough to be his daughter.

Absentmindedly, he tried to turn a ring on his finger he no longer wore.

And for the first time in a long time he thought about his wife and hoped she was safe.

He stood at the edge of one of the fields, eyes closed, enjoying the quiet. The air was brisk, birdsong filling the air as birds hopped from tree to tree. It was a perfect morning, except for the plumes of smoke dotting the landscape.

Somewhere he could hear the spinning blades of a helicopter. He did not hold out any hope of being rescued knowing that the military were abandoning their own men these days, as well as shooting civilians believed to be infected. How many people were left alive on the island, anyway? Were they locked-down in places they had fortified, or scattered all over, only to emerge and be picked off by Army weapons or dead teeth?

And why had no one else arrived at the house after the message he had left on the station doors?

"Because everyone's dead," he said to himself, the thought constricting his chest.

He returned to the farmhouse, checking the barns and storeroom on his way. He found nothing and saw no one, but he wanted to feel like he was doing something.

The kitchen door was open, Charlotte making sandwiches as Cole inserted batteries into a small portable radio, an empty television remote near the Irishman's hand.

The secretary did not look up as he entered, but Cole held the radio aloft as if it were a trophy.

"People maybe broadcasting," he said, slotting the last battery into place. "Maybe someone will know a way off the island."

"Maybe," Warrington said. "Or maybe the military still has all communications locked down."

Cole tried the radio. The small black box crackled into life, but he was rewarded with static. He turned it over in his hands before pressing a button. "It's got an auto-scan feature."

The static lifted and fell as the device searched for a live frequency. Warrington sat as Charlotte slid a plate of sandwiches between them.

"There's plenty of food here," Charlotte said. "Lots of canned stuff. We would be alright here for a few days."

"We leave tonight," Warrington said.

"I know," Charlotte said sharply. "I'm just pointing out that we have enough supplies to last us, if needed."

"Plus we're on a farm," Cole said, still staring at the transistor. "Doesn't tha' give us free license to grow our own food. An' eat the pigs?"

"Have you ever killed an animal?" Warrington asked.

Cole raised his eyes. "No, but I killed my twelve-year-old neighbour when she tried to eat me."

Warrington nodded slowly. "There's a difference between defending yourself and killing someone or something that wouldn't harm you."

Cole returned his attention to the radio. "It's all about survival of the fittest now, man."

"Is that what you'll tell anyone else that turns up?" The policeman asked him. "'Welcome, but if you slow me down I'll drop you like a hot brick'?"

"Isn't tha' what you'll do with me?" Cole said.

"Jesus Christ." Charlotte slapped a bread knife onto the table. "Will the two of you pack it the fuck in? We're the only living people we've seen lately, but right now I'd rather spend my time with the walking dead. At least they don't bicker and argue."

"No," Warrington said. "What they do is worse."

Throwing her sandwich down, Charlotte pointed a finger at him. "But at least they—"

A floorboard creaked above their heads.

They froze, Charlotte's finger aimed at Warrington, Warrington holding a sandwich in one hand, Cole stretching back on his stool. They all stared at the ceiling.

"I hope tha's just the house making noises," the Irishman whispered.

Footsteps thumped overhead.

"How the fuck did they get in?" hissed Warrington, popping the shotgun and checking its chamber.

"The upstairs windows aren't locked," Cole said.

"Well, the dead can't climb walls," Charlotte said, snatching the knife back up.

Warrington moved, halting at the bottom of the stairs, shotgun aiming upward.

The noise above ceased. Outside, sheep bleated and mud squelched—the sound pulling at Cole's attention.

He leapt from his seat and ran to the open door, slamming it shut as a zombie tried to throw itself into the kitchen. Locking it, he jammed in a deadbolt at its base. The thick wooden door vibrated as fists clashed against it.

"He's here," said Warrington.

"The Tall Man?" Charlotte asked, eyes wide.

"Who?" Cole asked, pressing his back against the door. He glanced at Charlotte. "You mean the tall, gangly fucker you were telling me about?"

Warrington cursed as he saw movement through the cracks in the kitchen windows. Had he been so lost in his thoughts outside he had not seen anything untoward? He dismissed the notion, knowing the Tall Man could have buried the dead in the mud if it so wished.

The din outside the door grew and Charlotte and Cole exchanged glances. Warrington was torn between helping them and going upstairs to investigate. He saw the door holding firm and it made his decision for him. "We need to get upstairs."

He started his ascent. The clattering and banging all around became maddening, but he could not force his body to move any quicker.

More sounds from the main bedroom, creaking and movement. In his mind, he tried to picture where the steps were coming from. By the window or the door to the hall?

He let out a low breath as he neared the top, shotgun shaking in his hands as he pointed it down the hallway. He could see the door to the bedroom was ajar.

His teeth chattered and his sweat was cold. He moved on, feeling like a child stumbling into the dark.

He reached the door, placing the shotgun barrel against it, and nudged it open. The noise of the hinges pained him as the racket escalated below. He could hear Cole and Charlotte arguing.

Pressing the door fully open, he took a step backwards, his shoulder blades touching the wall of the hallway behind.

He was terrified.

Ahead of him, the part of the room he could see was empty. The window inside the room was open, but nothing moved in view.

The blue carpet of the hall extended into the bedroom and he could see tracks of mud on it. Had Cole or Charlotte walked mud into the room?

The foot of the bed protruded around the door in front of him. He edged closer, blinking only to clear the sweat dripping into his eyes.

The room was empty. He relaxed and shoved the door wide open, the handle hitting the wall with a bang.

He stepped inside and could see no one. He lowered the shotgun.

He heard a noise above his head.

The Tall Man was wedged into the top corner of the room above the door. Its unnaturally long fingers dug into the coving around the ceiling, skeletal-toes digging holes into the wall just above Warrington's head.

The creature fell upon him before he could raise his weapon, knocking the wind from Warrington.

They collapsed in a heap, the loaded shotgun pinned between them as the Tall Man scratched at his face.

The pressure he felt as the creature grabbed his skull was immense. He screamed through gritted teeth, trying to pull himself free. The Tall Man hissed, its horrible mouth breaking into a grin, inches from his own face.

His head felt like it was in a vice and he closed his eyes as bursts of white exploded in his head. Warrington could not pull himself away ... he was going to die by the Tall Man's hands unless he found a way out.

He pulled the trigger.

The blast was loud, even though his ears were covered by the foul-smelling hands. The Tall Man released Warrington as it screamed in agony, a sound so inhuman it put his ears through extra torment. Man and beast separated, the shotgun falling from Warrington's hands as he stumbled back against the wall.

The screaming did not dissipate and Warrington had to open his eyes despite the pain; the world developed from a white haze before him. The Tall Man's pain-contorted face swam into view, staring down at a thigh left in tatters by the Remington's twelve-gauge buckshot. The flesh of its limb had been torn away and blood as black as tar oozed down its leg.

The Tall Man snarled, lips curling to show teeth like thick needles. Gone was the glee Warrington had witnessed moments before.

The shotgun lay on the floor between them, Warrington's glance at it bringing the weapon to the Tall Man's attention. It curled a lip at the sight of it, hissing loudly.

Warrington blinked the fog from his head and swooped to snatch the old Remington. The Tall Man moved slowly, still managing to reach Warrington before the policeman could bring the gun to bear.

A long hand dug into Warrington's shoulder and

he yelled. The creature's other hand grabbed the barrel of the shotgun and pushed it away from its body.

Warrington kicked at the beast, heavy boots striking its shins, but it did not let go. The policeman tried to pull the gun down and aim it at the Tall Man, but he could not match the abnormal strength of the thing.

The Tall Man loomed over Warrington, drool dripping on the policeman's chin. The teeth reappeared in a hideous grin as it forced Warrington onto his knees. It opened its mouth, fetid breath filling Warrington's nostrils as it moved close.

The policeman sank down, knees buckling, head throbbing, ears ringing, hope fading.

A thud shook the thing and it slumped forward, yellow eyes blinking in stunned shock. Another thud and Warrington felt the grip upon him weaken. From over the Tall Man's shoulder, Warrington could see a rolling pin arching through the air to strike the back of the beast's head again. As the Tall Man fell forward, Christopher Cole came into view wielding the kitchenware as a weapon.

The black orbs in the Tall Man's yellow eyes glazed over and Warrington pushed it away from him, wrestling the shotgun from its grasp.

"Kill it!" Charlotte yelled from behind Cole. They both looked terrified.

The Tall Man was bent down on one knee, propping itself up using the bed as a support. Warrington bought the shotgun level with its long, thin head—his own skull throbbing—and squeezed the trigger.

Nothing happened. Warrington stepped back as Cole shouted at him, "What are you doing?"

Warrington held up the Remington to show Cole the Tall Man's iron-grip had squeezed ruts into the barrel.

"Jesus," Cole said. "It's fucked."

The Tall Man stood, thin legs shaking as it hoisted itself upright.

"Move," ordered Warrington, throwing the now-useless weapon at his enemy.

Charlotte was already out of the hallway and running down the stairs as Cole followed. Warrington backed into the hall, eyes fixed on the bedroom. Thin skeletal fingers grasped the wood surrounding the doorway as the Tall Man staggered out, one hand clutching the back of its head.

Warrington fled.

Cole and Charlotte were in the kitchen when he caught up. The front door and boarded windows were under a relentless attack by dead hands, and all three kept their distance from the stairway.

"Now what?" Cole said.

Warrington put his hands under the lip of the kitchen table and grunted as he pulled the heavy furniture upward, head throbbing hard. Cole and Charlotte helped and the three of them hefted the oak table up and over onto its end, creating a barricade at the bottom of the stairs.

They moved to the lounge, Warrington pulling the door to the hallway shut. A window leaked light through the slats of its coverings, Cole peering between them.

"How many?" Warrington asked.

"Too many," Cole said quietly.

"Come on," Charlotte called, continuing along the hallway.

She stopped at the front door, Warrington having earlier hammered floorboards over the top and bottom of it.

"We're going out there?" Cole pointed at the door.

They heard the table in the kitchen fall over with a crash!

"We are now." Warrington gripped one of the floorboards and tore it away from the doorframe.

Cole grabbed the lower one and with Charlotte's help pulled it out with a squeak of resisting nails.

Charlotte's hand hovered over the key in the door. "Where's the police car?"

"Still around the side," Warrington said. "We won't make it. There's too many dead. We've got to run for it."

More chaos from the kitchen—more breaking wood.

"He's let them in the back door," Warrington said as Charlotte turned the key.

She threw the door open as the dead spilled into the hallway from the kitchen. None of the three still living looked behind them as they burst into the morning sun.

Outside, the dead they surprised were already struggling in the mud. Charlotte pushed at one as it made a grab for her, pitching it over on the wet ground. It clutched at Charlotte's blouse as it fell, dragging her down with it in a tangle of limbs. Warrington bent to help, but Cole beat him to her, grabbing Charlotte's arms and hoisting her to her feet as the zombie snapped its teeth at her.

Using patches of grass and thinner spots of mud to step on, they hurried down the driveway, mindful of the noisy pursuers emerging from the farmhouse behind.

"Have you got the keys for that?" Charlotte pointed at the tractor blocking the entrance of the drive.

"No," he said, pulling out a different set of keys. "But I do have these."

"My old man's car!" Cole laughed. "How far away is it?"

"Not far," Warrington said, running around the farm vehicle.

The dead were scattered across the road when they reached it, and Cole finished off the rolling pin on one of them. Warrington shoved another into a ditch before directing them to a cottage yards down the road. On its driveway sat the Capri.

"Give me the keys," Cole said as he moved for the driver's side.

Warrington curled a lip at him.

"I've been nicking this car from my dad for years," the younger man said, his palm out to the policeman. "I can drive this better than you."

Warrington slapped the keys into Cole's hand. Charlotte was already in the backseat as the two men climbed in.

Cole threw the vehicle from the 1980s in and out of corners and through any undead barring their way. Charlotte winced as each thud resounded inside the car, but Cole did not flinch.

"They are fucking everywhere," Cole said as he idled the car to a halt at a junction. Crashed cars blocked one exit while the other two were cluttered with approaching dead. "Where now?"

Warrington looked at Charlotte, who was staring out of the back window. "We need to go for a boat," he said, still watching her, waiting for a response. He got none. "Charlotte? It's time we got away from here completely."

She turned to him, eyes red and streaming.

"Aaron's going to the farmhouse," she said. "He'll follow the signs we left him."

CHAPTER TWELVE

Drury was smiling. The locket he had placed on the door handle of the police station was gone, and the message scrawled on the doors told him to go to Purton Mill.

He pointed at the XXX sprayed in swirling letters beneath the message. "See," he said to Zac, who sat panting at his feet. "I told you she's alive."

Drury shielded his eyes, trying to ignore the moans ringing in the air. He had learned the sounds usually meant there was food nearby. He had also learned that often he could not help those who were on the menu.

They moved alone or in groups along the roads leading in from the coast. At times their numbers were so great they seemed crammed too close together to move at all, spilling over cars and pushing past each other as more joined their ranks in answer to their feeding cries.

"Let's go, girl," he said, spying some of them wandering onto the police station road.

Drury stayed off the roads, using fields and pathways to navigate the way. The denim on his legs was soaked and labored his walk, although the brightening sunshine had warmed the fabric some. Man and dog moved away from the center of the town called Ryde and were walking on one of the many rural lanes leading in-and-out of it.

The dead were thinner in number outside of town centers. He guessed it was because the population-heavy areas equaled food, and it made him shudder.

Their trek led them further inland, towards Hangshaw. Drury tried several cars to try and speed their journey, but each vehicle was either incapacitated, penned-in, or had no keys, and the one time he did find a working vehicle, its rear end was stuck under a lorry and it would not break free.

He considered leaving the road and traveling via the fields, but the land was covered in rain, and he had had enough of being wet and muddy after the run from the bus crash which killed many of his friends. The thought made the lump on his head ache, and he wondered if the survivors of the crash were all still alive and if they had made it to safety.

He was almost relieved his parents were away so they couldn't see what the island had become, but the thought of another person pushed everything else from his mind.

Charlotte.

He hoped she was safe, and his heart had thudded hard in his chest when he saw the message on the police station wall. The knowledge of her being alive kept him plodding one heavy foot in front of the other.

The dog ran ahead, its energy boundless, although Zac's tongue seemed to hang lower with every mile they walked. Drury's body ached and the cold he carried and the strain—both mentally and physically—was telling.

The need to rest was great, but the need to find her was greater.

There was a mile left until the Purton Mill.

He did not like what he found there.

Drury grabbed Zac's collar and pulled the Rottweiler close. At the bottom of the driveway leading to the mill were a cluster of dead, moaning and moving in a herd. They were heading away from him and he did not want to gain their attention.

Zac growled and Drury soothed the animal, cupping its muzzle and stroking its head.

Somewhere close a car roared into action, followed by a crunch of gravel and the squeal of tires begging for purchase on tarmac. Had the people at Purton Mill fled the zombies and escaped in a car?

Maybe it was Charlotte.

He could see the Mills's farmhouse through the hedge on the other side of the road. Figures flitted behind the leaves, more of the dead moving down the muddy lane to the road.

One of the undead slipped on muddy feet as it reached the road and fell on its stomach, head pointing towards where they were concealed. Drury pressed himself further into the hedge until he felt sticks pierce his body. He pulled the dog in as far as he could, its growls growing harder.

She barked.

Drury held his breath and grabbed her by the snout, but it was too late. The mob was heading their way.

Drury slowly stood and was barraged with a hail of groans as the dead made for him, anger and excitement washing their gray faces.

He let go of Zac and turned, only to find the road they had traveled was now hedge-to-hedge full of the dead. They must have been close behind him for miles.

"Fuck."

They were penned in from both directions, and the hedges on either side had them entirely boxed in.

Drury took his chance with the foliage for the second time since falling through the hedge at the high school.

Protecting his eyes with one hand, he threw his body at the bushes, all fourteen stacked-stone of him crashing into the vegetation. Meeting resistance, he pressed his body harder. The branches scratched him, but he ignored the pain, even as he felt the waterproof coat he had looted rip to pieces around him.

The hedge started to feel endless. Time slowed and his mind tormented him; would the dead finally capture him after he got stuck in a fucking bush?

He burst through the other side so suddenly he was

caught off balance and fell into a field of cabbages.

Zac hopped around him, growling at the hole Drury had made as the dead gathered on the other side.

Blood dripped into his eye and he wiped it with his bare forearm, the coat sleeve having surrounded it lost somewhere within the hedge. The remainder of the coat hung from him in tatters and he tore it off, quickly taking count of the numerous scratches covering him.

A dead hand burst through the hedge.

He ran in the direction he had heard the car disappear.

His eyes were as heavy as his legs. Exhaustion was taking him. His downcast eyes stared at the mud blurring beneath his feet and he longed to lay down and sleep.

Zac bounded around his feet, urging him on.

They came to a gate after crossing the cabbage field. He saw a road, and the thought of treading on hard, flat ground gave him a second wind.

The change of terrain jarred his feet, but the sound and feel of trainer-to-tarmac was preferable to the strength-sapping mud. He passed a cottage and another farmhouse, but both looked empty and unfortified, and despite his tiredness, he did not want to find himself in a defenseless building surrounded by the dead.

He pressed on, drawn to a plume of smoke rising over the brow of the hill he ascended.

A clutch of small buildings were situated over the rise, one of them heavily on fire. A once-lush garden blazed in the sun, corpses smoldering on the road. Ordinarily, it would have been a sight to stop Drury in his tracks, but ordinarily had hitch-hiked the fuck out of Hangshaw a couple of days ago.

Drury jogged towards the burning building, but Zac slowed, whimpering.

"Come on," he said. "I'm hoping these things won't like a bit of fire."

They were yards from the cottages when he had to grasp the dog's collar and force her onwards, despite her resistance. The heat was intense and almost gave him second thoughts about getting any closer himself.

A porch overhung the door at the side of the cottage, designed to shelter a car that was not there, a thick hedge separating it from the property next door. The porch was alight, cracking and hissing as the flames engulfed it. The area was a tunnel of smoke and flames.

Drury gathered the Rottweiler up in his brawny arms even as it squirmed in his grasp. He clutched Zac so tightly he was afraid the dog would bite him.

"You're gonna hate me for this." Drury ran into the tunnel of heat and flame.

Ducking his head, he closed his eyes and ran, Zac's whimpering drowned in the noise and intensity of the flames. Blundering through, he opened his eyes to find his bearing, but the heat burned the moisture from them. He screwed them shut again, but not before he made out a bright doorway of light beyond the world of smoke of heat. He hurtled towards it, holding his breath, and holding the dog close.

They sprung from the hall of fire, smoke billowing from their bodies as Drury fell on the trimmed back lawn. Zac wriggled from his grasp, standing in the long grass and sneezing smoke from her nostrils as she shook her head. Drury rubbed his stinging eyes and looked the dog over. Smoke rose from her fur, but she did not burn, although Drury had to slap small flames from the cuffs of his own jeans. Well, at least they're dry now.

He sat next to Zac with a relaxed sigh, inspecting their bodies for burns, but they had been fortunate. A series of cracks and snaps and the porch was completely lost in flames. Drury was at once horrified at his idiotic run through the fire, as well as being impressed he had actually made it.

He scratched Zac behind the ears as the dog licked its singed nose. "I don't think they'll come through the flames."

They came through the flames.

The dead—unhampered by injuries or pain— stumbled through the heat, skin and clothes burning. They moved blindly, waving charred hands in front of them in an automatic effort to find someone to grab hold of ... someone to eat.

Zac growled as Drury was already scrambling to his feet. A flaming zombie moved towards them, its steps faltering as the fire sucked the strength from it. Black sockets seeped where the eyes had burned out, and torched lips snapped around a mouth billowing smoke.

More undead spilled through the burning porch-way. Drury called for Zac as he retreated further into the garden. The smell of burning rotting skin made him gag.

A chained metal gate separated the garden from a field and Drury had to lift the Rottweiler again to drop her over the gate. The boxer climbed over the gate as the dead—those that were not engulfed in flames—caught up with him.

He choked on the fumes and stench as the dead fell upon the gate. Spreading the flames among themselves they flailed at him, the gate being the only barrier between him and them.

Drury left them writhing upon one another.

The field was flat, and shade from the trees had kept the ground relatively dry and solid underfoot. They ran along the tree-line, cool air washing the heat from them.

They maneuvered over a stile cut into a hedge. A road stretched north and south, barren of vehicles and zombies. It felt like the first clear break he had had in an age.

Glancing back at the field, Drury saw the dead pursuing them. He wondered how they had unchained a padlocked gate.

He shielded his eyes from the bright sun, his attention drawn to the gate swinging open under the numbers of the dead. It looked like the bars had been warped, bent under pressure.

And then, in their throng, stalked a man head and shoulders above them. It was not just his size marking him out from the rest, but also his face; it was long and thin, pale, and covered in a smile so wicked it shook Aaron Drury with fear.

He pushed his aching and tired limbs beyond what he ever imagined he was capable of. He ran through thin lanes, dog by his side. Zac had barked incessantly as the Tall Man neared them, and Drury thought the dog might attack the creature, but once it was close enough they could see the malevolence in the creature's eyes the Rottweiler trembled, turned tail and fled, followed closely by Drury.

They slowed when Drury's lungs ached so bad he thought he would be sick. They had made good speed with no pursuers in sight, although moans echoed over the fields and hills around them. The dead always seemed to be close by.

He cocked his head, ear straining as he thought he heard an engine heading their way. Was it potentially the car Charlotte may have fled Purton Mill in?

It turned out to be a jeep, which almost ran him over as it rounded the corner with a squeal of tires, its rear-end kicking out to drag through the hedge on the opposing side of the road to him and Zac. The battered old vehicle skidded to a halt yards down the road from where he stood. He was unsure whether to hide, but he was sure he was too tired to move.

Two men rode in the open back of the vehicle, leaning over the roof of the cab aiming long, black rifles at him. The driver's door opened and a large man got out. Sweat coated his brow and his pepper-flecked beard shuddered as he thumped a foot onto the road.

The man swiped a flat cap from his head and squinted at the boxer and dog.

"Hold fire, boys," his voice boomed as he adjusted his belt, a handgun poking from the waistband. "This one's a live one. And male." He looked Drury over in disgust.

The men lowered their weapons, exchanging disappointed glances with each other.

"Please," Drury said, trying to catch his breath. "Help me."

"Seems like everyone needs help these days, boy," the man said in a thick rural accent, one common to the majority of farmers on the island. "What makes your problem bigger than anyone else's?"

"They're chasing me," the boxer said. "There's so many of them. We've got to get out of here."

The man stroked his chin, throwing a blue-eyed glance at his companions. "How many?"

"What?"

"How many are chasing you?"

"Why?"

"How ... many?" the man repeated slowly.

Drury looked at Zac for inspiration.

"The dog won't help you," the man snapped, his fingers hovering above his handgun. "How many are chasing you?"

Drury shook his head. "I don't know ... a lot. Twenty, maybe more? Probably more. And some big weird guy."

The old man's laughter was louder than the rattle of the jeep's engine. "There we go! We got ourselves some game!" He retreated into the cabin of the truck, revving the engine and leaving Drury in a cloud of diesel fumes as the men in the back of the jeep hollered and fired their weapons into the air.

"They think it's some kind of sport," he said to Zac as they watched the jeep disappear. "They'll get themselves killed."

The dog stood rigid as more shots rang out, ears cocked and nose sniffing the air. Drury shook his head and told the dog to follow. They left in the opposite direction of the game hunters.

CHAPTER THIRTEEN

The 1983 Mark Two Ford Capri Christopher Cole had taken from his undead father ran out of petrol on the outskirts of Hangshaw. Charlotte had been tired of the hills and fields before the dead had overrun the island, and now that she was stuck on foot, she detested the place even more.

"I'm sick of this," she said, moving along a public pathway, one off the main roads. "I'm sick of walking. I'm sick of people trying to eat me. And I'm sick of this island."

"No one wants to be here right now," Warrington said.

Cole walked behind the secretary, leather jacket over his shoulder, taking in the surroundings like he was on a Sunday stroll. "It's still a beautiful place," he said in his bubbling Irish brogue. "I mean, despite the blood an' all."

"You can stay here," Warrington said. "Enjoy the scenery all you want."

"No thanks," Cole answered. "I figure I'll jump on tha' wee boat wit' ya."

Warrington shut the Irishman's voice out as his mind worked on a plan. All he had concocted so far, though, was to reach Medina Quay—unfortunately through the center of the island again—and try and find a boat that may have survived the attempted mass exodus. If they found one that would be the easy part. It was going to be a lot harder to cross the Solent, especially if the Navy was patrolling and protecting mainland England. Maybe if they could get the attention of one such vessel they could talk their way on board. He was a policeman after all. That must count for something.

Charlotte had voiced what he himself was thinking; he was sick of running and being attacked. But would the mainland be any different?

"Wha' if the mainland is overrun wit' them things?" Cole asked, and Warrington told him to shut up. "But what if it is?"

"What if Aaron doesn't find us in time?" Charlotte asked.

"That's a lot of what-ifs," Warrington said, still walking. "What if we get a boat, escape, and find everything is peachy in Portsmouth? Will anyone thank me then?"

"Not if the Navy blow us out of the water," Charlotte said.

"What's worse?" Cole asked. "Being eaten or being blown up?"

"Being beaten to death by me," Warrington said, coming to a halt in front of Cole, fists clenched.

The Irishman stepped up to him, smile wide. "Give it your best shot, officer."

Gunshots stopped any potential rematch between policeman and criminal.

"The Army?" Charlotte asked as Warrington grabbed her arm and pulled her towards a hedge.

"I don't think so," he said as they squatted down. "Rifles, I think."

Cole stayed in the middle of the road, standing on tiptoes as he peered around to find the source of the gunfire.

"Get down, you prick," Warrington said. "They might not be friendly."

"Listen, anyone wit' a gun has to be shootin' them dead bastards, instead of us live bastards," Cole answered, waggling a finger at the policeman. "Besides, if it's a choice of being eaten, beaten, or shot, I'm going with a bullet."

Warrington lunged at Cole, gnarled hands making a grab for the Irishman who danced out of the way.

"Easy there, John," Cole said, his smile fading. "Let's keep things nice an' friendly. You don't want me breaking ya big nose again, do ya now?"

Warrington ground his teeth. Charlotte grabbed his arm, pulling him away and positioning herself between the two.

"Listen!" she said, head tilted. "Can't you hear that?"

His eyes still on the Irishman, Warrington heard more shots, closely followed by screams.

"Do we help them?" Charlotte asked.

Warrington stared at her, the anger diminishing. "No. If they have guns and they're dying, there's not a lot we can do for them."

Charlotte held his gaze for a moment before dropping it and sitting on a small embankment on the path, head in her hands.

"We can't save everyone," he said.

Gunfire rattled around them as they walked. Eventually the noise thinned out and was replaced by the sounds of different kinds of engines.

"Tha' way," Cole said, pointing towards a freshly-plowed field. Across the muddy horizon farmhouses were visible, and a plume of smoke choked the air as something exploded behind their sight.

A Land Rover crested the field accompanied by other 4x4s, all heading their way.

"Do we signal them?" Charlotte asked.

Warrington watched as the mud-covered farm vehicles carried men dressed in shirtsleeves or dungarees, firing rifles and handguns, in the direction from which they fled. Some look terrified, while others hooted and yelled in glee.

"No," he said. "I don't think it's—"

"Over here!" Cole yelled, standing as tall as he could over the hedge, waving his arms.

"Fucking idiot!" Warrington hissed, ducking back down and pulling Charlotte with him. "Get down!"

"They've already seen me," Cole said. "They're coming this way." He turned and waved again before pointing along the hedge at a gate. "I'll go and open tha' for ya!"

The leading Land Rover smashed through the gate, hitting the road sideways as thick mud sprayed from its heavy wheels. Cole rubbed his hands together as the vehicle halted before them, the door opening and a big man with gray hair and stubble leaning out.

"Get in!" he barked, looking at Charlotte. "No time for fucking about."

Warrington threw a poisonous look at Cole, but the younger man was already climbing into the vehicle, Charlotte close behind.

Warrington followed.

"What happened?" asked Cole as Charlotte was pushed onto his lap as Warrington squeezed into the cab behind them.

"Those shits tore my boys to pieces," the driver said, slamming a hand against the steering wheel. He looked through a dirty plastic window over his shoulder. "You all right, Frank?"

The silhouette of a man sat with his back against the window nodded, or his head may have been bobbing up and down as the Land Rover bounced along the road.

"No," came a faint voice.

Warrington looked at the driver who kept his wide eyes fixed on the road. The policeman noticed a handgun poking from between the farmer's thighs.

"They were there for the taking," the big farmer in the flannel shirt said, shaking his head. "Easy game. We picked them off." He looked at the three squashed passengers. "But they came out of the hedges … they came from everywhere."

"Like they were coordinated?" the policeman asked.

The man shot him a wide-eyed look. "You've seen it before?"

"We have," Charlotte said. "Ordered around by a scary-looking lanky guy."

"The tall thing with the teeth?" the farmer asked as he clipped a parked car, bouncing them around in their seats. "What the hell is he?"

"It," Warrington said. "And it isn't a man. I think."

The vehicle slowed to a more sane speed, allowing Warrington to properly look through the plastic window. There were two more old jeeps behind them, but the dirty window made it unclear how many people the vehicles carried.

"How many of you were there?" he asked.

The driver shrugged. "Fifteen? Sixteen? We're farmers and riflemen from all over the island, and when the plague broke out we got together and decided to do something about it." He shot a glance at Warrington. "Seeing as the police weren't up to the job. Plus, the fucking military were shooting anyone who crossed them, alive or dead."

The farmer slapped his hand on the wheel in frustration. "If I'd listened to that boy and his dog we might not have walked into those things with our bollocks swinging in the breeze." He wiped a hand across his brow. It came away bloody.

Cole noticed this and grabbed the door handle beside him.

"It ain't my blood, boy." The farmer snorted, but his laugh was brief. "I think it was my nephew's."

The farmer steered the Land Rover through roads

familiar to Warrington, and he realized where they were heading.

"All quiet out West Wight?" he asked. "Is that why we're heading this way?"

The driver nodded. "We should have stayed out there, plenty of open fields. We could've covered all areas."

"And boarded up your home," Cole said.

"Fuck that!" the man snapped, maneuvering around another upturned car. "Only an idiot would seal themselves up in a house like a tin of ham waiting to be eaten."

Cole leaned around Charlotte to aim a raised eyebrow at Warrington, but the policeman ignored him.

"At least in a house you would have food and defenses," the policeman said.

The driver flicked his eyes at him. "In the open we can pick them off, and we'll loot anywhere that we need supplies from."

Warrington wanted to pursue the topic, but kept silent. He did not think this man was open to discussion about rights and wrongs. He seemed like an old-fashioned, angry old man who had probably lost his farm and/or family in the outbreak.

The ups-and-downs of the rural hills smoothed and the fields around them grew in size as the trees thinned out. Ahead of them the sun echoed off the sea, and to the northwest white cliffs of a town called Freshwater stretched out of the water.

"How will Aaron find us out here?" Charlotte asked softly, leaning her head against the rear window.

She was answered with a slap on the plastic behind her, making her jump.

They all looked round and saw a bloody handprint squeak its way down the window. The driver picked up the handgun and loosed two shots towards it without warning, deafening everyone in the cab.

The Land Rover swerved out of control, hit an embankment and crashed into a tree. The tree splintered under the impact, but it was sturdy enough to stop the vehicle.

Warrington fell out of the cab, hands over his ringing ears. The driver got out a moment later, one hand on the bump on his forehead as he waved the gun at a figure thrashing around in the pickup's flatbed.

His companion lay on the metal flooring, twitching and spasming, blood soaking his clothes. A bullet had shattered the man's teeth and jaw, yet it snapped open and shut, fragments of teeth spraying the air.

The next bullet entered his eye socket and stopped him.

"Sorry, Mr. Allen," the farmer said, even though he could not hear his own voice through his pained ears.

The trailing jeeps pulled up by the crashed 4x4, armed men jumping out to inspect the damage. Warrington inspected them, all covered in blood, some supporting their allies, while others bore an array of rifles and shotguns in sweating hands. They were all wide-eyed with fright and adrenaline.

"You all right, boss?" asked a tall ginger youth. Teeth protruded from his mouth. Warrington felt his stomach turn when the youth licked his lips at Charlotte getting out of the Land Rover.

"All good, Mathew," the big man said, rubbing his forehead with his gun-holding hand. "I hope you got some room in there, 'cos we need a ride."

"I'll take the lady," said the driver of one of the jeeps and getting rewarded with some weak laughter.

Warrington stepped in front of Charlotte, who looked on in confusion. "We'll make our own way, thanks."

The men were caressing their weapons and Cole saw them.

The big man in the flannel shirt walked around the jeep to stand with his fellows. "Fine," he said, opening the pistol to check its contents. "But the young lady will be leaving with us." He snapped the gun closed.

"John...," Charlotte said with a voice that croaked.

"She comes with us," said Warrington.

"Shoot him, Mr. Low!" the ginger kid yelped, hopping from foot to foot, jabbing his weapon at them, making all three flinch.

The big man stepped forward and cracked the butt of his pistol on the back of the youth's head. The youngster stumbled, dropping his own gun and rubbing the back of his head with both hands. "S-sorry, Mr. Low."

Warrington saw the gun he dropped was nothing but a plastic water pistol.

More of the men laughed, their domination over the situation growing.

Cole stepped forward, smiling. "Now now, boys." The grin vanished as weapons were pointed at him. "Easy, fellas. We're all jus' trying to get along durin' these dark times, ain't we now?"

"Sure are," Low said, stepping towards him. "The way I see it, there's gonna be a whole new world after this shit has died down. People are gonna need to rebuild, to clear up the dead ... to harvest the land." Several men nodded. "This island will be the safest place in the country and we'll rule it. It will be a new country! But, like all kingdoms, there needs to be cattle … for repopulation."

Cole pointed at Charlotte, and Warrington could see the Irishman was sweating heavily. "You mean her?" Cole asked, and issued a short laugh. "She can't have babies, man. She's barren."

Low raised his pistol. "Then we'll use her for practice," he said, and several hunter-farmers agreed. "Now, be a good little pikey and fuck off."

"Pikey?" said Cole.

"There's no need for this," Warrington said, pushing Charlotte behind him. She shook as she clutched his hand behind his back. "Let us be on our way."

Low swung his aim from Cole to Warrington, pulling the hammer back. The other men jostled their weapons and more clicks echoed on the high road above the sea. "Give us the girl, or we'll take her."

Cole's mouth opened and closed.

Warrington shook his head, once. "No."

Andrew Low, a farmer on the Isle of Wight for over forty years, shot the sergeant of Hangshaw town.

The bullet passed through Warrington's shoulder and Charlotte Lewis heard it whiz by as she cowered behind him. A dark stain splashed the back of his dark shirt and his knees buckled. She caught him as his head rolled forward and she did something very unlike herself:

She screamed.

Cole moved for Low, but the farmer clubbed him with the butt of his handgun. The stunned Irishman dropped to his knees.

Low's companions moved.

Charlotte struggled as strong hands grabbed her arms and pried her from the downed policeman. Cole grasped at a leg passing him and was rewarded with a punch to his temple, filling his vision with stars.

Through a haze, he saw Charlotte punch Low before the burly man struck her in return, sending her to the ground.

She was screaming his and Cole's name as consciousness escaped him.

CHAPTER FOURTEEN

Aaron Drury had watched the three 4x4s weave across a field and disappear over the summit. Zombies followed the convoy, so Drury and Zac marched in the other direction. There was no sense in getting themselves caught up with the troublesome gunmen.

The moans faded with distance and Drury slowed to a lighter pace. He tried to remember the last time he had done anything other than run or fight lately.

They came across a blue single-decker bus, its emergency door open. Inside, Drury found a body slumped in its seat near the front. Everywhere was covered in blood, and the windows all around were starred and dirty with claret. The vehicle reminded him of his team's bus and crash. It made his head and chest ache for the hundredth time.

He spun as he heard yelling, trying to pinpoint the origin.

The shouting grew as he crouched behind the bus, peering out as he held Zac's collar.

Three people ran towards them, a large, powerfully-built black man leading them from a pursuing posse of the undead, a girl in her teens trying to keep pace with him, and an old lady who was brought down by the beasts. The old woman screamed loud enough to hurt Drury's ears.

He moved further behind the bus, tugging Zac with him. As the black man ran past, he spied the man and dog and skidded to a halt. "Get out of here, man! They're coming!"

Drury got to his feet. "You dick," he snapped. "Why not hang a dinner bell around my neck?"

The young girl rushed past them and they fell in behind her.

They trampled the thin lanes, sticking to the main roads as they found them, and bypassing small roads and alleyways, anywhere they might get stuck if they met oncoming trouble.

The girl was lagging behind them and stumbled over a curb. Drury stopped to help, but as he bent down, Zac stood at his side, growling.

"Leave her," the other man said, hands on his thighs as his barrel chest filled with oxygen.

Drury put a hand on the girl's shoulder despite Zac's growls growing into barks.

The girl lifted her head and dark drool fell from her nose and lips. Drury recoiled as her eyes glazed over before him. Her skin was cool and she reached out a light gray hand towards him.

"She got bit a while back," the dark-skinned man said. "Me and that old lady have been trying to ditch her."

The girl's head lolled forward, her hair falling over her face.

Drury's hand hovered near her, uncertain of what to do.

"You can stay here," said the other man as he turned away.

Drury hesitated until Zac's warnings shook sense into him.

Moments later, the dead girl rose to her feet and followed in the direction the two men and dog had taken.

"Name's Kerry," the man said. "Kerry Williams." He wiped a big paw down his dark forehead. "Save your jokes about my name. I've heard them all before."

Drury gathered hay into a large pile before falling into it with a loud sigh. Zac came to lay next to him, resting his chin on Drury's thighs.

"Is that your dog?" the bigger man asked.

"Nope," Drury said, scratching the animal's ribs. He inspected Williams who sat on his own hay bale. "I'm Aaron Drury and I'm looking for my girlfriend." The other man wore sharp trousers and a dirt-stained shirt covering his large frame. "What did you do before hell took over?"

"I'm a teacher," he said. "Or was a teacher. I'm not sure the world will ever be normal again after all this."

"Well, Kerry," Drury said, lying back in the hay with another satisfied sigh. "You won't be teaching anything while you're stuck up in this hayloft."

Williams wrinkled his thick nose and looked around. At his feet was a ladder they had ascended into the loft of a barn they had found down a side-lane. Drury had carried the dog up before Williams raised the ladder. They sank into the hay, keeping out of sight and silent until the dead had passed the entrance to the farm and its barn.

The girl who had followed them soon went past at a shambling run, arms flopping at her sides.

"Who was she?" Drury asked.

Williams shrugged. "I never got her name. There was a group of us from the high school. We'd hidden in one of the science labs when the attacks first started." He lowered his face and stared at his palms.

"Take your time," Drury said, hands behind his head as he sank into the straw. "We've all got our stories to tell."

Williams nodded. "Families came to get their kids." Silence for several moments. "We let a few of them into the school before we realized those who were bitten turned pretty damn quick. It was ... I saw mothers hugging kids ... even as the kids were biting them...

"It was our PE teacher who saw the link between the bitten becoming the dead, and not the biology guy!" Then he laughed—once, but with his face not sharing the humor. "Stupidly, we went higher up into the main school building, shoving desks and whatever we could against the doors. There were four classrooms at the top level. We heard a lot of screaming from two of them."

"How did you get down?" Drury asked him, as the dog snored quietly on its side.

Williams spoke with his eyes closed. "We had to fight our way out." His words so soft they were almost unintelligible. "I saw staff and pupils fall around me, but I ... I couldn't help them. The dead were everywhere. If I had stopped...."

Drury closed his own eyes. "I know the score."

Williams picked at straw between his legs. "What about you, man?"

Drury cracked his eyes a touch. "Like I said, trying to find my girlfriend."

"But you found a replacement?" Williams nodded at the Rottweiler and gave them a weak smile.

Drury said nothing.

Williams pulled at one of his ears, sliding down from the hay bale and sitting on the wooden floor. "I'm trying to find my brother. He's in Ryde—"

"Ryde's a hellhole," Drury interrupted. "I came through there to get to Hangshaw. That place is fucked. They had helicopters flying over it for some reason."

Williams stared at the hills outside of the barn, saying nothing.

Drury sat up a little, annoyed at himself for having no tact.

"I'm sorry," he said. "I'm sure he's safe somewhere and you'll find him soon."

Williams raised an eyebrow. "No. You think he's dead. Well that's fine, because if he is, then so is your girlfriend."

"Easy, fella."

"My brother has as much chance of being alive as your girl does." Williams brushed some straw from his close-cropped hair. "Do you even know where she is?""

Drury looked away.

"Well, then," Williams said. "I know where my brother is, and he's in Ryde."

Drury woke, but had no idea how long he had slept. He had abandoned his smashed phone and watch on his travels. Zac raised her head as Drury jerked himself upright, at first puzzled by his surroundings. Sunlight poured through the barn's doorway and Williams was nowhere to be seen.

He rubbed the sleep from his eyes and saw the ladder to the ground had been lowered. He picked the dog up and worked his way down the ladder before dropping Zac gently to the ground. She threw up dirty straw from under her paws as she ran outside to relieve herself.

Drury stood inside the hay-barn, waiting to hear if Zac growled, but the canine sniffed the air, investigated a flowerbed, and squatted into it. Drury exited the barn, sniffing the air himself.

"Bacon?" he said, and his stomach answered affirmative.

The clinking of kitchen utensils sounded from the open window of the farmhouse. A thin trail of smoke rose from the chimney stack of the building. The grounds all around were empty and quiet, but where the Purton Mill had been renovated and carried fresh structural work, this old farm seemed ancient in comparison, old brickwork and rotting-wooden window frames. Straw littered the mud in an attempt to soak some of the water out of it, and a set of vehicle tracks running mud onto the road suggested an empty home.

The back door of the farmhouse was wide open and Drury saw Williams moving inside. The broad man was bent over an open fire in a hearth, cooking bacon in a pan over the flames. Drury stood in the mud for a few seconds, wondering if he should stay with the other man, or if he and Zac should press on looking for Charlotte. The smell of bacon and the rumble in his stomach decided for him. He said hello as he walked in the doorway.

The pan shook in Williams's hand, clanging against the rock surrounding the fireplace. "Jesus," he said. "You scared the shit outta me!"

"I could have been one of the dead."

"The dead moan and groan and stamp their feet about," Williams said, sliding the frying pan onto a work surface. He filled slices of bread with the slabs of meat, muttering under his breath at Drury.

He put the sandwiches on the table as Drury closed the door after the dog had followed him in. They all sat down.

"I made extra for the dog." Williams dropped bacon onto a plate on the floor.

They ate quickly and Williams made a second batch. Turning the bacon over in the pan, he flickered a look at the boxer. "Why not come and find my brother with me?"

Drury finished his food. "I'm not going back into Ryde," he said. "I barely made it out last time."

"But you know where to avoid," Williams said, butter on a knife. He waved it at Drury. "I'll take us to where my brother lives and you can help me avoid the bad places."

"Everywhere's a bad place."

"Help me, man." Williams's eyes pleaded with him. "Help me find my brother and I'll help you find your girl."

"Why should I?" Drury asked between mouthfuls. "Why don't I just find her myself?"

"Because two pairs of eyes are better than one," Williams said, throwing Zac more bacon. The dog moved to sit by his feet. "Plus, I think I'm winning your dog over."

"She's not my dog."

"Well, she thinks she is," Williams said. "And from the way she was growling at that girl before she turned, I'd say you're lucky to have your own personal warning device."

Drury looked at the dog, tall and powerful, her black-and-amber coat covered in grime, yet she stood proud. How often had Zac saved his life by warning of approaching danger? Drury certainly felt a bond with the dog, a bond created through trauma and testing.

He clicked his fingers and the dog returned to his heel. He patted the broad ribs as Zac rolled onto her back. "What do you think, Zac?"

"Zac?" Kerry asked, eyebrows raised. "And there I was concerned about my own name."

Zac wriggled under his touch, springing to her four paws as her makeshift master slipped the rest of his sandwich between the dog's big teeth.

"You should've eaten that," Williams said, holding an empty bread bag between his thick fingers.

"My early warning system needs his strength as much as I do," he answered. "Plus, she'll smell trouble before we see it." He held a hand out to Williams who shook it heartily.

"Well, all right."

"I'll get you to your brother's house and then I'm out to find my girlfriend."

"If he's there, I give you my word we'll both help you find her."

The walk back to Ryde was usually short, but this time it was made longer by hiding from the undead who stalked the streets. A sign reading The Falcon lay trampled on the pavement outside the burnt shell of a pub, and they hid behind a van as a mob of the dead wandered through the wreckage.

"They don't have any coordination," Williams whispered as the horde eventually moved on.

"Trust me," Drury said, one hand over Zac's rumbling muzzle. "I've seen coordinated. They surrounded your school as the Army was...." He swallowed at the thought of the soldier shooting the civilians in the tennis courts. "Helping survivors there. The dead certainly had a plan of attack then."

"Fuck," Williams said, furrowing his brow. "That must have been after we broke out. "We passed the Army on our way out. I had no idea they were going to the school."

"Where did you hide?"

"Anywhere we could. We skipped from house to house, and I slept in the back of a car the first night, hiding under a bunch of coats ... not that I slept much. What about you?"

"Hid in an old lady's house before it got overran. I've lost count how many windows I've jumped out of lately."

"I've lost count of how many dead people I've killed," Williams said, and then stopped Drury with a hand on his chest. He pointed to a pair of bicycles tucked behind a low garden wall.

"Really?" Drury asked. "Doesn't that cancel out the sneaking-around-thing."

"Yep, but it's mainly downhill from here to my brother's place," Williams replied. "Bikes are quiet, and quicker than a dead thing on gammy legs." He lifted one of the bikes over the wall. Checking the tires, he sat upon it, one foot on a pedal, and smiled at Drury.

"You game?"

They rode the bicycles through the upper high street of Ryde, flashing past the undead who reached out at them. The beasts grew in number as they pressed deeper into the town, but Williams directed them down a long hill that turned away before they reached the town center, where a monotonous undead hum reverberated from.

St John's Hill had been one of the busiest on the island, but was now instead a mess of mangled cars and bodies. Houses on either side of the street were ruined, smoke rising over them like the weather Death himself may have summoned. From the top of the hill looking down, the ride held no appeal.

Williams's squeezed the brake lever on his bike to slow his descent and the noise the old contraption made scared them more than the undead did. The sound was not far off from a pig being slaughtered, making their position as loud as a foghorn on the Solent. Drury pulled the single brake on the bike he rode ... and it clicked against the handle.

"Shit." he said. At least my brakes don't make any noise.

Putting his feet against the ground, his speed was too great for his trainers to create enough friction to slow him. The patter of Zac's paws dwindled behind him as the gap grew, so he drove his feet harder against the tarmac.

He zig-zagged the bike among the cars, hoping to make it to the bridge at the bottom. The incline up the other side of the hill should slow him down.

The dead had other ideas.

One of them stepped out from behind a car, watching Williams fly by and not looking at the man plummeting towards it from behind. Drury, bike, and zombie collided spectacularly accompanied by the sound of breaking dead bones, followed by an uffff as the wind left Drury's body, and a skreeetttch as the bike slid along the road into the curb.

Williams looked over his shoulder and skidded to a halt. He dropped the bike and ran to Drury, who was wrestling with a dead man as they fought half-under a car. The zombie pushed its head towards Drury, jaws snapping. The boxer kept one hand on the thing's head and the other on its neck. Zac's teeth sank into the thing's shoulder, pulling it away from Drury.

Williams snapped the seat from Drury's wrecked bike, a long piece of tubing still attached to the underside. He waited until Drury had pushed the zombie's head a little higher into the air before driving the piece of metal into the zombie's skull, perforating the bone with a crack.

The beast fell limp, Drury shoving it away, getting to his feet. He thanked Williams.

"Did you break anything?" Williams eyed him carefully. "Get bitten?"

Drury patted himself down slowly. He had some nasty grazes and scrapes, and one knee was swelling fast, but he could not find nor feel any bite wounds. "No," he said. "I think I'm good."

"Think is not good enough," Williams said, stepping back and curling his huge hands into fists.

"Fuck you," Drury said. "If I'd been bitten the dog would be growling like he did at the girl you abandoned."

Williams regarded Zac who was following her master as Drury walked towards the bridge. The boxer picked up Williams's bike, holding it on its wheels for him.

"We don't need that," Williams said. "My brother's house is over the bridge and up the other hill, and I don't think either of us is gonna ride that thing carrying the other guy on the handlebars."

Drury let the bike clatter to the ground.

"That's not very discrete, either," Williams said.

Drury pointed over the teacher's shoulder. "Fuck discretion."

Behind Williams the undead were gathering in number, moaning and gaining pace as they approached down the hillside.

Williams pushed past Drury and started jogging. The boxer fell in behind, his knee aching with his other ailments. Zac stayed by his heel. All three looked over their shoulders as they ran.

The bridge was snarled with traffic. Cars had smashed into other cars, and zombies that had been trapped in vehicles hammered at windows as they passed. One zombie had been pinned between two vehicles, moaning so loudly at them the chords in its dead neck stood out.

The creature struggled and slapped its palms on the car it was pinned behind. As they neared, the undead creature's bloodlust grew and it gripped the car bonnet by the windscreen, dragging itself forward. With a wet, sucking noise, its torso ripped from its legs, and the upper half of the thing's body came free.

"Christ...," Williams said, hesitating at the sight. Drury shoved him with a: "Move!"

Behind them the dead pursued, their moans signaling to other monsters in the area. As the three survivors reached the crest of the bridge, they could see up the opposite hill. The undead were tumbling down towards them in their haste to answer the feeding cries.

"We're cut off," Drury said, his voice as strained as his body.

Now Williams pushed him, pointing to a construction yard at the mouth of a side road.

Pushing a zombie away, Drury reached the gates as Williams threw his own considerable weight at them, using one long arm to grab the top of the gate, and hoist himself up and over.

Drury followed, squeezing strength from his battered frame. His fingers poked around mesh and his toes sought purchase in the closed gateway. He dropped down, beaten, but jumped up again, this time holding his weight even as the thin metal gate-top dug into his hands.

He pulled himself up, arms in agony as Williams was already landing on the other side. Drury got his other hand on the top of the gate and heaved himself up, swinging a leg over as the dead reached him, smashing into where Drury had been only a second before. Their momentum rocked the gate and Drury fell without grace to the concrete ground on the other side, punching the wind from his chest.

Williams grabbed his arm, but Drury shrugged him off. "Give ... give me a minute," he winced, breathing deeply. His knee and back hurt enough to spark flashes of pain throughout his body. He could feel blood beneath his ripped jeans and it coated one of his hands.

The dead smashed themselves against the gate at the sight of blood and the living men. Williams moved down a short track leading to the other side of the yard. Drury thought for a moment the black man was going to leave him where he sat.

But Williams jogged back, grabbed Drury under his arms and hauled him up.

"Wait," Drury said. "What about Zac?"

Zac barked back an answer as she squeezed her bulk through a gap by the hinges of the gate, a gate buckling under the weight of the dead throwing themselves against it. Drury patted the animal, and then leaned on the dog as his vision swam.

"We gotta go," Williams said, grabbing Drury's arm to steady him.

The mesh-gate creaked under the weight of the dead.

A store opposite the open storage area flanked the alleyway, the dead at the gate behind them, and a courtyard opening in front. Two forklifts sat in the yard's center, clearly used during a normal workday to move the building materials stacked around the yard. The back of the courtyard was separated from the houses lining the back wall, security spikes glinting along the top to deter intruders.

Drury sat heavily on some cement bags, breathing harshly. He spat on the ground and saw blood in it. He looked to see if Williams noticed, but the other man was too busy investigating the far wall.

"His house is over there," he said, nodding at the charcoal roofs jutting above the bricks. "On the new estate."

Drury put a hand to his side, his face spasming as he touched it. "I've broken some ribs."

Williams black eyes stared at him. "You gonna slow me down?"

Drury shrugged. "I'm sure you'll leave me if I do, Williams. Just like you did that girl."

The black man ignored him. "We need to get over that wall." He nodded at the forklifts. "Or maybe smash our way out on those things."

"Have you ever driven a forklift?"

Williams shook his head.

"They're not like stealing a bike," he said. "And they're about as fast as them." He nodded at the gate coming away on its hinges.

"Then we go over the wall," Williams said. "Help me stack things up against it."

The teacher grabbed a bag of cement and misjudged its weight, grunting under the exertion, veins in his thick arms pulsing. He waddled his way towards the wall and dumped the bag, kicking up cement dust around him.

Drury pulled himself into one the forklifts and started it up, glad it had its keys in the barrel. He used the vehicle to pick up palettes of materials and stack them on top of one another by the wall. The pile was hastily arranged and leaned precariously to one side.

"That's a mess," Williams said as Drury slid out of the forklift cab, clutching his injured side.

"If you'd like I'll take it down and do it again."

The gates buckled and the hinges fell from their brackets as the dead forced their way through.

Williams clambered up the wood and bags as Drury followed. Zac stood at the bottom of the pile, whining.

Drury dropped back down and picked her up, almost throwing the animal towards Williams. The dark man hesitated before grabbing the dog by the pink collar and helping it to the top. He reached down for Drury's hand.

Drury cried in pain as he was hauled up, his side on fire. Tears filled his vision as he collapsed next to Williams, Zac pressing a rough nose against his cheek.

He stroked the dog once and told him he was alright.

"Obviously not," Williams said as he straightened, the movement making the stack tilt further. He took off his waistcoat and threw it over the spikes crowning the wall.

With slowness and pain, Drury removed his tattered waterproof jacket and passed it to Williams. The dead fell over and around the forklift and against the stack of materials, shifting it again.

Williams placed Drury's coat over his on top of the spikes and lifted himself up onto the top of the wall, hands holding onto the spikes beneath the clothes. He pulled himself up carefully, but quickly, slipping one foot between the sharp protrusions. Gently positioning himself between the barbs, he beckoned to Drury.

"How far is the drop?" Drury asked.

Williams looked down the other side of the wall. "Not that bad," he said. "There's a shed below."

Drury put his arms around Zac, who did not flinch—the animal growing used to being hauled around—and handed him to Williams. The black man took the dog and dropped her over the other side.

"Hurry," Williams said as the moans threatened to suffocate them.

The undead crawled over one another as they scaled the makeshift mountain, one ghoul managing to grasp Drury's heel as Drury sought Williams's hand. The big man waited until the boxer had a hand and foothold among the spikes before letting go of him and dropping down to the shed roof, narrowly missing the dog.

Drury pressed his toes between the spikes, pulling himself up while the pain in his ribs threatened to sap his waning strength.

His arms ached and his head pounded. His lungs dragged in as much air as they could, but it was his mental strength that moved him upward. A zombie grabbed his trailing foot and they engaged in a grim tug-of-war. He flicked his foot out, but the demon held fast. Drury panicked, waiting for teeth to sink into his ankle.

Williams tugged at his forearms in sudden support. Between them they pulled Drury upward, although he slipped in his haste, and the spikes tore at his thigh and stomach as he tipped forward. He yelled, but the pain shocked him into action and he hoisted himself unceremoniously over the top of the wall and the spikes, only to fall over the other side.

He hit the soft asphalt of the shed roof and fell through it, Williams jumping down a moment before Drury struck. Zac had already made her way off the roof using the lower wall beside it.

"Hey, man," Williams said, opening the shed door and finding Drury in a heap amongst the tools and broken plants. "You okay?"

No reply. No movement. Blood tainted equipment all around his body, Zac nuzzling the young boxer, but still he did not move.

Hands slapped against the wall above them and Williams shook his head.

"I'm sorry," he said.

Zac watched him go.

CHAPTER FIFTEEN

The sun burned Cole's eyes as he opened them. It took him a moment to find it was asphalt under his cheek, but the pain in the back of his head was sudden. Bile rose in his throat as he lifted himself up and he put a hand to his chest as he waited for it to pass. Swallowing the vomit back down, he pulled his other hand from the back of his head and found it bloody.

How long have I been out for? he thought, and then the realization of the horrific new world he was in hit home.

His head spun, his eyeballs throbbed. He squinted and found Warrington lying on the road nearby. Cole dragged himself slowly across the road to the policeman.

Warrington lay on his back in a pool of blood flowering beneath him. Cole lifted Warrington's shoulder to investigate the back of the wound and immediately wished he had not.

He sat back, waiting for the fog shadowing his mind to clear.

Was Warrington unconscious or dead?

He put a hand on the other man's chest and finally felt a heart beating faintly once he had quieted the thunder in his own head. He relaxed a little as he watched Warrington's chest rise and fall. The policeman's face was pale, but he looked peaceful for the first time since Cole had encountered him and Charlotte.

Charlotte.

The thought of her flipped his stomach, feeling guilt at not having saved her. It tore through him.

He could still hear her screams in his ears....

Right now he had to concentrate on getting off the road. The dead could appear at any moment. Or worse.

Andrew Low's Land Rover was still at the side of the road, front end wrapped around the broken tree. Water dripped from under the bonnet into a large pool, giving him an indication that he had been out for a while, which meant Warrington had been bleeding out for longer than he feared. The front wheel of the Land Rover nearest to him was flat to the ground.

Slowly getting to his feet, Cole got into the open side of the jeep and tried the key.

The vehicle came alive, the noise shocking Cole bad enough he turned the engine off instantly. Firing it up once more, he put it into reverse and pulled away, the tree snapping entirely and the bodywork of the 4x4 groaning under the duress.

It returned to the road, wobbling as it sat back on an even surface. Hissing escaped the bonnet and Cole knew they would not get far in the vehicle, but he hoped it would get them to a small village he knew nearby.

He looked down at Warrington, the prone man pale and bleeding. Cole got out of the cab and opened the boot. The rear was full of tools and bags, but tucked into the side was what he was searching for, a first aid kit.

Cole returned to Warrington, opening the kit as he knelt beside him. He had to inspect the severity of the wound and ripped Warrington's shirt from his body. It was the first time Cole was glad Warrington was out for the count.

He had seen bullet wounds in films before, and some of his fellow inmates in prison had carried gunshot scars, but he had never seen a fresh one. The front of the older man's shoulder was a large bruise with a small hole in the center where the bullet had entered, but the back of his shoulder was a mess. A larger hole there leaked blood and bone fragments onto the tarmac.

Cole was unsure if the lack of blood coming from the wound was a good sign or not. Either Warrington had lost all the blood he could or maybe the bullet had not caused as much damage as he feared.

Either way Cole had to dress the wound. He applied his basic medical knowledge and gauze to the front and back of it. His hands soaked red with blood, more so when he had to tape the dressing on, and then awkwardly wrap all the kit's bandages around Warrington's shoulder and upper torso.

He sat back, surveying his handiwork. The center of the dressing was already stained with blood, and maybe it was his imagination, but the color seemed to be returning to Warrington's face.

Cole opened the door of the Land Rover and dragged Warrington to it. The policeman groaned as Cole held him under the arms, but the Irishman could afford him no comfort. He had heard groans other than Warrington's nearby.

Cole remembered hearing that St. Mary's hospital was a complete mess and should be avoided at all costs.

Had Warrington or Charlotte told him that?

He considered driving to his parents's house, as they were both dead, his father having killed and converted his mother. Cole wondered who had given his dad the bite marks that covered his arms. Maybe it had been young Jesse from next door, the young girl Cole had decapitated with a shovel.

He had seen her in the back garden of the place as he fled, picking up the shovel laying in the dirt of the new patio he had been helping his father build while Cole was housebound on curfew.

He lifted his Jean trouser leg and looked at the tag around his ankle, the irony of his being tracked during a time such as this made him chuckle.

"I'm sure your boys'll be out lookin' fer me," he said over his shoulder to the unconscious Warrington.

With the hospital out of the question, where else could they go? Who else was alive? With no communications or obvious places of safety, Cole began running through all the areas he knew on the island which might shelter people. There was a castle in the center of the island, surrounded by an empty moat, but he had a feeling a lot of people would have been drawn to it, and if they'd shut the gate, he could be sat in a car park full of undead.

During the World Wars the island had been fitted with armaments along its coastline to bombard enemy ships sailing into the Solent. The old battlements were still in place, although the weaponry had been dismantled decades ago, and the areas were now tourist attractions for the locals to play in the sun. If he could get in through the old gates he might be safe there.

Safe, but in the cold, dark, deserted corridors of an underground maze of tunnels. He shuddered

"The forts!" he exclaimed to himself as the thought struck him.

Off the coast of Ryde, and further around the east coast near Bembridge, were two forts. They had been decommissioned after the second World War, but one had been converted into a hotel, complete with tennis courts, multiple bedrooms, a large kitchen, a dock, and a helicopter pad.

"Perfect," he said to himself.

The Land Rover's engine chugged loudly, and the temperature gauge was as far to the red line on the right as it could go. Cole was no mechanic, but he knew they were not going to get much farther.

They?

He looked back at Warrington, covered in sweat and blood-soaked bandages. His skin was sallow and his eyes dark. He looked like a zombie.

What if you don't need to be bitten to turn? he thought, and the occasional looks he threw over his shoulder became more frequent.

"Hey, officer," the man from Ireland asked. "Are ya still wit' me?"

Warrington moaned.

"If you're turnin' into a fuckin' zombie, I'll ditch

you right here," Cole said, his attention away from the road, causing him to grind the 4x4 along a low brick wall.

The impact slid Warrington from the seat and onto the flooring of the vehicle behind the front seats. He cried out in pain.

Cole sighed. "Zombie's don't do that."

The vehicle lasted less than a mile before shuddering to a halt next to a village sign reading SHORWELL. Cole dipped the clutch and allowed the vehicle to coast down a winding hill and into the center of the village. He stopped yards away from a pub, its windows boarded and cars strategically placed to block the car park. There was no lights or sign of movement from within the building, although anyone would be obstructed by the shuttered windows.

Cole drummed his fingers on the steering wheel as Warrington moaned again.

He thought back to the time he had tussled with Warrington, which had led to Cole's imprisonment. Cole had told the court it was an accident, a result of the struggle during the arrest, and—truth be told—it was an accident, a flailing elbow had caught the older man's face.

"I should leave you here," he said to Warrington.

Cole wiped his forehead, sighed, and took off his leather jacket to lay it over the policeman. He got out of the car and went to the boot where he had seen the plastic sheet while searching for the first aid kit.

He dug out the dirty blue fabric and unfolded it. It covered most of Warrington's body as he lay between the back and front seats.

Cole locked the Land Rover and headed for the pub.

The closed shutters revealed nothing. He was not even sure what he was looking for, although proper medical supplies would be a start. He briefly hoped there were survivors inside, although after their encounter with the hunters he was unsure if that was a good idea.

The world was becoming a worse place by the day. Society and morals had been left in the gutter.

It looked like his only option was to save Warrington and try to rescue Charlotte.

He recalled Warrington's words about ditching Cole at the first opportunity, and the urge to go back and shake the policeman awake and point out that he had not left Warrington almost overwhelmed him.

It would do neither of them any good. They needed to find supplies and shelter. Cole did not want to be stuck outside in a broken Land Rover when the dead turned up.

The doors of the pub were sealed, barricaded shut from the inside. If nothing had gotten in, then surely there were people inside. Probably hiding.

Rounding the building, he found a side door and knocked. The small car park adjacent to the pub was crammed with cars. He looked them over as he waited for a reply to his knocks, mentally noting those with keys inside, and then dismissing them when he realized there was no hope of getting them free of the logjam around the car park.

No answer so he knocked again, a little louder. He held his breath as he thought he heard movement within.

"Hello?" he called out, pressing his mouth to the door. "Is anyone in there?"

He was being louder than he dared and looked around. It was a bright, beautiful day, but without any signs of life.

Cole circled the building and entered a beer garden at the rear. Picnic tables that once seated customers were upturned and positioned against a back door and the rear windows of the pub.

Still there was no signs of break in, either from the undead, people looking for shelter, or looters. He hoped there was somebody inside who may know of Andrew Low, or where he and his cohorts would be hiding, in turn leading to Charlotte.

He wondered what fate was befalling her right then, but stopped himself. He could not do anything for her until he'd got Warrington somewhere safe, armed himself, and then....

And then what? March into Low's band of merry men, kill them all, and rescue the girl like an honest-to-gosh hero? What if he never found them? What if they killed him first?

"Shush, Brain," he said as he continued around the structure.

A circuit of the building revealed nothing. The place was sealed shut as far as he could see, which meant survivors were definitely inside.

He stepped deep into the garden and surveyed the top floor, but all the curtains upstairs were shut.

Back at the Land Rover, Cole opened the boot

after a cursory examination revealed Warrington was not dead. Or undead.

He found a canvas roll among the rubbish and pulled it out. It was heavier than it looked and the clank of metal inside told him it was what he had assumed, a tool-bag. He looked inside, nodded, closed it, and hung it on his shoulder before securing the vehicle once more.

Cole returned to the side door of the pub where he pulled out a chisel from the tool-bag, wedging it between the door and the frame where he knew the locking mechanism to be. He was about to strike the butt of the tool with a hammer when he hesitated, removed his long-sleeved T-shirt, and bunched it up on the end of the chisel. Striking it with the hammer deadened the noise, but not much. He looked to see if his commotion was attracting attention.

Christopher Cole stood on the gravel of the car park alone, sweat coating his tattooed body.

He returned his attention to the door, refitting the wedge into the now-widening gap and struck it. It took numerous blows, but finally the lock inside snapped and clattered to the floor within. He heard and saw no signs of life. Or death.

Cole tried the door. It barely moved as something blocked it from within the pub. He managed to budge it a centimeter before finding a fruit machine pressed against the other side.

Putting his shoulder to the door, he leaned into it, the machine moving a little. He squeezed his fingers into the opening and tried to shove the gambling apparatus out of the way. A smell invaded his nostrils and he turned his head to retch.

Pushing his eye to the gap, he peered inside. The

sunlight broke into the room and spilled across part of a bar. Empty bottles of alcohol and a basket once full of crisps and confectionery sat in the bow of the sun. His mouth watered. He pushed harder against the door.

It moved slowly, the noise achingly loud, but necessary. Soon he had a wide enough margin for him to fit his body through, hammer and chisel raised in defense.

The inside of the public house stank of death. Blood and gore covered the carpet and tables, body parts littering the floor around corpses. There were eight in total, and each skull was beaten to a pulp. He couldn't tell the sex of two of them. A broken glass ashtray lay by one body, and a small axe was embedded into another's face. He had no idea if they had been dead or undead before being butchered.

The scene made Cole reconsider investigating further, but without supplies and medicine Warrington might not live much longer.

Trying to step lightly, he shuddered as his feet sunk into the bloodied carpet with a squelch. He took some chocolate bars from the basket and slipped them into his pockets. Deeper into the room his bare skin chilled and he put the tools down on the side of the bar so he could put his T-shirt back on.

Cole leaned over the counter and found what had been a barmaid face down with smashed bottles around her fractured head. Whatever had happened in here had been bloody, violent, and horrific.

Dropping the chisel Cole wrestled the axe from the skull. The sound the bone made when it cracked open startled him. He put a hand to his stomach and was glad it was not full.

The axe was small, but heavy, and had been used to chop the logs stacked next to a fireplace before it became a crude weapon. Its dull blade was covered in blood, brains, and splinters of bone.

The axe gave him some security and he swung it in an arc as he rounded the bar to the hallway behind it. It led to the bottom of a stairway, Cole fighting instinct to call out. Instead, he listened, heard nothing, and moved on.

The ground floor of the building was empty save for a blood-splattered kitchen. There were no bodies in it, though, so he returned to the stairs, placing one foot on the bottom before giving himself a moment to gather his wits. He ascended slowly, axed raised, treading on the outside edges of each stair to absorb his weight and sound.

He heard noises above. Judging by the sloppy sound he knew what it was, but felt he had to investigate, anyway, in case someone was trapped and alive somewhere.

He found the zombies all in one room—a master bedroom—feasting on the flesh scattered over the bed and floor. Blood painted the walls, almost touching the high ceiling in places. Cole could not distinguish how many corpses were strewn between the demons, such was the carnage.

There were five undead, each crouched on the floor, tearing flesh from bone with sounds that made him gag. Each of their faces was awash with gore, their jaws hungrily scissoring back-and-forth as they tore at their food.

One of the ghouls spotted him and hissed, spraying blood from its lips. The noise caused another to look up from its meal, its milky eyes enlarging at the sight of new flesh.

They came at him, but he was ready, pulling the door of the bedroom shut. He leaned back, arms stretched and hands around the doorknob, his weight pulling the door closed. Fists pounded upon the other side, shaking the door in its frame.

Cole was glad the animals were too feral and stupid to figure out something as simple as a door handle.

The door handle turned in his grasp.

Cole let go and ran down the stairs.

Hurrying through the bar, he could hear them falling down the carpeted hallway, a succession of thuds growing louder as they scrambled over one another.

Cole squeezed back through the doorway to the car park and ran into air so fresh he gulped it in, glancing over his shoulder.

The sound of crunching gravel spun him and he found more dead converging ahead of him. He guessed they had heard him smashing his way into the pub minutes earlier.

One of the creatures was close enough for him to hit with the axe, the blunt blade caving in its skull like a coconut, except with a lot more red blood than white milk.

Cole pulled the tool free, taking in stock the number of the dead coming towards him, and those coming from all around, such as the beer garden. Up the road leading away from the building he could see a dead man staggering towards him, following the drones of its comrades.

Cole ran away from the Land Rover in the opposite direction.

It took him an hour to circumnavigate the roads of the village and arrive back at the vehicle. He shielded his eyes from the sun as he looked towards the pub. The dead milled around the cars in the car park, and occasionally one would stumble in or out of the public house through the door he had left open.

Checking the coast was relatively clear, he carefully opened the back door of the vehicle and found Warrington where he had left him, breathing weak and his skin still pale.

Cole rubbed the stubble on his face. He looked around for inspiration and saw it hanging from a sign above a building further up the road:

VET'S.

Warrington groaned as Cole dragged him from the 4x4. The dead heard the noise and moved in their direction like a flock of deadly birds.

Cole pulled the policeman along the road towards the veterinarians. The entrance was unlocked and he dropped Warrington onto the carpet inside the reception. The Irishman threw the bolt at the top of the mercifully double-glass windowed door, and then pulled down a blind over it. Hoisting Warrington up, he struggled past the reception desk, along a hallway, and into an operating theater as the dead noisily gathered outside the front door.

The theater was spotless and a contrast from the images of death and destruction which had soaked Cole's senses of late. Instruments lined a tray and a gurney was covered in long blue tissue-paper. Cole lifted Warrington onto the table before sinking to his backside on the floor, panting and rubbing the back of his aching head. The lump by Low's handgun throbbed as blood pulsed through him after all the exertion.

He pushed the door of the room closed with his foot to muffle the pounding from the reception door.

Warrington moaned, rolling his head to one side to look at Cole through bloodshot eyes.

"Don't you start," Cole said.

Cole massaged his eyes with his palms, puffing out his cheeks. Wobbling to his feet, he stood over Warrington to re-inspect the gunshot wound. The bandage was saturated with blood, so he peeled it off, the policeman groaning throughout.

"Luckily," Cole said. "If you were gonna turn into one o' them, I think ya would'a done it by now. Safe to say it's the bites that cause death … and, er … not death."

Thankfully the bleeding had slowed a little. Cole chewed his lip. He rummaged in the drawers and through the shelves, piling bandages and equipment onto the gurney as he found the items he thought might be useful. He turned over vials of medicine in his hand until he found one which brought a wry smile to his face. Another search found a stockpile of syringes.

Warrington's eyelids fluttered as Cole spoke his name, inserting the point of one of the instruments into the vial. The Irishman tore at the remainder of Warrington's shirt sleeve, leaving the shirt hanging from the policeman in shreds. He wiped at a spot on Warrington's upper arm with some cleaning alcohol.

"I'm going to give you a lil' something for the pain, officer," Cole said. "You're gonna be living in a world I've frequented several times ... Ketamine. And this is what we call a K-Hole...."

Warrington's moans subsided soon after the drug weaved its way into his system, allowing Cole to concentrate on fortifying the veterinarian building.

The barrage against the shop door had petered out, but he dragged a filing cabinet against it for peace of mind. Past the reception and through the corridor was a kitchen adjacent to a toilet, and an emergency exit which he checked was secure. An empty office made up the rest of the ground floor.

He secured all the windows before returning to the operating room. Warrington was still, his slowly rising chest the only signs of life. Cole peeled open one of Warrington's eyes and found it vacant and glazed.

Cole washed the wound again before picking up a surgical needle and thread.

The gunshot wound on Warrington's back looked

as good as Cole could get it once the excess blood was carefully cleaned away. Claret still seeped from it, so he washed the wound once more with a jug and water from a sink. The policeman did not flinch as Cole sewed the wound together as best as his amateur skills would allow.

"Gotta love ketamine," Cole said. He soaked some gauze in the jug, wrung it out, and placed it on Warrington's forehead. He balled up the policeman's bloodied and tattered shirt and threw it in a waste-bin.

Retiring to the kitchen, Cole cursed the lack of electricity as he stared longingly at the kettle. He ate a packet of biscuits from a cupboard and drank half of a bottle of milk from a fridge. A walk around the premises revealed everything still secure, and peeping from between the blinds of every room showed that they were still surrounded, but the dead were thinning out.

Cole sat in the waiting room, scanning a copy of an animal magazine before tossing it aside and turning his thoughts to where he did not want them to go: Charlotte Lewis.

They had been separated for a few hours now and Cole had no idea how long he had been out after Low had struck him.

What horrors awaited the secretary in a land that was already horrific? The thought of her striking features and thin body in the hands of the hunters made him bury his head in his hands.

If only he could have done more....

He jumped to his feet, angry at himself. He looked around the room for something to take his frustration out upon, balling his fists and swearing loudly. A moan silenced him.

It came from the operating theater.

Cole swallowed. Hard. His throat clammed up and he had to clear it before he was able to call Warrington's name. He was answered by another groan.

Cole looked for a weapon, but all he could find was the kettle in the kitchen. It was then he realized he had left the axe in the Land Rover when he carried Warrington to the vet's.

Cold water from the kettle sloshed onto his feet as he edged towards the theater, calling out the policeman's name again.

Warrington was still on the gurney, but had managed to roll onto his side, pale visage facing the door. Putting the kettle down, Cole gently rolled Warrington onto his back, checking that his stitching was holding together.

Cole eyed the vial of ketamine. "I'm not sure I should give you anymore," he said, stroking his chin. "We wouldn't want you becoming a drug addict now, would we?"

CHAPTER SIXTEEN

Charlotte Lewis was dimly aware of being on her stomach, face squashed against dirty slats in the back of a pickup truck. A rough hand on her back kept her low, but sometimes the hand slid towards her backside to touch her inappropriately. The first time it had happened she had tried to speak to the owner of the hand, but was answered with a strike to her head which dizzied her. She could still taste the blood from her split lip.

She recognized the voice of Andrew Low nearby and was then hauled up and over the side of the pickup, falling heavily to the ground. Her head ached and she kept her eyes closed. The ground beneath her hands was dirt and stones. She opened one eye and pressed fingers to her temple. Blood seeped from a wound and she thought she might be concussed.

She squinted as a man stood before her, recognizing the red flannel shirt of Low. He tucked a hand into his belt as the other waved the gun he had shot Warrington with at her.

"F-fucker," she said, spitting blood on his boots.

One of those boots connected with her head and then everything disappeared.

Somewhere in her mind a little voice told her she was being dragged through the mud, losing one of her trainers on the way. She lifted her head, eyes aching as a shed loomed before her. The little voice gave her an: Uh oh, this doesn't look good.

The man pulling her limp body opened the door, a dim light-bulb swaying inside the shed revealing a clutch of women and young girls, huddled together or in pairs, holding onto one another for dear life.

Charlotte wondered what was going on, but the little voice in her head told her to go to sleep, and that her head hurt dreadfully, and she could do with being unconscious for a while.

Before she could comply, she was thrown inside the shed, hitting the wooden floor hard and sliding to a stop at the knees of a dirty, middle-aged woman. Bottom lip trembling, the woman scampered away as far as the cramped conditions would let her.

None of the other occupants moved to aid her, so Charlotte lifted herself up as the shed door was closed and locked behind her.

It was dark inside the shed, but a couple of chinks in the wooden panels around them allowed glimmers of light into the room. The faces around her were scared, and many were marred with blood, black eyes, or split lips. Except for the middle-aged woman, there were five other girls, all around her own age. One girl lay on the ground beside her, unmoving. Charlotte stared at her until a girl leaned towards her, dirty-blonde hair falling in her face as she whispered:

"She isn't going to turn," she said. "One of those monsters"—she indicated the door with her head—"punched her out cold because she kept screaming."

"Why was she screaming?" Charlotte asked but received no reply.

"They don't want the dead coming here," another girl said after a pause.

Charlotte blinked, wiping blood from her eye. "What the hell is going on?"

"Hell?" asked the blonde girl. "I wish we were in Hell. It would be better than being here."

Charlotte saw all the girls were in their underwear, some in even less.

"Oh," she said.

Hours later, two men entered the shed, one of them turning on a light and putting his finger to his lips, smiling. The second man pointed a rifle at Charlotte and motioned for her to get to her feet. "Time to go, new girl."

She shook her head. The first man grabbed her by the hair and hauled her upward, making her yell. His knuckles caught her flush on the cheek, starring her vision and silencing her.

"Shut it," he hissed and dragged her from the

shed.

The other women cowered in silence as the light was turned off and the door locked.

Only a few hours ago, Charlotte had thought the world could not get any worse.

She was wrong.

So horribly wrong.

The first man beat her when she resisted, and the second man beat her because he wanted to. After another man joined them, her mind detached itself from the physical world and lost itself somewhere she did not need to think or act.

Time meant nothing, but eventually the black blurs around her dissolved as something she recognized as the sun filled the skies behind them. Her eyes would not focus, and her body ached. Another light flickered on the edge of her vision, and she felt solid ground under her. The yellow light died and time slipped by until gentle hands came to hold her.

"M ... h...." Her bleeding lips moved, but would not form words. She had gone beyond pain and now felt like a burnt-out fire. She tried to move, but nothing in her body would respond to her hazy thoughts.

"Shhhh," a voice said to her, and she felt a hand stroke her hair. "Sleep if you can. It's the best place for you."

She did not sleep, but she did lose consciousness.

CHAPTER SEVENTEEN

Garden instruments and splintered wood poked Aaron Drury's body when he finally awoke. The Rottweiler lay beside him, lifting her head at the man's movement. Excitedly, Zac jumped to her paws and licked Drury's face. Drury pushed her away, ruffling the dog's head absently as he looked around to get his bearings.

Above him smoke drifted across the sky through a hole in a shed's roof, and he slowly pieced together what had happened. The top of the building yard wall was visible, and he could hear moans emanating over it. A hand slapped on top of one of the spikes lining the wall, two of the fingers slicing off and falling into the shed with him.

Sitting up, he pulled long splinters of wood from his backside and thighs, marveling at the luck he had had in not piercing any arteries. He picked out as many as he could find before getting to his feet. He was a mess; blood covered his ripped clothes and he had scrapes and grazes from crashing the bicycle into a zombie.

He left the shed, looking around the empty garden. "I guess the teacher didn't fancy sticking around?" he asked the dog, who growled in the direction of the wall.

The undead had not scaled the wall yet, but their moans did. He could see his and Williams's coats covering the spikes and the hand impaled upon them. It wriggled, minus its two fingers, and then a zombie's head appeared, staring down at Drury, and issuing a long, low moan that was echoed all around.

He tapped his thigh for Zac to follow, wincing as he did so upon discovering another cut to add to his injuries.

They emerged into a housing estate composed of gray and lifeless flats and buildings. They approached a car-park acting as a courtyard for the area, and found the dead milling around it in numbers.

Drury skidded to a halt, very aware of the blood seemingly seeping from his every pore, drawing the dead towards him, their faces contorted in bloodlust.

He spun to find an escape as a growl rumbled in Zac's throat.

A shrill whistle rose above the growing commotion, his eyes scanning the buildings before movement above the dead creatures caught his eye. A big black man hung from an open window, waving a towel in long, sweeping arcs.

"Williams." Drury smiled, surprised but gladdened.

The dead barricaded the gap between him and the school teacher. Drury took deep breaths, focused on a gap in their numbers, put his head down, and ran, trusting Zac to follow.

The dead clutched for him, some of the quicker ones managing to get their hands upon him, but he tore himself free. He used his build and momentum to burst through, knocking many of them on their backs. He punched others, years of training in boxing gyms making weapons of his fists.

Drury sped for the block of flats just ahead. Williams was no longer at the window, but he could see the front doors were now open. To one side of the doorway was a group of the undead, all bent down on the floor, tearing and feeding upon something. He could not see who or what it was, so he kept running, thankful for whatever distraction it was.

Zac ran through the doorway, Drury closing it behind them. Instead of a lock, there was a mash of splintered wood where the door had been previously forced open. He abandoned any hope of reinforcing it in the little time he had.

Stepping over abandoned suitcases and items of furniture, he reached the bottom of a stairwell and pushed open the separating door, running into a dead tenant.

The beast was unsurprised, but also slow to react. Drury's arms became pistons and he smashed his hands forward into the dead man's chest, forcing him back with such power he heard the thing's spine snap against the railing behind as it tumbled over and down the stairway leading to a cellar floor.

The zombie spasmed where it lay, jaws snapping as it feebly waved its arms at Drury.

"C'mon," a voice hissed, making him look up, and he saw Williams bending over a railing a floor above.

Drury and the dog ran up the stairway, following

the black man into an apartment on the first floor, Williams locking the door behind them. He indicated for Drury to be silent, and Drury placed his hands around the muzzle of the dog, whispering soothingly to it.

The teacher showed Drury into a lounge covered in children's toys. Williams stepped on them without a thought and peered through a pair of curtains.

"They're coming in downstairs," he said. He tiptoed back to the main door and dragged a heavy chest of drawers against it. Drury helped him.

They waited. Outside the door, they could hear shuffling and moaning as the undead filled the stairwell. An occasional slap against the door startled them, but without any visual sign of food, the dead returned to their aimless wandering.

Drury turned to Williams. "I don't know if I should be pissed at you for leaving me, or thankful that you saved me."

"I was gonna come back for you," Williams said, walking back into the lounge.

Drury stood in the doorway regarding the other man. Adjoining the lounge was a kitchenette, and he entered it. He was thankful the water was still working in the buildings and ran the tap gently to splash water on his face. The amount of grime and blood that dropped into the sink concerned him.

He found a bowl under the sink and filled it with water for Zac. The dog lapped at it noisily as Drury explored the cupboards. He found some tinned fruit and a spoon, and ate.

"Is this your brother's place?" he asked as he slipped a peach segment into his mouth. "Sorry if I'm making myself at home."

Williams was back at the curtain. He shook his head. "No … he lives on the other side of the square."

Drury frowned. "I think I saw one on fire over there." Drury watched the back of Williams's head nod.

"I figure he got away before it burned."

Drury dug deeper into the tin. "So, who's place is this?"

Williams said nothing, keeping his vigil at the window.

"Kerry?" Drury said as Zac sniffed the air and headed for a closed door leading further into the flat.

The man turned to him, sweat coating his colored-skin as he shrugged. "I don't know."

The spoon paused at Drury's mouth. "You don't know?"

"I don't know," Williams said. "I saw this place was empty—"

"From across the other side of the car park?" Drury asked, frowning.

Williams stared at him, brown eyes against blue.

Zac scratched at the door …

… and was answered with a thump from the other side. The Rottweiler jumped back and growled.

"Who's in there?" Drury asked, pointing his spoon at the door.

Williams remained in place, staring at Drury.

Drury pushed himself away from the kitchen counter. "Who's in there?" he asked, louder.

Williams moved, holding a hand out to placate him. "Quiet," he said. "They'll hear you."

His voice was answered by a louder bang.

"Who the fuck is in there?"

"Ssshhhh!" Williams said. He looked like he was

about to fall to his knees and beg. "Please be quiet. It … it was just some girl."

Zac's growl rose as the moaning outside the front door grew at the sounds they made. Williams's gaze shifted between both doors, sweat dripping from his nose and chin.

"What do you mean some girl?" Drury asked, his voice causing blows to both doors.

Williams put his hands on his ears and shook. Drury moved to the door Zac growled at, his eyes always on Williams.

The door handle on it turned slowly before he reached it, was released, and then turned once more.

"Zac," Drury called the dog away from the door as he himself backed up, entering the kitchenette. He took a carving knife from the draining board as the dog moved to his side. Williams squatted on his haunches, hands covering his ears. Drury heard him talking rapidly under his breath.

The door to his right creaked open. A young woman emerged. Her skin was gray, but with a pinkish tinge. Her eyes were glazed but not as milky-colored as the other zombies he had seen. She's only just turned.

She hissed as Zac stepped in front of her and barked, the blows upon the outer door vibrating through the room. Drury ordered the dog quiet and the dead girl's head snapped towards him. Her mouth drooled as she thrust her hands at him so fast he thought they would shoot from her arms.

He moved quickly, swatting away her hands with one palm as the other hand swung the knife over his shoulder and towards the top of her skull. A split-second moment of thought screamed at him, What are you doing to this girl? but his body was in survival mode, and survival mode had kept him alive so far.

She jerked her head and the knife slid down her scalp and embedded into the base of her neck. It did not seem to pain her, and her hand snaked up and grabbed Drury's wrist. The two engaged in a tussle.

Drury pushed her backwards, aiming her towards the room she had entered from, but she bounced off the doorframe and they found themselves pressed against each other. Her mouth snapped at him and he had to put his hands on both sides of her skull to keep her away.

The knife in her neck sawed back and forth over his knuckles and he gritted his teeth at the pain, hissing at Williams to help.

Drury was slowly forced backwards by the uncanny strength of the girl and the pain in his hand, and he tripped over the dog biting at her legs. Man and zombie went down in a heap, Drury managing to maintain his hold on her. Spit, drool, and dark-blood sprayed him and he squeezed his lips to prevent any of it from falling into his mouth.

The girl's teeth almost bit his nose. Zac pulled at her jumper and between them they got the girl off of Drury so he could scramble away. He glared at Williams for his lack of aid.

The man was sat on his backside, shaking his head.

"Help!" Drury said, spitting blood from his mouth as the girl leapt upon him again.

Drury held her by the wrists as she tried to bite him.... Until she saw Williams.

The pressure from the ghoul lessened on Drury as she hissed at the black man. For the first time since the dead had begun to walk, Drury saw a look other than vacancy, anger, or hunger on a dead face.

This was a look of fury in its purest form.

The zombie screamed, and without air in her dead lungs it should have been a physical impossibility, but the dead girl in his clutches let out a sound that made Aaron Drury fear for a life other than his own; he feared for the man she howled at.

As she lifted herself from Drury, he saw a wound pumping blood from her chest onto his. With her attention elsewhere, he shoved her away. The dead girl landed on her side, eyes not leaving Williams who was busy getting to his feet.

Drury watched as the zombie crawled towards Williams, who stared at her, head shaking, mouth agape.

"I'm sorry," Williams said, sinking back into the curtains. The weight tore them from their fittings and they fell in a heap around the man.

Drury pounced on the girl's back, pulling the knife from her neck. She clawed at the carpet between her and Williams, ignorant of Drury in her intent on reaching the dark man.

In the space of a breath, Drury saw into Williams's soul, and saw a blackness brought on by a dark new world. In that breath, he wondered if he was becoming as bleak, or if he could save his humanity.

Drury pressed the knife into the base of the girl's skull, shoving it up towards the top of her head and leaning his body into it. The undead scream ceased as the blade sunk through her brain. Drury shut his eyes until she moved no more.

He sucked in breaths through his teeth, eyes on Williams. The teacher was pressed against the big bay window of the apartment, curtains wrapped around him.

Drury squinted his eyes against the sun shining in through the bare windows. "You want to tell me again who's place this is?"

Williams cleared his throat, finding words hard to come by. He closed his eyes, tilting his head back, and only spoke when Drury addressed him again.

"I saw her behind the curtains," Williams said, nodding down at the body the boxer sat astride. "My brother's place was on fire, man. I didn't know where to go … then I saw her looking at me through the window … so I ran over here."

Drury stayed silent. Zac grunted and released her teeth from the girl's dress once she was satisfied there was no more threat.

"She let me in and told me to be quiet … but those two were making all the noise!" he said, eyes wide. "She was pretty beat up, and she'd been bitten."

Drury looked at the handle of the kitchen knife protruding accusingly back at him. "So you killed her?"

"The dead followed me," Williams said, a big finger shaking at the girl before jabbing it at Drury. "Man, you should be thanking me for saving you! I thought we'd be safer as a pair. We're both big fellas. Plus, we got your dog."

Dead noises increased in the hallway.

"You killed an innocent woman," Drury said. He looked down at her, his mind replaying the look on her face and the noise she made when she had spotted Williams. "And she was angry at you...."

He stopped, his attention drawn to a playpen. In it and around the lounge floor were scattered children's toys. He looked over his shoulder at half-made bottles of baby formula lining the kitchen counter.

"You said: 'Those two were making all the noise.'"

Kerry Williams was unmoved for so long Drury lost track of time. They stared at each other, unblinking. Drury squeezed the handle of the knife in his hand, feeling it grind against the girl's skull.

"Where's the baby?" he asked, and the instant he asked, he knew ... he knew what the dead were eating below the window of this very apartment.... What it was that had distracted the undead so much he was able to run by them.

"You cunt," Drury said.

He pulled the knife from the dead mother's head as Williams stood, producing a similar knife from the back of his jeans, the blade smeared with blood. Drury could now see Williams's big, dark hands were peppered with crimson.

"You sure you wanna do this?" Williams asked, his voice strengthening as he kicked the curtains out from under his feet.

"You're a murderer."

"Everyone's a killer these days."

Zac stood beside Drury, growling, but at a living person for once.

"At least those fucks don't kill through choice," Drury said.

The three of them moved in the same instant; Williams kicked out as Zac pounced, sending the dog sprawling with a whimper.

Drury charged forward, knife before him. The blade grazed Williams's ribs as he wrapped an arm around Drury's neck and sank his own knife into Drury's back. Drury tried to ignore it, shrugging his shoulder with enough force to make Williams leave the weapon buried inside.

The boxer stuck his own knife into Merchant's stomach as the black man rained punches on his face. He heard a growl and saw a flash of black and gold as Zac bowled into Williams, sinking her fangs into his thigh.

Williams swore through his own teeth. Drury pushed the knife into him as far as he could, almost losing the handle in the process. Williams punched Drury's head downward, reaching over Drury's hunched form to pull the knife from the boxer's back.

Drury fell back as the bigger man slashed at him with the bloodied knife, slicing open one of Drury's palms as Drury defended himself. Drury's other hand still clutched his own knife. The blows to his head had made Drury groggy and his legs buckled as he retreated. He fell against the kitchenette worktop separating the rooms and Williams advanced on him. Brown eyes wide, Williams's prepared to windmill the knife at the dazed man before him.

Drury breathed hard, his head clearing, but his muscles not responding to the screaming from his brain. Move! Make those feet dance! You've been training for fights all your life, and now you're gonna get cold-clocked by a guy two weight divisions above you, but moves slower than a fucking zombie? The voice sounded a lot like his dead boxing coach.

Drury was gassed, and all he could do was watch as the teacher leaned back, ready to throw the knife into an orbit whose trajectory would end somewhere around Drury's skull.

Zac had other ideas.

She jumped again at Williams, her teeth taking one of Williams's big bear-like mitts between them. Williams howled and tried to decapitate the dog, but the animal wriggled so much Williams missed his mark, instead creating a long slash down the Rottweiler's midriff. The dog did not release its grasp and Williams stabbed at it again.

Williams was bent over trying to kill the dog, leaving his side exposed to Drury. The dazed boxer moved automatically, plunging the knife into Williams's stomach so deep even the wooden hilt was barely visible.

Williams knees sagged and he gasped. His hand grew limp and let go of the knife he was slicing at Zac with. It fell with a thud. The dog released its grip on Williams's hand, sensing the battle was almost over.

Williams sank to his knees, confusion upon his dark face.

Drury stood beside him, wounded hand steadily dripping blood onto the dead girl at his feet, the other pressed against a slash across his chest.

"You killed a mother and her child," Drury said. He looked down at the girl. "They'd survived the dead and took you in ... and you threw her child out of the window and then you killed her."

Williams winced as his fingers touched the end of the weapon protruding from his waistcoat. He made no noise as he pulled the blade from his abdomen, just gritted his teeth, instead.

He dropped the knife. Blood soaked Williams's clothes, pouring in gushes from the wound.

He looked at Drury. "You...." He paused to wipe blood which was now trickling from his mouth. "You're not gonna survive this...," he said, his words bubbling. "You're ... weak...."

Drury said nothing as Williams fell into the pile of curtains and died. Drury picked the heavy body up and pushed it through the open bay windows. He did not watch it hit the ground outside.

His legs finally gave out after the duress of the fight, the exertion, and the blood-loss and he fell onto the sofa, eyes and mind swimming.

Zac nuzzled him, whining and trying to lick Drury's injured hand. Two savage knife wounds opened up the dog's side, yet the dog seemed more worried about her master's condition.

Drury inspected his hand and could see sinew and bone through the gashes in his palm. A pain in his back reminded him of his other injuries and he could feel the fabric of his shirt soaking through with his own blood.

Using his good hand, he pulled his T-shirt off, crying out in pain as he did. His face ached and he could feel bumps around his eyes and cheeks where Williams's huge paws had pummeled him.

He threw his saturated top over the dead girl's face and it stuck to her with a slap. Drury struggled into the kitchenette, pulling open drawers and cupboards, exploring them as well as using them to keep his balance. He found a simple first aid kit and some superglue in one draw.

He showed the adhesive to Zac, the dog constantly at his heel despite her own wounds. "This isn't going to be very nice." He slid down to the Lino-flooring, leaving a streak of blood down the kitchen cupboards.

Zac sat before him, whining quietly as the pounding on the flat door shook the dressing table against it.

CHAPTER EIGHTEEN

Charlotte Lewis's body ached when she woke. Her mind was foggy and she had the vague notion it was not allowing her to remember what had….

She remembered.

She knew why her body was swollen, bleeding, and in serious pain. She assumed she was back inside the dark shed, a cool, thin breeze against her bare skin. Despite the bruises on her arms, she traced her body, only to find she was wearing only her knickers. They were soaked, as were her legs, and she did not know if it was with urine or blood. Or something else. She did not want to know right now. She had to get out of here.

She pressed a hand to her forehead and tried to hold back the tears, but some escaped, spilling down her cheeks to her ears as she sobbed.

"Please," said a voice. "You have to be quiet. If you don't bring the dead, you will bring the men."

"And that's worse," whispered another.

She sat up and managed to hold in a cry of pain.

Around the small building, the whites of five sets of wide eyes gleamed at her, all tired and terrified. Charlotte tried to talk, but her throat was dry.

"Here," one of the women said, and a small bottle

was pressed into her hand. "Don't drink it all. There isn't much left."

Charlotte sipped at the water. Her throat and jaw ached as she swallowed, and she pressed lightly against one of her cheeks, finding an eye almost swollen shut.

Light strained through the slats of the shed they were caged in and they saw hints of the men moving outside. They, too, whispered, but there was humor and quiet laughter in their conversations.

Her head still aching—but clearing—she could now make out the five frightened faces. Their ages were indiscernible in the gloom. Two of them huddled together, wrapped in each other's arms. Charlotte thought one of them was only a youngster, possibly early teens. The girl had a similar black eye and a vacant stare.

"We have to get out of here," Charlotte croaked, staring at the girl.

No one answered.

"I'm not staying here," Charlotte said, standing on thin legs which wobbled underneath her.

"Please," one of the girls hissed. "If they hear you they'll come for us all!"

Charlotte hesitated, one hand reaching out to find the door handle of the shed. One of the huddled girls sniffled and another whimpered.

She lowered her hand. Her body burned, but her mind raged. "We have to get out of here … all of us."

"We've tried," one said.

"How hard?"

A sob was stifled behind a hand.

Charlotte closed her eyes, to both think and to try and blowout her headache. Her mind attempted to formulate an escape, but, instead, images of the horror she had recently endured flashed behind her eyes. The groping hands, her skirt torn from her, the flash of an open palm or closed fist against her—

Charlotte shook her head, and setting her jaw, she bunched her fists. "I am not staying here." She peered around the gloom. "There must be something in here we can use?"

"And fight our way out?" another voice said.

"How long have you all been in here? It can only be a couple of days," Charlotte said. "Assuming those arseholes started farming you girls as soon as the shit dropped on the island. Whatever hell you've been through since then is only going to get a lot fucking worse."

A girl gasped, but not at Charlotte's words, but at the sound of men's voices approaching.

Charlotte spoke through her teeth. "I haven't survived this long just to die in a fucking shed like an animal."

She dropped to her knees, scrabbling over the ground to find anything she could use. She brushed against a bare leg, and at the touch the owner recoiled with a gasp.

No one offered to help her. Charlotte's blind groping found two girls huddled under a workbench, and she felt up the wooden leg of the furniture to its top. Her fingers passed through sawdust and devices she did not recognize, until her fingers grasped something familiar.

She sat down, her breath echoing in her ears.

"W-what are you going to do?" asked a voice.

Charlotte's tone was flat but angry. "I'd rather die fighting than live in fear."

Clasping the pliers to her chest, she sucked in a

lungful of air, and screamed: "Come on then, you fucks! Was that all you got? Call yourself men? I can still walk!"

The girls whimpered, cried, and begged her to be silent.

Boots thudded towards the shed.

CHAPTER NINETEEN

No matter how hard John Warrington retched he had nothing left in his stomach. He looked into the vomit-stained sink, half expecting to discover the lining of his stomach in there, or at the very least some blood. The pain from being sick had lessened the pain of the bullet wound in his shoulder, but now that ached again savagely.

Leaning against the steel sink, he turned on the taps to wash the mess away. A mirror above the basin showed him a pale, sweating man, with sunken eyes, looking years older than he was. It took a moment to realize it was his reflection.

Turning his body, he examined the dressing on his back in the mirror. It was stained with his blood. He touched the entrance of the bullet-wound on his upper chest and almost vomited again through pain. He clutched the sink to hold himself up, waiting for the feeling to pass.

He looked in the mirror again and thought his reflection looked like a zombie.

Stumbling to the gurney, he lay down to stop the room from spinning. Closing his eyes, he dozed for a while.

The sensation of bile in his throat woke him, and the pain in his shoulder caused his body to twitch. He pressed his palm against the wound, the pressure making him focus.

A single syringe and vial on a trolley told him he had been sedated at some point. He rolled the glass container around in his fingers, reading KETAMINE on its label.

"Son of a bitch," he said.

"No need for name callin'," Christopher Cole said, leaning against the door-jam.

Warrington threw the glass jar at him, but it smashed on the wall feet away from the unflinching Irishman.

Cole raised an eyebrow. "Y'know what?" he said. "You're one ungrateful man, sheriff."

"You gave me horse tranquillizer," Warrington croaked.

"What I did do was pick you up off tha' road, fight a shitload of zombies, get you in here, patch you up, an' then I gave you horse tranquillizer," Cole said, jabbing a finger at him.

Warrington examined the dressing once more, the arm of his injured shoulder clutched against his stomach so he could investigate it without moving too much. "You did all that? And this?" he asked, raising his elbow slightly. He winced.

Cole nodded.

Warrington looked away. "Thank you."

Cole held a green first aid kit towards Warrington. "I found it in tha' office," he said, moving to sit on the gurney next to the policeman.

Warrington looked blankly at the kit in his good hand. "Where are we?"

"Shorwell. In a vet's."

"Oh," he said, nodding slowly. "Explains the ketamine."

Cole reached out and withdrew bandages from the box. "We need to make you a sling, but first I'm going to have to change tha' dressing."

Warrington body slumped. "It hurts."

"That's because you've been shot."

The policeman sat upright, setting his teeth against the movement as his memories replaced the pain. "Where is she? Where's Charlotte?"

It was Cole's turn to look away. "They took her," he said, beginning to remove Warrington's bandages.

"Do you know where?"

"No."

Warrington thought the other man was on the verge of tears, but then he groaned, putting his hand to his forehead as his own wounds cried for attention. The sickness the ketamine made him feel added to his woes.

Cole slid off of the gurney and wheeled it towards the sink, positioning Warrington by it. The older man did not move as Cole unraveled the dressing.

Feeling the air upon his injury, Warrington looked down at the small hole the bullet had made in his upper chest. He tried to look further over his shoulder at the exit-wound, but the injury and pain prevented him from doing so.

"How's it look?" he asked weakly, nodding over his shoulder at his back.

Cole washed a ball of cotton under the tap. "Not as bad as you'd think," he said. "Don't get me wrong, it ain't pretty, but I've cleaned it out an' washed it with disinfectant."

"Glad I was out for that part."

Cole picked bits of gauze from Warrington's skin, the policeman flinching and sucking air through his teeth.

"Tha' sickness is the ket," Cole said. "You've been in a k-hole." He held his arms out like a circus ringmaster. "Welcome to the wonderful world o' the junkie."

Warrington ignored the remark. "We have to find her," he said as Cole rewrapped his chest and shoulder.

Cole nodded. "Aye, but we need weapons an' manpower. They're armed an' they outnumber us."

"And we don't know where they are."

They stopped talking, listening to the irregular moans beyond the building. Warrington felt a numbing sensation glaze over his body as Cole's makeshift medicine flowed through him. The Irishman stood against the sink, eyes unfocused as his mind wandered.

Cole left the room, returning with a dark blue sports jacket. "This was behind the reception desk. Put it on and I'll make a sling for your arm over it."

With help, Warrington managed to work himself into the top. Cole zipped it halfway up his chest, then wrapped the policeman's injured arm tightly against his body in a sling he made from bandages. There were not too many medical supplies for normal people in a veterinarian's.

Cole admired his handiwork. "Not bad."

"Why didn't you leave me behind?"

Cole shrugged. "I guess I'm not a bad person after all," he said, half-expecting a laugh from Warrington. He did not get one.

The policeman picked up a towel Cole had left on the gurney, wiping his face with it.

Cole filled a plastic cup and handed it to him.

"How long will this last?" Warrington asked.

"The ketamine? Not too long. I only gave you a dose to dull the pain. I ... er—"

"What?"

"Well." Cole smiled wryly at him. "I found some morphine after, an' I should probably have given you some of tha', instead."

"I don't know whether to laugh or cry."

"I'll try an' find some laughing gas," Cole said with an exaggerated look around himself. "I don't want you crying all over me. People will talk."

Warrington shook his head, a small smile creeping across his face.

Cole leaned back against the sink. "So," he sighed. "How are we gonna get her back?"

The smile on Warrington's face was short-lived. "We have to find out where they're keeping her. We need men, guns, transport—"

"And for all the zombies to fuck off," Cole added. He cleaned his hands with a sanitary wipe. "First, I need to give you some more painkillers."

Warrington's head shook. "I can't be groggy if we've got to go outside."

Cole withdrew a plastic tub from his pocket. "I got painkillers, an' I think ye should have a wee shot o' morphine."

The policeman took the tablets and washed them down. He experimented with moving his shoulder.

"Gimme the morphine," he said, once he knew he was not going to faint.

Cole injected him with a small amount. Warrington's shoulders relaxed as the lines around his eyes thinned.

"It still hurts."

Cole helped him to his feet. They entered the reception room and Cole pulled back the blinds covering the entrance door.

"There's a few around," he said, peering outside. "Mainly standing still … jus' swayin' about. I think we can get past them, okay. An' there's all those cars by the pub we could try."

Warrington slumped across a row of seats bolted to the blue carpet. "We don't need the hassle of getting a vehicle." His voice was drowsy.

Cole glanced at him. "Oh, are ya up for a cross-country run, instead?"

Warrington closed his eyes and slowed his breathing, his mind trying to find ways of teaching his old body to deal with the pain.

Cole watched as the afternoon faded through the blinds. The dead stood in the road, milky-eyes staring at nothing as they waited for sound or movement to indicate their next prey. A few of them did wander without purpose, bumping into cars or each other, teeth snapping until they learned it was not fresh flesh on the offer. Somewhere an explosion boomed across the fields and villages on the west side of the island, a cloud of smoke drifting across the sky, stronger than the many others painting the horizon. The dead shuffled from their positions, heads high as they sniffed the air, wandering in the direction of the explosion and the accompanying smoke trail. Cole wondered if they could actually smell. Or think. He knew they did not feel pain ... or at least none of them had shouted when he drove things into them. The young girl living next door to his parents had continued trying to bite him even as he pressed his weight against the shovel that was slowly piercing her skull. He shuddered, wishing for the cigarettes he had stopped smoking when he was released from prison.

The explosion outside intrigued him. It could mean other survivors. They might need help, or they may know of the farmer and his lowlife friends who had taken Charlotte. Or maybe it was the bastards themselves....

Cole took off his leather jacket and lay it over Warrington, the policeman either fast asleep or unconscious. Cole envied him either way. He watched over him a moment before leaving the veterinarian's through the back door.

The early evening was muggy, the sun fighting against the strengthening darkness. Cole rolled up the sleeves of his T-shirt and rubbed absentmindedly at the red-and-gold flame tattoos covering his forearms. They were splattered with blood, although he did not know whose blood was whose. Some ... most was probably Warrington's, but other specks he must have picked up along the course of the hellish past few days.

He crouched by the corner of the vet's building, watching the undead as they trekked away towards the explosion. The sound of gunshots hastened their progress, their moans increasing.

Could it be the hunters who had taken Charlotte?

He padded down the road behind one of the

straggling zombies. He ducked behind cars and walls whenever it paused its walk. He investigated the cars he used as cover, but there was nothing worth salvaging. The best he could do was arm himself with a steering-wheel locking-bar. It was thick and heavy, but better than nothing. He also found an open-faced crash helmet next to an abandoned scooter which he put on. The extra security comforted him a little, and did not dampen any sound too much in his ears.

The zombies poured on ahead, leaving the straggler behind. One of its legs threatened to collapse under each step it took. The limb looked like it had been crushed at some stage in its dead lifespan.

Cole ran up behind it on tiptoes and swung the bar down at the ghoul's head. The first strike sent it to the ground, the second and third crushed its skull. The metal bar rattled with the blows, some of the plastic parts of it shattering and showering the road around the mangled head.

He wiped sweat from his eyes and looked around, concerned at the noise he had made, but nothing moved towards him.

Continuing to use cars as cover, he darted from vehicle-to-vehicle, getting closer to the pub. There was more undead around it than earlier, but he hoped they were all moving in the direction of the smoke plume, instead of the building. Even though they we all headed for the same place, he did not want to get caught up on a countryside walk with a dozen undead.

He waited behind a camper-van, watching. A zombie scratched for something amidst the gravel of the car park, occasionally stuffing its hand in its mouth.

It was sucking blood off the stones.

The hunger of the beasts frightened Cole. They

were relentless killing machines, unnerved by injury or the threat of harm. Thankfully, they were not intelligent, otherwise the living might be utterly doomed.

Hurrying around the van and up into the back of a pickup truck, Cole crouched and watched the dead moving ahead of him. The sun dipped behind a row of tall trees, the last rays washing over the Irishman. It was a beautiful moment after so many full of horror. He hoped Warrington would not blunder out of the vet's to come and enjoy it with him.

Everything around him stopped so suddenly he froze along with it.

The dead ceased their movements, standing or crawling to a halt. Even the zombie with its dead lips around a stone. The breeze felt as if it had stopped, too, and Cole let out a breath he had not realized he was holding.

The thud of his heart filled his ears as every one of the undead sprawled before him turned to face him. To stare at him. Stunned, he was unable to summon the effort to hide, his eyes peering over the cab of the pickup. Were ... were the dead looking at him?

Something moved behind him.

Christopher Cole turned.

The Tall Man grinned.

The pain in Warrington's back and shoulder woke

him as the sedatives wore thin. He stared at the clock on the reception room wall until he could focus on it to see how long he had been out, but then realized he had no idea what time it was when he had passed out.

The room spun as he sat upright on the waiting room bench, his good hand clasping the edge of the seats that he was laying across. Cole's leather jacket fell from his body. He called out for Cole, but got no response.

Waiting for the initial pain to subside, Warrington gingerly moved to his feet, his good hand against the wall for support. He slowly walked around the medical center, but could not find Cole in the building. The back door was unlocked and Warrington assumed he must have left through there on an errand.

Maybe to try and track Charlotte down.

Warrington returned to the operating theater and sat on the gurney, trying to organize his thoughts through the burning in his shoulder and back, the pain scorching its way through his drug-induced haze.

The gunshot wound ached and sweat poured from his body. The vial of morphine blurred in his vision on the portable table beside him. He knew the drug would dull the pain and discomfort, and he knew he did not want to be meddling within the realm of drugs he believed were for recreational fun for people like Cole.... But he longed for release from the pain.

He closed his eyes and sucked in his breaths, the act hurting his back. He knew that despite the injury he had to stay as level-headed as possible. The meds would dull not only his pain, but also his mind.

In the reception, he lifted the blind away from the front door. Dusk fell outside, coating the road heading left-and-right from the vet's in a smoky glow.

Near the bottom of the hill to the right sat a large pub surrounded by a mob of the undead. They were unmoving, but ... were they standing in a circle around something?

Warrington pressed his cheek against the glass for a better look, the coolness easing his discomfort. He could see more of the undead. The gathering was bigger than he first thought, and they were definitely surrounding something.

If it was a human, they would be attacking. He lifted his good arm to lay a hand on the bolt securing the door. He swallowed against the pain, debating whether he was going to be sick or pass out, or both.

He did neither as he saw Cole arch above the heads of the dead and land on the windscreen of a car. He heard the smash of glass from behind the closed door.

The Tall Man stood straight, towering above the heads of the undead, moving towards where Cole lay prone.

The demon jumped up and crouched on the roof of the car, jabbing at Cole with a long finger. The Irishman was covered in blood, barely moving, and Warrington forgot his pain as he slapped his hand against the doorframe. "No!"

The Tall Man picked up Cole by his leg and threw him again like a rag doll. Cole crashed against a camper van and crumpled to the tarmac. The Tall Man hopped down and stood over Cole, the assembled dead turning their heads to watch, although not a one of them moved from where it stood.

Warrington grimaced as the young man was grabbed by an ankle and tossed into the middle of the road. The Tall Man strode after Cole, long legs bending outward in a way that would have seemed comical if the creature which owned them was not so hideous and foul.

Tilting its head, it gazed down at Cole.

And then looked straight up at Warrington.

The policeman dropped the blind in fright, hoping the beast had done nothing more than glance in his direction. He cracked the blinds open again. The Tall Man still looked his way, now pointing a finger at the veterinarian's.

Warrington's throat was so dry it hurt to swallow, the pain in his body dulling a touch as adrenaline started to....

Adrenaline.

Warrington hurried his aching body back to the operating room. With his one hand, he tipped drawers of vials onto the counter and searched their labels until he found one marked ADRENALINE.

He picked up the syringe, uncaring if it was clean or not.

Right now a dirty needle was the least of his worries.

CHAPTER TWENTY

Charlotte ran, her bare feet thudding upon dirt as she blundered her way through branches tearing at her skin. The sound of booted feet behind her spurred her on.

She was not sure how many of the pursuing footsteps belonged to those living or those dead, but she did know it had all gone spectacularly to plan outside of the shed.

Charlotte had been dragged out by a man who shoved her down the side of the small, wooden building. He unfastened his trousers as he pushed her to her knees. She used the needle-point pliers she kept concealed against her abdomen to puncture one of the man's testicles as he advanced upon her, laughing. The laughter turned to a scream as blood poured through his fingers. She snatched the hunting knife from his belt and stuck it deep into his thigh before she fled.

Andrew Low burst from the house at the other end of the garden to inspect the screams. His huge frame bounced as he ran to the injured man, silencing him with a boot to the face. Already the moans of the dead were filtering towards them, drawn to the wails.

Charlotte glimpsed one of the savage farmers lining her in his gun-sights. She put her head down and sprinted, uncaring of the stones against her bare feet as a bullet ricocheted off a truck, striking a gas container on a table of assorted supplies next to the shed.

She ran for the trees behind the makeshift prison as the sound of punctured metal threatened to burst her eardrums.

She heard Low swear loudly at the shooter as the tree-line welcomed her. The dead man she ran into was not as welcoming. She bowled the creature over and jumped over it as it flailed its arms and snapped its teeth at her.

More human shouting from behind, moans growing in size before her. Slowing her run she peered into the trees. The fall of evening added darkness to the surroundings, but she could see figures moving in the shadows among them.

Despite Low's orders she heard more gunshots from the area of the house as the dead gather towards it. Another loud bang and woof of flames told her the gas canister had exploded properly. The light of the flames filtered through the trees, illuminating the ghouls around her.

Charlotte kept low and rushed through gaps where she could find them. Her fear of the undead was nothing compared to her fate at the hands of the living.

A scream tore through the trees, followed by more gunshots. Low no longer ordered for quiet.

The secretary ran, covering her face as twigs snapped against her. She could see the flush-green ground of a meadow ahead in the dying daylight.

She burst from the trees and into the long grass, the difference from the lashing branches against her arms into open air causing her to stumble. She fell into the reeds, their coolness enveloping her torn body. She closed her eyes, bare chest heaving and tears falling into her ears.

The rhythm of heavy boots neared, but she felt had no more strength left to move.

The urge to live fueled her.

She tried to get to her feet, her legs buckling as she sprawled into the grass again. She lay low, panting, hoping her pursuer would not see her.

"Get up, you little slut."

Fuck.

Low aimed a shaking handgun at her. His face and bare forearms revealed scratches from the trees like her own, except he did not look as if he had been gang-raped and beaten by a group of backward farmers.

"You fucked-up my operation," he said, face red and sweating. "That place was tight as a drum and we could've ridden pretty much any shit-storm out there."

She scurried backwards on her elbows, Low taking steps forward to match her movement.

"You made a mess of Reuben and his bollocks," he said. "His yelling dragged them fuckers from everywhere. He was still crying when they ate him."

"Good," she said.

Low stared at her. "I don't know how many of my boys you got killed with your little stunt," he said. "I just lost me some good friends."

Charlotte's swollen cheek throbbed. She did not attempt to cover her nakedness from him. "All the world lost were a few dirty inbred rapists."

"They were my friends!" he snapped, thrusting the gun at her, making her flinch. "And you got them killed."

"Good!" Her eyes were as wide as his.

The farmer shook, the gun never leaving its target. She felt the fear leave her body. "I'm glad they're dead," she said. "There are enough monsters out here already without the living turning on each other."

Low's eyes narrowed. "And what about your pals you left in the shed? If the blast didn't kill them, the dead will."

Charlotte's eyes watered. She had no words. She hoped to the other girls were dead from the explosion. They were worse than dead if they survived. Why hadn't they run with her?

Low looked around the meadow, keeping the gun trained on her. He walked the tree-line, grass parting beneath his thick legs as he listened to the gunshots in the woods grow less frequent.

"You're not looking at the bigger picture," he said, the redness in his face fading. "This is a 'brave new world,' where only the 'brave' and the strong will survive."

"Where's the bravery in rape?" she asked, her words hard and crisp.

"A coward wouldn't do it," he said, and she had to look away from the hunger in his eyes. "Can you not see that nothing will ever be the same again? We have to build towns and defenses to keep the dead out. We'll need to repopulate and grow soldiers and armies—"

"By keeping women like farm animals in sheds?"

"Only the first generation," Low said, talking to her like a child. "The more girls we breed, the better we'll be able to bring them up knowing their sense of place.... Their sense of existence."

Charlotte stared at him. "They'll be nothing more than cattle."

"Isn't that what we all are, anyway?" he asked, jerking the gun at the trees. "But now the food-chain has changed some. Now survival of the fittest has never been truer."

"How can you all become such savages?" she asked. "The island has only just become infected. It was a few days ago. Where's the humanity you had then?"

Low smiled and it scared her. "Man has always been a savage," he said. "Look what happens when a little law and order goes out the window. You get riots in London when a local youth gets shot, and young men fight the nights away in towns the world over."

A zombie—an old man—crashed out from the trees. It blinked its glazed eyes at its new surroundings.

The white patches of Low's dirty teeth shone in the low light. "Look at it, pathetic, slow, diseased. A victim of its own hunger." He turned to her. "All the same issues a living man has!" His own observation made him laugh

The dead man had turned towards Low's voice, a murmur rising in its throat. It cast its glance between Low and Charlotte, hissing at them.

Low leveled the pistol at the creature's face. "It's a mindless thing, young lady," he said, eyes still on the dead man. "But it's relentless. A relentless killing machine. Cut off its arms and legs and it will still try and eat you."

The zombie went for the closer of the two—Low. It moaned as it moved, quicker than Charlotte had expected. The hunter shot it through one eye. The body hit the ground and Low stepped cautiously to it.

"Gotta be careful," he said, nudging it with his foot. "I've seen the fuckers bite after being shot like that."

Charlotte chanced a look over her shoulder towards the other side of the meadow. As she tried to guess how long it would take her to get to her shaky feet and run for its safety, she heard Low's boots crush the grass towards her.

"I'm going to have to start my little empire all over again," he said, standing over her. "I'll have to round up what's left of the boys … if there are any left. I don't think it will be too hard to recruit others."

Charlotte wanted to close her eyes and sink into the reeds, but fear of the man towering over her stopped her. He reached down and grabbed her arm, pulling her towards him. She cried in anguish and terror, so he hammered her across the nose with the hilt of his gun.

Her eyes watered as blood flowed from both nostrils. She put up a hand to stem the blood, but Low threw her back on the ground.

She was dazed, eyes blinking to clear the tears as Low put a heavy knee on her chest, pushing the air from her body. She beat feebly at his leg, but the farmer struck her again, this time on the side of her head.

The wetness of blood pouring from the wound seeped into her ear as she was granted her previous wish to lay back in the long grass. The world became a haze, the reeds stretching towards the heavens as they framed a Low-shaped mass.

"Like I said," she heard a zip unfastening somewhere far away. "I've got to find a new place to call home ... new men ... new cattle." He pinned her hands over her head with one big hand. She offered little resistance. "And you're gonna be the bell cow."

The last of her clothing—her panties—were ripped from her waist.

"The ... gun..." she said, her eyelids fluttering.

"What? No," he said. "I'm not gonna shoot you, sweetheart."

"No," she croaked. "The gun ... the dead...."

His eyes widened at her words. He held up the gun, staring at it dumbly, knowing that by shooting the zombie it would have rung a feeding bell to the dead within the forest around them.

He raised himself up out of the long grass.

They were already in the meadow, staring at him. Four of them, covered in death-inducing bites, faces contorted in hunger and anger. Their soul-sapping moans encircled the meadow and disappeared into the woods.

Charlotte's head cleared enough for her to know she was in trouble ... more trouble than she was already in. The pressure on her wrists relaxed as Low's attention was diverted. She pulled a hand free to wipe the blood from her eyes. She winced as she brushed against her broken nose.

Low slowly lifted his weight from her, fighting to hold his trousers up with one hand, the gun in the other flicking between each zombie.

Why isn't he shooting ... ah, he hasn't enough bullets.

Low fired at the nearest of the undead as they all moved forward at once, the shot disappearing into its ribs without any acknowledgement from the creature. With one hand holding his trousers together he lined up another shot, this time catching the zombie in the neck. Still it did not slow down. His next two shots had about as much effect as the first two.

The farmer went down amid a flurry of gray hands and a string of obscenities from himself.

Charlotte moved while they were distracted, spitting out blood oozing into her mouth from her shattered nose. A zombie lifted its bloodied head from

Low's neck and watched her. She froze, unable to breathe, but it dipped its head and tore at Low's throat.

Charlotte gasped and choked on the gulp of air she sucked in, but she managed to roll onto her front and crawl towards the opposing tree-line.

She did not look back until she reached the other side.

One of them was staggering towards her. Its mouth open and closed on some part of Low's flesh, blood soaking its face and chin. Glassy-eyes and gray skin disguised the person it had once been. Now it was one of the relentless killing machines Low had described. It cut through the grass at her, moaning as its jaw hung low from its face. She wondered if she had known the person before they had died, or if she had ever passed them in the street. Its face was so gray and broken she could not tell what the person-before-the-zombie would have looked like.

Charlotte Lewis finally gave up. She had been raped, beaten, chased, and attacked by humans and the undead for three days and she had nothing left in her tank.

The dead man advanced on her, breaking into a disjointed run as it hissed its excitement at the new meal.

Charlotte did not scream. She did not close her eyes.

But she did flinch when a bullet evaporated the zombie's face.

From behind her, soldiers strode from the trees, firing at the dead and taking them down with military-trained precision. The first row of troops dropped to their knees as their brothers emerged behind them. The four undead in the meadow dropped, and another soldier shot the undead Andrew Low as he got to his feet. More evil creatures poured into the meadow to be dispatched by the soldiers.

Charlotte noticed they wore two different types of uniform, some wearing stars and stripes badges on their arms, and others she recognized as British military uniforms. One of the local boys knelt beside her. She was too weak to cover her nakedness, but the man did not look at her like the hunters had. He kept eye contact with her, talking with a firm and quiet tone.

"Ma'am," he said. "Wait...." He stared at her. "You're Charlotte, right?"

She stared at him, and nodded.

He took off his helmet and smiled. "It's me," he said. "Private Hayward. We met at the Yarmouth ferry port."

She did recognize his face. It warmed her some, but she was too dazed, beaten, and tired to engage in small talk.

"I need to know if you have been bitten," he asked, face now stern.

She shook her head. The pain made her press her hand to her bleeding face.

The soldier looked around the meadow as more shots were fired. Shrugging a pack off his back, he took off his jacket and held it to her. "Put this on," he said. "We're going to get you out of here."

She flinched as Hayward reached out a hand, so he slowed his movements, talking to her quietly all the time. She allowed him to help her to her feet. He wrapped the thick jacket around her.

"Who ... who's we?"

He smiled at her again, an act that seemed strange upon anyone's face in these times. "The combined forces of the US and the UK."

A tall, broad soldier who stood and watched over them during their entire exchange turned and smiled at her. "Looks like y'all needed our help again in a fight," he said in a thick, American drawl she could not place.

Charlotte's legs trembled as she took a step, both soldiers catching her as she stumbled, wrapping arms around her waist.

"What's your name?" she asked for the lack of anything better to say to the Americans. Her mind tried to adjust from almost being killed by Low and the dead, to being saved by gun-toting soldiers who had all but ridden in on silver steeds.

"Sergeant Aaron Bell, US Marines, ma'am," he said, turning her away from the death in the meadow. "Can I ask your name?"

She had to think about it for a moment. "Charlotte," she finally said as they led her away. Bell released his hold on her, but Hayward was more than able to take her weight. Bell walked two yards behind them, scanning the woods all around.

She looked back at the soldiers who were double-tapping the zombies in the grass. She became aware Hayward was talking to her, but she did not hear what he was saying. He repeated her name until she responded.

"What? I ... I'm sorry...," she stammered.

"Don't apologize," he said, shouldering his main weapon and unholstering his pistol.

The sight of the gun shook her and her legs went from underneath her. Bell swooped forward and took down a zombie that had appeared a few feet away from them as Hayward held her upright.

The sound of the gun so close to her made her scream. Hayward held her close and she allowed herself to be propelled along.

"It's okay," he said. "We're gonna get you back to the chopper."

"To the mainland?" she asked as they moved on.

"Is that the bigger island?" Bell grinned.

He had a smile which would normally have proved infectious. "Alright, are we going to England?" She did not think it would be possible for herself to smile any time soon.

Hayward ducked them under a branch, his eyes scanning the area as more soldiers passed them by in the direction of the meadow. "I'm sorry to say England is probably as fucked as the island."

She dragged her feet, forcing Hayward to stop and face her. "What do you mean?" she asked. "It's not just the island that's infected?"

He shook his head, pulling her gently to urge her on. "The plague-virus-whatever spread fast. All of England is in pretty bad shape, and it's cutting through Europe already."

She closed her eyes and let him lead her.

The whole country?

The trees around them disappeared as her bare feet struck tarmac. Around them soldiers dashed in all directions. More of them filed out of dark-green military trucks, following orders barked by men who looked sterner and meaner than the grunts they bellowed at. These men were more organized and in greater numbers than the troops she had encountered before. It gave warmth to her cold form.

Bell and Hayward guided her to a jeep where a man swathed in bandages was either asleep or unconscious. Hayward motioned for her to get in, but she paused, eyeing the man already in the vehicle with suspicion.

"It's safe," he said. "He's been shot, not bitten. Get in and I'll drive you to the evac zone. From there you'll be taken to a safe zone."

"There's such a thing as a safe zone?"

"Anywhere is safer than here, ma'am," Sergeant Bell said as she climbed in.

Bell took the wheel of the jeep, driving it away from the bustle of men and clanking of weapons as Hayward settled in beside her, squashing her against the prone soldier on her other side.

Charlotte looked over her shoulder, now-familiar plumes of smoke rising all over the horizon as they ascended a hill. She looked towards the woods she had escaped from, the fire caused by the exploded gas canister spreading through the trees.

She asked Bell if there was a list of survivors available somewhere of who might be at the safe zone.

"No, sorry," he said. "But at the camp you'll be able to chase up your friends, if they've made it."

"How far is the camp?"

"There's one here on the island we will stop at briefly," Bell answered. "But the main ones are over in England. That's where we'll try and get all the survivors to."

She sank back as far as she could into the rigid seat, her exhausted body uncaring of the lack of comfort.

"Bell," she said, her eyes growing heavy. "You do realize we're in England? The Isle of Wight isn't a foreign country."

"It is to me, ma'am."

CHAPTER TWENTY-ONE

Drury's body was held together by super-glue, tea-towels, and sheer determination. He had almost screamed when he saw the tendons and tissue in the palm of his left hand, and had bitten down on a spoon as he glued the split skin together. Zac whimpered as he applied the adhesive to the dog's equally as injured side, but the Rottweiler did not move as Drury stuck her back together.

"You're tougher than me, Zac," he said, patting the dog gently, but even this movement opened up the knife-wound on his back and he felt blood begin to run down his skin.

He tried to look over his shoulder, but could not see where the wound was. Filling a cup with water, he tipped it over himself to wash where he thought the wound and blood were mainly located.

A mirror in a small bathroom showed him the slit was at the base of his shoulder blade. Using the reflection, Drury managed to seal the injury with glue. He stood still while it dried. It was uncomfortable but it held.

In the lounge, Zac sat on a rare patch of carpet not saturated with blood. Drury wondered how much was his, how much was the dog's, the dead girl's, and Williams's.

He stood in one puddle of crimson, inspecting the bruises and cuts on his torso, trying to keep his glued-hand immobile, holding it in the air by his face. His good hand touched at an eye almost swollen shut, his tongue tracing a thick split in his lip as Zac hunkered down with a low whine.

"Time to go," he said, sad he had to make the dog move from its comfortable spot.

He looked out of the bay windows and saw a dead Kerry Williams wandering around the courtyard amid the throng of his new brethren.

"Looks like you don't need to be bitten to become one," he said, spying the still-bleeding wounds on the big man. "You just have to die."

As the dead moved around beneath him, he heard a sound from above. It was the same sound he had heard in Ryde a day-and-a-half before, the sound of helicopters. They flew low overhead, four of them.

"The Army," he said to Zac as he saw crests on their tails. "Let's go and get ourselves saved."

He could find no clothes to fit him in the dead girl's wardrobe—unsurprisingly—so he kept his dirty, blood-soaked jeans on. He did not want to try putting his bloodied shirt back over his wounds, and did not want to get fabric stuck to his glued stitches, so he remained bare-chested. The weather outside was calm, if darkening, and he figured he could pick up more clothing on his journey. Scavenging/looting was not so much as frowned upon, as having become a way of life these days.

He put his hip against the drawers covering the front door, shoving them away. The dog looked up at him as they listened to shuffling sounds on the other side of the door. Drury pressed his body against it, cracking it open.

There were two undead outside, drawn to the door because of the noise of the moving drawers. One of them moaned as it spotted Drury peering out, while the other launched itself forward.

He opened the door as the zombie struck it, the beast falling into the room, crashing to the floor. Drury stepped over it as he shoved the second dead man over the stairway railing. The wounds on his body opened and closed, and he hoped he had enough glue on them to keep them together long enough for him to find safety.

He ran down the stairs, Zac in tow, and kicked the dead man at the bottom of the stairwell as it gathered itself to its feet.

Zac bounded through the still-open front door of the apartment building, Drury on her heels for a change. The dead all around turned towards them, the square filling with moans that overshadowed the fading helicopters.

Drury sprinted for his life in the general direction the aircraft were headed.

CHAPTER TWENTY-TWO

John Warrington stepped out of the veterinarian's into the fading sun. He looked up at it, enjoying the last of its heat against the cold sweat covering his face. His eyes flickered as he fought to keep his eyelids closed. He gave up, instead surveying the dead assembled before him. They stared, but did not approach.

Christopher Cole lay crumpled in the road between him and the dead, blood plastering his swollen face.

"Cole?" he asked, and the dead stirred.

Cole coughed a tooth onto the road and waved feebly at him. He tried to talk, but choked on blood.

The Tall Man stood behind Cole and in front of the dead gathering, a serrated grin blossoming its face. The monster scratched a long fingernail over its chest, ripping the thin fabric of what may once have been a shirt, slicing a cut into its own torso. It bled very little, but what it did bleed was thick and jet black.

Warrington remained a step outside of the open vet's door, wondering if the building would offer him any protection if he decided to hide back inside it. The undead watched him, unmoving, but with the wide-open eyes of hunger. He was not used to seeing them so placid. He assumed the Tall Man was keeping them at bay for whatever reason. Probably not a good reason.

"You followed me?" he asked the gangly creature.

The Tall Man stepped over Cole, its shattered hip slowing it, making its movements more erratic and hideous. If that were possible. It looked at Warrington through half-closed, curious yellow eyes.

Warrington regarded it with an expression as blank as the dead faces around him. "You took the shotgun-thing pretty personally, huh?" He nodded at the hip of the beast, damaged in their previous encounter at the Purton Mill.

The beast snapped its teeth at him, the smile gone, replaced by evil.

"Let him go." Warrington pointed at Cole.

The Tall Man tipped his head inquisitively.

"You want me, you let him go," the policeman said.

The beast peered from Warrington to Cole, studying him before placing a foot on the downed man's ribs and shoving him to Warrington. The Irishman slid and rolled along the road, crying in pain as he stopped at Warrington's feet in a crumpled heap.

Warrington crouched beside him, holding his injured arm close to his body in its sling. Cole's face and torso was swollen and lacerated from the Tall Man's fingernails. A bone in one of Cole's arms poked through his tattooed skin. He was a mess.

"Get inside and lock the door," Warrington said.

Cole tried to lift himself on his good arm, crying

out in pain. The dead wavered around them, a low moan bristling through their numbers until a sharp hiss from the Tall Man silenced them.

Warrington helped the stricken man to his feet, but as he stepped towards the open door of the building, this time the Tall Man hissed at him.

Warrington closed the door behind Cole, who stumbled and caught himself on the seats as he entered the relative safety of the reception area. He turned to speak to Warrington, but the policeman had the door shut before Cole could tell him whatever the policeman was doing was a bad idea.

Warrington already knew it was.

He turned back to the un-dead crowd, rolling his injured shoulder to see how much movement he had. It was not much.

Warrington could not help but retreat back along the road as the beast took long, uneven strides towards him. His heart hammered as he raised his good fist in defense. The beast swatted it away, catching Warrington around the throat with one large claw. Cold fingers dug into Warrington's skin, cutting off the air to his lungs.

Warrington kicked out, the agony in his shoulder and risk of suffocation pushing him to panic. His foot struck the dead man repeatedly, his last kick before his vision went black connecting with the broken hip. The Tall Man jolted a step back, releasing its grip.

Warrington staggered, sucking air into his raw throat. Blinking tears from his eyes, he rubbed at his neck. And then he charged the creature.

The Tall Man did not expect the attack, Warrington's good fist striking him in the mouth. The policeman felt a knuckle break under the impact. The

Tall Man swayed back and spat broken teeth from its mouth. Warrington moved forward again, but a skeletal hand caught him on his good shoulder and put him on his backside.

Awkwardly, Warrington got to his feet as the long creature attacked him again, the force so great Warrington was unsure if he lost consciousness for a short while, as one moment he was preparing to strike the creature, and the next he was lying on his back in the road again.

Shaking his head, he pushed himself up on his good arm. On the other side of his body the gunshot wound pulsated beneath the bandages.

"Is that all you got?" he said, spitting blood on the road.

He backed away again as the Tall Man's bony feet slapped the ground towards him. The beast kicked him, catching Warrington in the stomach and sending him into the surrounding dead. The undead men and women fell under him, but none attacked or bit at him despite their anxious moans of hunger. Warrington scrambled to his feet, pushing away at gray limbs and faces to put distance between himself and the undead crowd.

Searing flames in his side indicated broken ribs, and his breathing came in ragged gasps. "Come on, you fuck," he coughed, blood flecking his chin.

The Tall Man moved for him. Warrington waited until it was close enough so he could pull a surgical knife from his belt to bury into the creature's chest. The Tall Man looked down at the blade, pulling it free without a flicker on its face. It held the object up, examining it before flicking it away.

Warrington retreated, staring at the wound he had

made, at the blood slowly seeping from it.

The two fought, or rather the Tall Man rained blows upon Warrington who staggered under the onslaught.

The dead parted as he was driven backwards into them. His good arm blocked the swipe of the Tall Man's long nails, the fabric of the coat he wore shredding to reveal a magazine from the vet's waiting room wrapped around his forearm in defense.

Swaying on his feet as the breath of the dead warmed his neck, he taunted the Tall Man.

"C'mon, you ugly fuck."

It bore down upon him, Warrington spinning and heading for the small church doors away from the pub. He kicked open a gate leading to the main building. Bodies littered the cemetery, shot or destroyed beyond rising again.

He ran to the doors of the church. The Tall Man followed along the path, waving an open hand at the building and grinning.

"No, I know you're not scared of this place," Warrington said under his breath as he pushed open the doors. He stepped inside, leaving them wide open.

Bite-covered bodies littered the pews. Each body carried a puncture mark in the side of the head. A vicar lay at the foot of an altar, a long bloodied ceremonial knife embedded in his own chest.

Warrington wondered if it went against God's Will to kill one's own flock—unless under extreme circumstances—but the sound of nails clicking upon wood told him the creature was in the pews behind him.

The Tall Man slowly hurdled the seats, arms and legs (and damaged hip) working like a giant spider as it traversed the pews. The policeman adjusted his footing and braced himself, his gaze fixated on the Tall Man's yellow eyes.

As it pounced at him, Warrington produced another blade from within his sling. He caught the creature in its chest, penetrating the thin skin with ease. The beast stood before Warrington, hands on either side of the policeman's shoulders, long fingers snaking around his back as Warrington looked up into its face.

Warrington almost gagged at the smell of its foul breath as the Tall Man loomed over him. It regarded the knife in its chest as it had the first blade Warrington had sunk into it. Warrington's hands still gripped the hilt of the surgical implement. So the Tall Man pushed forward, burying the knife further into its own body until Warrington was forced to let go of it.

Warrington was forced to retreat, the demon's claws gripping tightly onto his shoulders, the injured one sending waves of pain through his body.

His chest shoved the knife past bone and tissue as their bodies touched. He tried to pull away, but the creature held him fast.

"A knife through the heart ain't gonna cut it, huh?"

The Tall Man shoved him to the ground, Warrington crying out in pain. He crawled towards the vicar's body.

The beast was upon him, spindly hands on either side of Warrington's head as it leaned over him, hissing, drool threatening to fall into the living man's mouth.

Warrington gazed up as the beast smiled down, and then threw his good arm around the beast's neck, hugging him so their bodies were together.

The Tall Man pulled its head back and regarded

Warrington with bemusement, but the man buried his face into the Tall Man's neck. When it realized the human was not going to let go, it panicked a little.

The beast pushed itself to its feet, Warrington's strength running on reserves as he clamped hold with his good arm and legs. The Tall Man lost balance at the unexpected turn of events, toppling into the pews. Wood crackled under the strain, echoing around the small church hall.

Still the policeman held on.

The creature thrashed against the seats, battering Warrington between it and them. The pain was immeasurable, but to release his grip would mean death.

The Tall Man stood, claws slicing the policeman's back. Warrington's stomach pressed against the knife in his enemy's chest. He slipped his arm from its neck, wrenching the knife free at an angle to render a tear up the ghoul's body.

The beast screeched, Warrington shutting his eyes at the sound. He pulled the surgical knife free, snaking his arm around the Tall Man's head, slicing deeply across the top of its back at the base of its neck.

The Tall Man pulled back its head and hissed. Warrington pulled his injured arm free from its sling, yelling in torment as he did so. In his closed fist, he held a vial of ketamine from the vet's office.

Stabbing the knife hard into the top of its spine, Warrington used it as a lever to pull himself up the creature's body. Whatever damage he had done with the knife had finally seemed to hurt it. He crushed the medicinal vial in his other hand, plunging the broken glass and liquid into the Tall Man's mouth, ramming it down its throat, lacerating his hand against the sharp teeth. He pulled it free before losing his hand completely.

The creature examined Warrington, large yellow eyes blinking at him. Its throat bobbed up and down as it struggled with the fragments of glass within.

Barking out a cough, the Tall Man finally pulled Warrington from its body, slashing its claws down the man's face in annoyance.

Warrington screamed, his face and a punctured eye dripping down himself. The creature threw him against the altar and the world grew hazy around the policeman.

His vision faded in and out, Warrington could not tell if the pain in his shoulder or his eye was worse. He coughed blood on the ground.

The Tall Man's chest oozed black blood from the knife wound. It held a hand to its throat as it choked on glass shards. With one foul, retching motion, it spat glass from its mouth, the same black blood spraying the pews all around it.

It stared at the mess, then at Warrington, hissing. The sound bubbled, black tar-like blood exploding from its mouth. The Tall Man clutched at a pew, doubling over in pain.

Warrington could not focus his eyes after the impact against the altar. His lungs struggled for air, and he wondered if he had punctured a lung, but the pain from his burst eye was incredible. He raised his bad hand to it, the movement making his bullet-wound throb. His body was a complete train wreck.

The Tall Man choked on more glass. It scratched at its throat, tearing fissures with its nails as it tried to dislodge the glass inside.

With one loud, rib-wracking cough it expelled a

lump of black phlegm-and-glass, clutching at its chest as its eyes closed, black tears streaming down its high cheekbones.

Warrington pulled himself up by grasping the top of the altar, his face soaked in blood. He held his other arm against him to try and ease the pain of his wound. He found it hard to focus, and fought to stay conscious.

The Tall Man stepped forwards, placing a hand on a pew to steady itself. Its long head swayed and its other hand tried to grab at the next pew, but missed.

"Is it working yet?" Warrington asked.

The ghoul looked at him, fighting to keep its eyelids open.

"I knifed your chest ... see if you bleed...," Warrington said, standing straighter. "Once I knew you did ... I gave you a whole fucking vial of Ketamine."

The damaged pew the Tall Man leaned on gave way with a crack. It fell over the seats to lay some feet away from Warrington, staring up the policeman. Its cracked lips moved, but only black blood flowed from them.

Warrington limped towards the Tall Man. The pain of his ruined eye sent waves of blackness over him, but he used it to focus away from the other breaks and lacerations throughout his body. He clenched his fist, feeling one more surge of the adrenaline he had injected himself with back at the veterinarian's pump through his body.

Ketamine and adrenalin? He was sure Cole would have been amused.

The beast swatted a hand at Warrington, missing by a distance.

Warrington looked into the Tall Man's half-closed

eyes. He could hear the dead once more outside, their moans washing over the small church.

"Looks like I've broken your little spell," he said, picking up the longest piece of splintered wood he could find at his feet.

The Tall Man raised itself up and leaned back on the seats, hissing. Its mouth opened and a long, pink, black-stained tongue flicked out at him.

Warrington plunged the wood through its right eye.

The Tall Man fell silent, its head drooping forward as the policeman pulled the thick splinter from its skull.

He nudged its head back up and drove the stake through its other eye.

Warrington staggered back to fall on his rump with a cry. Every breath he took hurt, and his ruined eye felt like a constant explosion on his face.

He slumped at the foot of the altar and closed his remaining eye, feeling consciousness slipping away from him.

The dead filed into the church.

"Let...," he whispered with a small smile.

"Let us pray...."

CHAPTER TWENTY-THREE

Aaron Drury's broad jaw wore a grin as he watched the helicopters hovering low above a field a mile or so away. He momentarily forgot his damaged hands, grasping Zac's big head between them and shaking the dog roughly as she wagged her tail. He almost patted a super-glued stomach with a super-glued hand, but caught himself in time.

"We are getting the fuck out of here, Zac" he said as they jogged through the open gateway into an adjacent field.

The aircraft filled the air, large, military-grade vehicles, rising and falling nearby to each other, probably breaking any safety restrictions about how close aircraft could fly near to another. It was a full-fledged rescue mission. Drury could hear the shouts of men as propellers spun and gunshots echoed towards him.

Beyond the trees, hedges, and buildings, fire and smoke raged through the town of Newport.

Drury slowed to a halt, trying to peer through the smoke encompassing the area.

Are they burning the towns? he thought just as a zombie bowled into him from the side.

He slipped, falling face-first into the mud, churned-up by military vehicles and the boots of soldiers. The zombie-girl thrust forward to bite the back of Drury's neck, but Zac leapt at it, sinking her own teeth into the join of the zombie's neck and shoulder.

The Rottweiler pushed her front paws against Drury's upper body to pull at the dead girl atop of her master, tearing a chunk out of its neck. Drury managed to roll around beneath it, putting his hands to the face of the zombie and holding it back.

The dead girl scratched at him with broken fingers, its nails gouging his neck and face.

Ignoring the flashing pain in his bandaged hand, he struck her with his fist, but the action did very little. He grabbed her head in both hands and jerked her away from his face, burying his thumbs into shrunken eye sockets. He felt some of the glue in his hand come unstuck, but with the aid of his dog they forced the dead girl off of him, and Drury shoved its face into the mud.

The boxer scrambled free, getting up in time to avoid another undead girl drawn to the confrontation. More and more of the undead in the immediate vicinity lurched through the mud towards them.

Drury slipped as he fled, managing to gain traction to evade clutching hands.

He broke free, Zac's growls ceasing as the dog bounded after him.

Drury put his good hand to his throat and found it was bleeding from the dead girl's grasp. He hoped the plague was passed through saliva and not fingernails.

Or he was really fucked.

He slid through the boggy conditions, wiping mud from his eyes after tripping over a mangled body in a

Jody Neil Ruth

puddle, an old man crushed by the wheels of some large vehicle. He got to his feet, Zac's growls coming to him over the noise of the helicopters flying above. His knife wounds ached, and he felt blood seeping from them.

Was the virus airborne? With all his exposed injuries, would he turn into a zombie? Was he already becoming one?

He shook the thought away. His steps thudded into the ground, slower-moving than before, but still making progress. He avoided the undead if he could, most of them heading for the commotion of the helicopters and soldiers nearby.

Civilians filtered out of military trucks and headed towards the awaiting helicopters. Drury unintentionally slowed his progress to scan the faces to find Charlotte, but could not see her. Soldiers in bio-hazard suits hustled the people forward as soldiers shot the dead pursuing them.

He realized he was in the line of fire.

He slowed to a jog. If he moved forward he might be shot, but staying put meant being eaten alive.

A dead child moved way too quickly over the mud. He timed it perfectly, binging his fist down across its forehead. It writhed in the mud, baring its teeth at him with a snarl.

Drury smashed his foot into its face. Repeatedly. He stamped until the skull caved, crying out in frustration with each blow. He was so close to safety, but completely entwined in danger. Zac watched, tail between her legs, eyes darting among the undead who were noticing Drury as a nearby accessible food-source.

Zac barked once. Drury looked up, seeing the

trouble surrounding them.

He stepped back, fists raised. Zac at his feet, shoulders hunched and nose down as he rumbled a threat of his own to the undead.

Drops of rain splattered the dirt around them, cooling Drury's face as they came. He bounced on his toes, finding a foothold in the mud, and boxed the first dead man to reach him.

He moved between them, beating them back with flurries of punches. Zac defended her master, biting at legs and ankles. One stumbled over the dog and Drury snapped its neck with his knee as it tried to rise.

Bare-chested, bandaged, and super-glued together, Aaron Drury fought, but despite all of his power and quick reactions, he was outnumbered.

One zombie came at him from the side and they went down. He elbowed it in the eye before connecting with a left-hook, shattering its cheekbone along with another of his knuckles. Drury scrambled to his feet, trying to check for bites, but he could not tell with the mud and blood already smothering him.

The knuckles on both hands were smashed, but he felt no pain. He cracked another ghoul into the mud and spun for the helicopters. The number of undead were forcing him that way. He would have to chance a bullet or two.

He could not see the vehicles, but could hear them over the crowd of the dead around him. Even Zac had become lost among them. Did he hear the dog barking nearby? He strained to hear above the whoop-whoop-whoop of the rotor blades and the undead groaning.

He whispered to Charlotte that he wished he had seen her face one last time.

Aaron Drury fought.

"We have to move, now!" yelled Sergeant Bell as he led Charlotte Lewis to a helicopter. The powerful blades spun above them, drowning out sound and keeping the rain from their heads.

Charlotte barely heard him. She had his Army jacket zipped loosely around her small body, her bare feet slapping the mud as she ran. The sergeant was shouting into a walkie-talkie for someone to wait or that he would personally shoot them himself. Private Hayward jogged behind her, his rifle sweeping the way they had come. He fired rarely, but when he did, she had to force herself not to scream in panic.

The American grabbed her arm and dragged her on, apology in his eyes as he forced her through yet more torment. Her fatigue and sore body begged for respite but there was none. If she slipped, he was there with a strong arm to right her. "We don't get on that bird we're stuck here for good," he had told her.

He stopped suddenly and she ran into the back of him, flinching away as her broken nose glanced off his shoulder, starring her vision.

Bell had his pistol drawn, nodding to the edge of the field they stood in. "They're through," he said, putting a hand across her.

She could not see what he was talking about due to the previous flash of pain across her face, but she knew what he meant. She could hear them, their noise louder than the hell already around them.

The dead broke through the hedges and from between the trees. All around the sound of gunfire increased, blending with the yelling and screaming of soldiers and the sounds of the undead, until it became a sound threatening to madden her. Bell turned, shouted, and grabbed her, but she could not hear what he was saying.

The dead were drawn to the commotion of the civilians and soldiers who were, in turn, making a commotion because of the advancing dead.

Bell let loose a shot, the dead almost on top of them. The shooting became staggered as bullet-ridden men, women, and children fell upon the soldiers who were trying to protect the living. A fleeing soldier—senses destroyed by the horror around him—knocked Charlotte off her feet, into the mud.

Bell picked her up again. "The 'chooks are leaving," he shouted, pointing with his gun as a military helicopter took to the air. "We're running out of time!"

"'Chooks?" she asked, wondering why the answer to her question was so important to her. Maybe it gave her something to focus on other than the pain.

"Chinooks," said Bell, pulling her after him.

They ran through a minefield of soldiers fighting the undead, either with guns or hand-to-hand. There were too many to help, so Bell dragged her through the battle, Hayward close behind.

Helicopters took to the sky all around, one having too many dead hanging onto its wheels, thumping back down to the ground. The dead fell in a wave around it and the Chinook successfully took to the air once more, the pilot escaping with his cargo of civilians unharmed, if a little shaken.

Everything blurred around Charlotte. Screams and moans soaked her as her feet felt like they would finally stick in the mud, making her a free meal for the hungry dead. She pressed a baggy-sleeved arm over her face and sucked in air to scream as the panic finally took over.

And then the ground disappeared from under her.

Bell had her over his shoulder, the man still running, kicking, and shooting the dead. Her world bounced up-and-down and her nose poured blood down his back. Hayward ran behind them. He had lost his rifle at some point, now using his pistol to fan any threats nearing them. The young man's wide-eyes caught hers and he gave her a weak smile.

Gunfire was replaced by the thundering rotor of an Army helicopter. Bell set her down on her feet next to it.

"We made it," he yelled, motioning for her to get on board.

A Marine leaned out of the helicopter, shaking his head and shouting at Bell. Bell yelled back, but she could not make out what they were arguing about.

But she could make out the figure of a man moving through the mud and the fighting to stand a few feet away from her. He was a big man, completely covered in blood and mud, his torso and hand bandaged. Mud caked his face, and only one eye was visible, the other swollen shut. Bizarrely a dog stood beside him, barking at the helicopter.

Charlotte tugged at Bell's arm but he paid her no heed. The mud-covered figure moved forward on shaking legs, the unbandaged hand reaching out towards her, the bones of his knuckles glinting through the mud.

Charlotte snatched the gun from Bell's hand and shot the blood-and-dirt covered figure advancing on them.

The Marine in the helicopter stopped shouting, looked at Charlotte holding the weapon, looked at the fallen man in the mud, and gave her a thumbs up. Bell took the gun and lifted her up, the other Marine pulling her and then Bell and Hayward onto the aircraft.

Charlotte Lewis fell into a seat by the door, looking down at the man on the ground. She felt a pang of sorrow for the muddy Rottweiler standing next to him, gazing up at the helicopter.

Zac watched until the aircraft disappeared into the rainclouds.

The dog curled up next to the body of her master, uninterested in the undead and soldiers battling around them.

She pressed her nose against an outstretched hand, whimpering.

And then Zac lifted her head, stood, and took a step away from the body.

And growled.

Book 2:
Land of The Dead coming soon...

About the author:

Jody can be found driving trucks all round England. Say 'hi' if you see him and give him another excuse to procrastinate from writing during his breaks!

@jodyneilruth on Twitter

www.facebook.com/jodyneilruth

www.jodyneilruth.com

Also By Devil Dog Press

Caldera By Heath Stallcup

Indian Hill Series

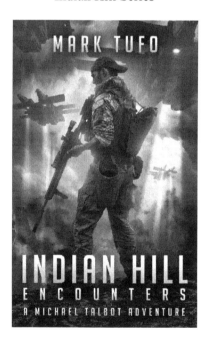

All That Remain By Travis Tufo

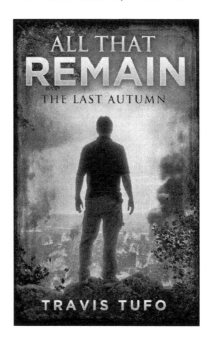

Prey By Tim Majka

Vodou by Brandon Scott

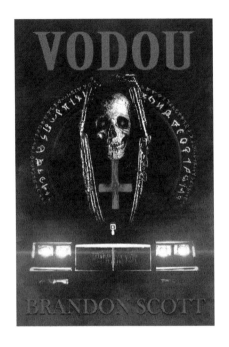

Redemption & Revenge by Nicholas Catron

Made in the USA
Middletown, DE
25 November 2021